ASHES OF ATHENS

JERRY AUTIERI

1

The hard butt of the crutch cut into the crook of Curio's arm as he hobbled toward the opened door. It tapped on the mosaic floor, a faded Greek pattern of ochres and browns that were dull beneath a gritty layer of dust. He bit his dry lower lip as he struggled to maintain his dignity. His left arm already tingled from the pressure of the crutch. He held his right arm away from his side as he proceeded across the floor toward the opening. The milky whiteness framed within it seemed like the entrance to another world.

Perhaps it was, in a sense. He had spent weeks in bed, agonizing at any motion that affected his abdomen. To his dismay, that was any movement short of blinking his eyes. However, today would be a long-awaited victory after a hundred failed skirmishes with his frailty. He was heading for the light and the outside world.

"Maybe you should continue to rest. Don't strain yourself." Cecelia's silvery voice was full of worry. She stood behind him. Though he could not see her, Curio knew she stood with her small hands extended to steady him at the slightest tremble.

"I don't need rest. I need air and activity. The doctor said so."

He immediately regretted the irritation in his voice. Cecelia had cared for him better than even his mother would have. She doted on his every need without complaint or delay. She slept beside his bed and awakened whenever he did. Especially in the first weeks when his pain had been unbearable, she held his hand throughout and begged the gods to ease his suffering. He sighed and resolved to be more patient.

"You can do it, Curio."

Galerius's silhouette reappeared at the door. He had stepped outside into the unpaved Athenian roads and now stood with both hands on his hips. Though Galerius and his twin sister, Cecelia, were both considered adults at fourteen years, Curio still balked at their familiar speech. He was a veteran centurion, after all, and should be accorded the respect of his rank.

"Of course I can do it! I learned to walk a long time ago. For the love of Jupiter. Will the two of you stop making such a fuss? I'm just going outside for a walk to the end of the street. It's nothing to worry about."

The pungent scents of the city sharpened as he wobbled closer to the door. The wound to his stomach had caused him terrible weakness in his left side. The use of the crutch took pressure off his midsection and allowed him to begin rehabilitating his weakened muscles. A few months ago he could have run backward up a mountain while singing. Today he couldn't cross a dusty mosaic floor without his knees buckling and his breath coming short. That humiliation hurt worse than the crawling pain in his gut.

Upon reaching Galerius, Cecelia applauded from behind, inhaling with breathless admiration for this least of Curio's achievements. Galerius grabbed him by the shoulder and squeezed it with pride.

Curio would have waved it all off but was gasping from the effort. He wondered what the doctor had been thinking when he suggested walking would benefit him. He had barely just begun to sit upright again. Now he was supposed to rebuild his strength? Sweat matted his forehead by the time he paused at the doorway.

"You did it!" Cecelia rushed up behind him, and Curio turned to offer her a smile.

She was shorter than he was, with lustrous brown hair and a round face that looked a bit too much like her father, Cilnius. Yet her joyful smile made her radiant. Her pale gray stola seemed to glow in the shade of the small room as she fluttered around him.

He was about to deliver another crabby retort when he caught himself. Cecelia deserved his gratitude, not prideful rage. So his trembling lips formed a small smile that he hoped matched her sincerity.

"I did, and I owe it to your care. I'll never be able to repay you for what you've done."

Cecelia's hazel eyes widened and seemed to gloss with tears as she brought her small hands to her chin. She blinked at him as if she had been struck in the head, and Curio realized that he must have been too stinting in expressions of gratitude for her to react like this.

Galerius relieved the awkward moment with a laugh. "All right, sister, clean up our room while I take your perfect man up the street."

Cecelia's dumbfounded smile turned to a glare at her brother standing in the doorway. Yet when she looked at Curio again, the smile returned and her big eyes widened again.

"Don't push yourself. The doctor said light walking only."

"Right. I promise not to take Galerius on a march around Athens." Now, he turned back to the young man in the doorway and squinted at him. "But I will get him marching soon enough. In three years, you'll join the legion. I'm not sure that's enough time to get you into basic shape."

Galerius stepped back to allow Curio space to exit the first-floor apartment. The doctor owned a number of these apartments that he rented to patients who needed extended supervision. From what he had learned vicariously from Galerius's explorations, they were not even equal to the poorest Athenian houses. The Greeks lived in small compounds with a tiny central garden. As a people, they did not seem to spend much time in their homes, yet enjoyed more living space than a Roman of a similar economic class would.

Before he could take his first step outside since Varro and Falco had brought him here, Cecelia's warm hand grabbed his arm. She gave a firm tug, brooking no resistance until he turned. Her face assumed the seriousness that only enhanced her charm.

Her smooth palms slid under his tunic and sought the wrapping around his torso. She plied back the tunic enough to examine the binding and tested its strength before stepping back with a nod of approval.

"You're more thorough than the doctor's orderly," Curio said, causing Cecelia to blush and shake her head.

Now, he turned into the street where Galerius stood waiting for him.

Though he was more than ten years Curio's junior, he was still taller. At fourteen, he had just barely traded his child's clothing for a man's tunic. Yet the dark hair around his lip was even more prominent than Curio's. He had always regretted his thin and sparse beard. Even when he had lived like a barbarian in the Iberian wilderness, he hadn't grown a beard to match his wild state. Falco had teased him for it even years later.

Yet before he stepped out the door, he paused to scan the blue sky that folded all around the ancient city of Athens. He was walking again, where only a few weeks ago he doubted his survival. Walking into the street was such a prosaic moment, yet he felt like this was a milestone. It was as if he were stepping back from the threshold of death.

He missed Falco and Varro. He wished they were here to encourage his recovery and to fill the long hours with nothing to do but stare at the rafters over his bed. At this moment, he wished they could see him walking out into the light, even if he leaned on a crutch that made his arm numb.

"We won't be long," he said over his shoulder to Cecelia.

"Please be careful. Galerius, don't let him fall."

Waving away his sister's concern, he nodded to Curio.

He paused, feeling the itchy tightness where the enemy had punctured his gut. The gods had guided that spear, weaving it between his organs and bones and preserving his life. Had that enemy blade twisted a fraction in either direction, he would have certainly died.

Now, Curio set his sandaled foot into the road outside the apartment. It tingled, though he knew that was his imagination. In two more hesitant steps, he was fully out of the apartment and bathed in warm, early autumn sunlight. He leaned on his crutch to ease the pull on his side.

The city seemed to suddenly spring into life, as if it had only existed as an idea before Curio had stepped onto its streets. The roads flowed away in a grid pattern, evenly laid out but formed of unpaved dirt. The buildings along the roads were built from mud walls on stone foundations and covered with beige plaster in various states of repair.

The Athenians were out in force. Everywhere people of every age conducted their daily business, their voices raised to a dull quiver in Curio's ears. He was always struck by the Greek's choice of bright colors and patterns for their tunics, even on their poorest folk. Clumps of pedestrians flickered through the spotty light between buildings, their multitude of colors flashing like the tail feathers of an exotic bird.

Far across the undulating city streets rose the massive stone block where the Acropolis was a smokey blue smudge.

"Let's go there," Galerius said, chuckling. "That's a good first walk."

"I would like to see it before I leave," he said, still straining to discern more detail. However, smoke haze from a thousand hearths, and the dots of birds wheeling through the sky obscured additional detail. "I also want to visit Minerva's temple."

The owl head tattoo on his left arm not only stood for Servus Capax but also represented the goddess. Perhaps Minerva, the patron goddess of this city, had speeded his recovery because of it. He felt obligated to venerate the goddess for her aid.

"Well, you better call it Athena's temple if you want the Athenians to understand you. They're a bit prickly with us Romans. Come on.

Let's walk to the end of the street and back. That's good enough for your first time outdoors."

Unfortunately, the street was not flat but rose at an incline that he might not have noticed when he was in better health. As he stared at it, the rise seemed to grow into a mountain.

"Let's go uphill to start," he said. "It'll be easier for you to carry me downhill."

Galerius tilted his head. "There's an uphill to this street?"

He led the way, leaning on his cane for support. Behind he heard Cecelia call out a final time. He would've looked back and assured her. However, the uneven and unpaved roads demanded his full attention. Ruts and potholes filled the timeworn streets. The late morning sun pooled these with blue shadows, but he knew how insidious they were for a man in his condition. He would sprawl out on his face if his cane caught a single rut. Never mind the potential to reopen his wounds, the humiliation would be unbearable.

"We're coming up on crowds ahead," Galerius said as he approached Curio's side. "These Athenians are just as rough as Roman crowds. If you want to go a different route, I'll find a clearer one."

Curio snorted and glanced up from the road long enough to see he had only traversed two small buildings up the slope. His arms were already trembling and sweat flowed into his eyes.

"This is fine. Just watch the pedestrians for me. I don't trust them to notice my condition."

The gentle incline fought him as he continued ahead. The tapping of his cane drove him mad and the squeeze of it against his armpit chaffed.

But he was walking! The realization that he might reach the top of the street filled him with vigor. His strides lengthened, even if he grunted with the strain.

Galerius matched his pace. The young man's nerves were evident in his silence. Curio had discovered his erstwhile caretaker could talk about anything for any duration. He was truly the son of a merchant, gifted with a natural rapport and gregarious nature. So when he simply strolled beside Curio without comment, he knew how tense he was.

"I think I'm going to make it!" He couldn't keep the excitement out of his voice. "I honestly thought this hill was going to beat me."

"Don't say it," Galerius said. "You're Centurion Curio, the hardest and toughest of them all!"

He was too caught up in his glorious victory to correct Galerius. Had Falco heard that description he would've collapsed in laughter. So he stumped along until reaching the cross street.

Now he was in a different situation. Going up the road, there had only been sparse traffic, and most of it was on the opposite side of the street. Now he approached a congested crossroads where both buildings and traffic were thicker.

"We can turn around here," Galerius said. "You're dripping with sweat."

"What? It's warm outside. That's all. I bet I could reach the top of this hill and still be good to descend." He paused to squint beyond the crossroads to where the dirt streets threaded toward distant stone walls. His sight was never good with distance, and he saw only the vaguest colors of pedestrians intermingled with their dull buildings and clumpy trees.

"It's your first time outdoors," Galerius said. "Let's go back before Cecelia gets worried."

Curio hobbled to a wall surrounding a small building and rested against it, Galerius following.

"Too late for that," he said. "She's been worried since I was wounded."

Galerius gave a sly smile. "Oh, she's been worried for you since you became my father's guest."

It seemed a lifetime ago that Cilnius had mistaken them for enemies of Rome and imprisoned them in his villa. Both Galerius and Cecelia followed him after he and the others gained release, even stowing away on their transport ship. They were a cunning pair, though naive to many matters of the adult world.

"Well, she can wait a bit longer," Curio said. "It's not my nature to give up when there's fight in me yet. A crowded street won't defeat me. Are you ready, Optio Galerius? Your centurion has given you a command."

"A promotion so soon?"

Curio shoved off from the wall, checked his footing, then started forward.

Upon entering the traffic of the crossroads, his balance immediately tottered. Galerius steadied him by the shoulder. People and animals flowed around him in a confusing rush. Dark-eyed women with water jugs balanced on their heads regarded him with skepticism, glancing at his cane as they passed. Men with heavy beards glared at him for slowing their progress through the street. Some quipped in Greek as they stepped around him.

"I'm fine," he said above the swirl of conversations and traffic noise. He was only at the edge of the street. His goal for reaching the top of the rise now shrank to successfully crossing the street.

"This is too much for you. You can't pause in the middle of traffic." Galerius pulled at his tunic sleeve. "Let's head back before you're hurt."

Yet Curio was in no mood to retreat. The crowds were like the pressed lines of battle where men lived or died by their skill and determination. The faces in the crowds were all Greek, easy enough to see them as Macedonian pikemen trying to push him back. He had faced that terror before and could face it again.

He launched into the street, right foot clapping the packed earth and left foot and cane thumping after it. The hard butt pushed against his side as he wheeled into the flow of traffic in both directions. His heart raced and his wild imaginings began to feel more real with each step forward. Death to the enemy!

The aggravated citizens of Athens avoided him as he pitched across their length. He felt out of control, and by the time he reached the center of the street, Galerius was with him and directing others away from him. He knew he was like a drunk uncle on a feast day, determined to have his way no matter the cost to anyone else. But Galerius kept him safe until he dodged the traffic without incident.

Reaching the opposite side, he turned and laughed as Galerius pulled him back toward the buildings. An old man stooped and leaning on his cane passed him with an inscrutable stare. Curio wondered if he appeared like that to everyone else.

"I did it!" His heart thudded and his breath came hard, but he admired the crowds crisscrossing in front of him.

"Great," Galerius said, not disguising his irritation. "Will you be able to do it again when we go back?"

He pushed off the wall and out of the shadows, staring at the street again with renewed fear.

"Well, I hadn't thought about that part."

Galerius snorted. "Fine. We can wait for traffic to thin. It won't be this busy all the time. Besides, you need a rest. You're dripping sweat."

Curio felt the lines of wetness streaking down his back. The pain in his side was an itching ache. While it was a sign of healing, it was no less maddening in its persistence. His legs and arms trembled from the strain. But his heart soared with the dark birds arcing through the clear skies.

"I suppose you're right. Though I don't want to stand around here. People will see the cane and think I'm a beggar. Let's keep moving, though we can slow the pace. I've never seen Athens, not like you have."

Galerius helped Curio wobble around, though he didn't need it. Still, he knew Galerius took his charge to watch after him seriously. Spirits lifted from his small victory, he gave a smile.

"You and your sister have turned out to be a gift from the gods. Maybe the two of you are gods in disguise, eh?"

Their laughter drew looks from those passing nearby. They both turned and started up the street, and Curio had to focus on his footing again.

"Athenians," Curio muttered as he navigated the hard-packed road. "Can't they pave their streets?"

"I've not found a paved one yet," Galerius said. "This place is ancient. You should see some of the buildings I've found by that place they call the Acropolis."

They fell into conversation about Galerius's explorations of the city as Curio stumbled along. Galerius walked before him as he talked animatedly about ancient ruins, statues, and exotic women who tempted him into their rooms.

"Of course, I ran away from them."

"You did? Were they frightening?"

Galerius turned as he led them up the street into more traffic ahead. It seemed there was some sort of backup that had gathered a crowd. Galerius continued to walk backward as he imitated a hideous face for Curio.

"They were like the Medusa. Their eyes were wide and their hair flew around like snakes!"

Curio laughed, then his cane caught on a rut and he pitched forward.

Walking backward, Galerius was not prepared and barely caught him before he hit the ground. The two of them were off balance and now pitched backward as Galerius overcompensated.

They crashed into a tall, broad-shouldered man in a shockingly white tunic.

The three of them now stumbled forward, and at last, Curio slid onto his face at Galerius's feet.

The stranger cursed and Galerius shouted Curio's name. For an instant, he feared his wounds had reopened. Wetness spread beneath him, but then he realized it smelled like sour wine.

"What are you fools doing?"

The stranger was a Roman and he swore fluently in Latin. Curio rolled over on his side, now looking up at the sky and then at Galerius and the stranger disentangling themselves.

"Sir, I am sorry. We tripped in the road."

"Tripped?"

The man seemed like a giant from Curio's perspective, though nearly any adult he knew was taller. He hovered over Galerius, his face red and eyes bright with a look Curio knew all too well. It was the face of the battle-mad: eyes too bulging, veins too prominent, and a fixed expression of endless rage. He had seen it in the faces of legionaries who had served long years on violent campaigns in Macedonia and Iberia.

The raging stranger wiped at his white tunic, now stained the color of a bruise from spilled wine and dirt.

"You ruined my tunic, you oaf!"

Galerius shrank beneath the bellowed curses. "Sorry, sir, I will have it cleaned."

"You will?" The Roman looked down at him, then to an alley between buildings. "Well, in that case, you'll be cleaning your blood off it too."

Before Curio could stand, the Roman cuffed Galerius into the alleyway.

And Curio lay on the dirt road, helpless to act.

2

Galerius struggled against the Roman dragging him off the street into the shadow of a narrow alley. Curio squirmed as he tried to stand, but his cane had fallen out of reach. Uncaring people flowed around him, and an impish boy kicked Curio's cane farther away. He laughed and trotted off, pleased with his mischief.

Feet shuffled around him, and everyone seemed more concerned with whatever had blocked the street ahead. Curio's weak voice drew no attention.

"Help! We're being attacked!"

Then he realized he called out in Latin, and the average Greek had little care for any place beyond his city. Whatever attention he did draw was dismissive. He was a dirty cripple squirming in the dirt and a foreigner as well.

He tried to stand without his cane, but the pain in his stomach flared into heat. It flattened him onto his stomach as good as if he had been tied to an anchor.

Pointing at the alley, he again cried for help. But the crowds were fixated on another drama that now drew their angry shouting.

Galerius struggled against the burly Roman as he threw him

against the wall. It was a shamefully lopsided contest between a man in the full bloom of his strength and youthful Galerius, who lacked the promise of developing muscle.

"You fucking pig! You made me look stupid and ruined my tunic."

Curio heard the slur in his speech. The man was a belligerent drunk.

"I'll pay for it. I'm a Roman citizen. Release me! You can't do this to me!"

But the fellow Roman bellowed laughter. "Fuck off, you brat!"

Holding Galerius by his collar, the Roman punched him in the jaw. His heavy fist thudded against flesh.

Galerius collapsed in the Roman's grip as he drew back for another blow.

"Coward!" Curio shouted as he wormed closer to his crutch. More people were rushing to the scene in the street, and their shouting and cursing drowned out the smaller violence unfolding in the alley. He decided the Athenians would not help and stopped shouting.

Instead, he at last grabbed the crutch and swept it to his side like a lost child. He heard the meaty thumping and Galerius's whimpering as the drunk Roman continued to rave about his tunic.

Yet even with the help of his cane, Curio could not rise from prone. The agonizing torture of his stomach wound kept him flat on the street. Yet he continued to struggle until he cried out in pain and nearly fainted.

He could not watch, preferring to keep his face to the road, smelling the muddy dirt mixed with spilled sour wine. The heavy thuds now sounded wet, like a fist piling into raw meat. Galerius stopped crying out, leaving Curio to imagine the horrible beating unfolding just beyond reach.

Eventually, the Roman cried out in frustration, and the sounds of beating stopped.

Curio turned his head and tested the cane again, only to find himself stunned into stillness from the fire-bright pain in his guts.

The Roman heaved and rested against the alley wall. Galerius lay at his feet, a crumpled and bloodied mess. For a moment, Varro thought he was dead, but then he rolled aside with a moan.

"Fuck, you're weak." The Roman shook out his fist as he regarded Galerius. "Maybe you've learned your lesson now. Watch where you're going."

As frail as his voice was, Curio filled his lungs with hot breath and shouted.

"He tripped because of me, you coward! Fight me and I'll teach you a few new lessons."

The Roman's ire now shined on Curio lying in the road just outside the alley. It was as if he finally noticed him splayed out on his face, struggling uselessly with his cane to resist an injury that anchored him to the ground. He stepped across Galerius as he closed on Curio.

"What's this? A cripple?"

"I'm not a cripple! I am Centurion Camilus Curio and you'll surrender to me now!"

As the Roman drew closer, Curio swiped at him with his cane. The blow was as useless as a child's slap, and the Roman did not acknowledge the cane striking his muscular calf. Instead, his bleary eyes fixed on Curio.

"Look what you made me do! I knocked over a fucking cripple!"

"You didn't touch me!" Curio again batted at the Roman's legs, his rage enflamed but unequal to his strength. The wooden shaft thumped harmlessly against rock-hard muscle.

The Roman again looked down the front of his tunic and raised his thin brows in surprise. He touched the blood speckled across the wine and dirt stains. Curio was not certain the stains had resulted from their collision. This beast was horridly drunk and could've soiled himself previously. He staggered around to face Galerius prone in the alleyway and kneeled beside him.

"You will pay for what you've done," Curio said. "As soon as I can get someone's attention."

Yet the crowd remained focused on what seemed like an overturned cart with men standing atop it and arguing while spectators cursed them or encouraged their dispute. No one paid Curio any attention, being that he was beneath anyone's sight.

The threat made no impression on the drunk Roman. He stood up and put a hand to the back of his head as he stared down at Galerius.

"Eh, he's not dead. Just playing it up for sympathy." Now he reached inside his stained tunic and produced a small satchel. He flipped open the cover and rummaged through it.

Galerius shifted once more, but Curio could not see him clearly between the Roman's legs. At least he had survived the savaging.

"Here's coin for a doctor. Plenty of Greek doctors on this street. Healers of all sorts here. Go get patched up. And remember to watch where you're going. I've got to find Sextus now."

Sparkling silver coins chimed as they fell around Galerius. The Roman, his slurred and rough voice now chastened, mumbled something before returning to the street. He paused before Curio, his narrowed eyes flicking to the cane in his grip. He seemed to make some sort of calculation and then decided he would not risk getting closer.

The callous Roman stepped around him and walked off toward the traffic jam.

"Bastard! I'll find you." Curio stabbed his cane skyward. The violence of the gesture ended any other dramatic threats with a shrill cry of pain.

In any case, the Roman seemed to have forgotten everything and elbowed his way through the crowds of onlookers surrounding the overturned cart. The men atop it had now come to blows, and cheers and betting erupted among the worst of the onlookers. Others seemed to want to end the violence, but could not mount the cart. The Roman vanished into the midst of this chaos.

Galerius moaned louder, and Curio realized he was calling for him.

"I'm right here," he said. "Hold on. Let me try to get up."

He had only ever stood up from bed or a stool. Rising from the ground was impossible, as his abdomen flexed and twisted with the frightening threat of reinjuring himself. Yet he could not leave Galerius to bleed until one of the heartless Athenians decided to help. They were too consumed with their sport to notice two ruined foreigners crawling in the shadows of their alleys. If anything, they might make matters worse.

So Curio again strained to use his cane to pry himself upright. If he could sit up, he might lever himself to his feet. While he flailed around, Galerius had already flopped onto his back and unfolded his body.

His nose still jutted above his face. Curio was glad it had not been flattened but it might have been broken. He had seen men killed in battle when a shield slam sent their nose bones through their brains. However, the feral Roman seemed to have been wildly inaccurate in his pummeling. Curio would have to get closer to examine him, but to do that he would have to stand. So the struggle renewed.

"Stay."

Galerius held up a hand, and with the other touched his nose. His voice was thick and viscous. A broken nose. Maybe other bones in his face were likewise broken.

"You're wounded, Galerius. Just lie still and don't make anything worse."

"Same for you, Curio."

To Curio's surprise, Galerius sat up as if he had only been napping. However, his face dripped blood and one eye was swollen shut. Curio could not get a good look at the extent of his wounds, but he seemed better than he should be.

"What a brute," he said, his voice nasal but steadier than Curio would've expected. "I think I lost a tooth."

He then spit blood that dribbled down his beige tunic, which was now dark with mud and blood.

"I'll get you to the doctor. Just be still."

Curio had pure intentions, but his struggle was genuine. His wound fought him, threatening to tear and fill the wrapping Cecelia had checked full of fresh blood. He gasped as he again failed to rise.

"Take your own advice," Galerius said through his bloodied nose. "I'll get both of us back to the doctor."

He watched in helpless frustration as Galerius peeled himself up from the alley floor. Bloody drool hung from his face as he paused on hands and knees before standing. He steadied himself against a wall with one hand and touched his brow with the other.

"I stopped fighting and tried to protect my face instead. One of my father's friends was attacked by a black bear once. He said he curled up and pretended to be dead, and the bear eventually left him alone. But it still took a giant hunk out of his leg. He never walked again, but he lived. I figured that was my best strategy with that beast."

"It seemed to work," Curio said, turning aside so he did not have to look at Galerius's face. "I've fought bigger and smarter enemies than him a hundred times over. I could've spun him around and immobilized him before he ever landed a punch. But...."

"I'll be fine," Galerius said. "It looks a lot worse than it is."

"Let a doctor decide that. I've seen men walk off the field making light of their wounds, then they die in their bedrolls at night."

Galerius groaned, and at first, Curio thought it was for his story. Then he turned to see him picking the drachmae off the ground, and collecting it into his pouch.

"What a drunk," he said. "First he beats your face in, then pays for a doctor."

"At least I got something for my beating." Galerius stood up, then tottered over to Curio.

His face was red and swollen on the left side, and his nose twisted. Black bags puffed out beneath both eyes, and his smile was dark with blood.

"I don't think you lost a tooth," Curio said. "But your nose isn't going to be your best feature."

Galerius shrugged. "I'm sure women will marry me for my money one day, anyway."

Getting Curio upright was more challenging than either of them thought. Every tug and push sent Curio spasming in pain. Eventually, their struggles in full view of the public caught the attention of two middle-aged men who had a better-developed conscience than their fellows. These men easily got Curio to his feet and put his crutch underarm.

They spoke Greek, which Curio did not learn as a child. That was for upper-class children, and he had come from a Class V family. Still, he understood their concern for Galerius's injuries. They wanted to take him to the closest doctor, but he managed to convince them they had one down the road. To Curio's relief, both men escorted them away from the traffic accident and ensuing brawl, which appeared to be spreading to the crowd. With enough finger-pointing, the two Athenians delivered them back to the small apartment where Cecelia worked inside.

"She's going to be mad at me," Galerius said.

"I don't think she will," Curio said. "She'll just be concerned for you until the doctor reviews your injuries."

"Not mad about me. Mad about your fall. You're not her husband yet, but she's already thinking like your wife."

While the two Athenians conferred together, one eventually gesturing he would go fetch the doctor, Curio rested on his cane beside the doorway. He blinked in astonishment at Galerius, who smirked at him through his swollen face.

"What are you talking about?"

"Come on, brother. You don't see it?"

Heat came to Curio's face and he stammered. "Your father promised her to another man already."

The door opened and Cecelia leaned out of it, wiping her palms on her pale gray stola. Her forehead shined with sweat and her smile at Curio fell away when she saw the kind stranger who waited for his friend to return with the doctor.

She then looked from the stranger to Galerius, who gave a red smile.

"We ran into some trouble. Don't worry. Curio is fine."

Cecelia flew out the door, and unlike Galerius's jocular prediction, she rushed to him first. Her small hands fluttered like two panicked sparrows around his face, uncertain whether she should touch him.

"For the love of Jupiter, Galerius! You were just taking Curio to the end of the street."

"Well, we did that. It was quite a success. Up until we ran into a drunk who got upset with us."

"Upset? He broke your nose!" Cecelia's voice trembled on the edge of tears.

"It's not broken. Just bent. It doesn't hurt that bad."

"It is broken. You sound like you've put your fingers up your nose. And your face is just hideous. You can't go around starting fights, Galerius. What will happen to me without you?"

"But I didn't start it!" He held up both hands and looked to Curio.

Both Curio and the kind stranger watched with expressions caught between empathy for Cecelia's dismay and humor at Galerius's plight.

Yet Curio saw the other stranger leading one of the doctor's orderlies from down the street. It was the young woman, probably a slave, who had been tending his wounds in between the doctor's visits. She carried a woven basket covered with white linens.

"And why didn't you help him?" Cecelia now whirled on him. A golden lock hung from her pulled-up hair and dangled in front of her eye. She puffed it aside as her cheeks flushed pink. "My brother is the most important person to me. What trouble did you get him in?"

"Well, I fell—"

"You fell?" She put both hands on her head and spun back to Galerius. "You were supposed to prevent that."

Galerius was probing his nose and wincing when he jumped back at the surprise accusation.

"I caught him. But we both fell. What else could I do?"

The other stranger had wisely left them to Cecelia's rage and joined his friend leading the medical orderly. Cecelia continued to interrogate both Curio and Galerius, never letting either finish a thought before demanding a new explanation. It seemed to take the orderly and her two escorts an hour to cover the final distance, and Curio was glad when they finally arrived.

"My brother needs help." Cecelia led Galerius by the arm toward the young woman. She was a little older than Cecelia, and Curio could hardly recall her name. For most of her administrations, he had been half-conscious and later he was too embarrassed to ask for her name. He remembered it as Kinara and hoped that was correct.

"I can see that." Kinara had a Greek accent that Curio felt strangely attractive. Normally, the sound of mispronounced Latin disturbed him.

The other two strangers spoke through her, saying they were leaving and wishing them well. Curio and the twins both conveyed their thanks. Galerius tried to offer some of the coins he had picked up after the fight, but both laughed and refused.

"Bring me a stool," Kinara said to Cecelia. "It is brighter out here to conduct an examination."

Cecelia did as bidden, and Curio drew closer to watch. He ignored the slow burn around his itching wound and the pulse of aches that ran along his side. He did not want to know how bad he had made things.

"Shouldn't the doctor examine him?"

Kinara raised her thick brow and her dark, shimmering eyes flicked to him. Her lip seemed to curl a moment before she answered.

"The doctor's daughter is not good enough? I've been taking care of you since you were on the edge of death."

"I didn't realize," Curio said, stepping back. "I thought it was strange that he'd have a woman as an orderly."

"Are you going to comment on my age too?"

Cecelia returned with a stool, which she set out for Galerius. He had been standing at rigid attention like a soldier on review hoping his disordered kit would not be spotted. He now sat when Kinara gestured for it.

Curio rubbed the back of his head. "Well, you're old enough to be married. I just assumed you were a slave."

"Not everyone follows society's rules," she said. Her voice was deeper than the sparkling melody of Cecelia's. "My father has no sons. I'm his youngest daughter, and I'm too smart to be married."

Both Galerius and Curio laughed aloud and Cecelia covered her smile. But Kinara did not join them. Instead, she pressed the side of Galerius's nose and made him leap with a cry of pain.

"Broken, I'm afraid. I'll have to set it for that to heal correctly. You Romans have famous noses. We need to preserve yours."

Galerius paled. "Wait, what does setting it feel like? Is it going to hurt?"

"Just a pinch." Kinara gave Curio a knowing smile. "Let's move to the bed. Master Curio, would you mind lending your bed to your friend for a short time?"

They herded Galerius indoors and set him on the bed, where Kinara guided him onto his back. She also suggested Curio and Cecelia wait outside while she worked.

Once outside, Cecelia looked fearfully after her brother.

"It won't hurt too much," Curio said. "I've seen men get their noses busted in battle and a friend will set it back for them."

"Is it that easy?" She folded both arms and looked inside. Curio balanced on his crutch and closed the door behind them.

"Easy enough if you only want to breathe freely. Kinara will do that and keep his good looks intact."

The streets had cleared of traffic. Perhaps the chaos farther up the street had caused pedestrians to take new routes. They both stood in patient silence, staring into the street. Cecelia wrapped both arms tighter around herself and frowned.

"What happened? You weren't gone long."

He explained their encounter with the drunk Roman, and by the end, Cecelia had her hands on her hips and shook her head.

"To think a fellow Roman here in a foreign city would do such a thing. And no one helped you until the end. Where did that brute go? If I could find him, I'd break his nose too."

Curio could not help but laugh, yet knew Cecelia was serious. He found even her angered face charming and he realized he was staring at her when she looked expectantly at him.

"Oh, well, he stomped off and said he had to go find Sextus."

Her small hand flew up to the base of her neck and her eyes widened.

"Sextus? Do you think it's the same one who works for my father?"

"That would be impossible. What would he be doing here?"

"Looking for me and my brother, of course."

Curio laughed and set his hand reassuringly on Cecelia's shoulder.

"And how would he know to search Athens? Even we didn't know we would come here. So how could he know?"

She nodded, but her expression did not shift. Curio squeezed her shoulder again, and at last, she looked up with a smile.

"Of course you're right. It's a common name. But my father is beloved of Fortuna, or so he says."

"Then so should his children be. It's not the same Sextus who works for your father."

"Thank you," she said, suddenly blushing and turning away. "You make me feel safe. I'm sorry I yelled at you earlier."

For some reason, Curio blushed as well.

Then the quiet moment was broken when Galerius shouted in pain.

3

Curio and Cecelia grabbed the door at once, blocking each other's way. The wood door rattled in the jamb before one of them pushed it open. Cecelia was the first through. Curio could only hop behind her since he relied on his crutch, leading him to curse under his breath.

Inside the small apartment, dark-haired Kinara bent over Galerius atop the single bed. His feet poked out from beneath a blanket, each pointing rigidly toward the ceiling. He had just screamed but now was silent. A pile of blood-smeared rags sat on the floor by Kinara's sandaled foot. Curio couldn't help but notice the gentle curve of her calf and dusky skin poking from her stola as she stretched out tending Galerius's wound.

"Is he all right?" Cecelia rushed to the opposite side of the bed, but Kinara ignored the question.

"He just had his nose reset." Curio entered, drawing the door closed clumsily with one arm while balancing on the crutch. "Probably shocked him more than anything else."

Kinara continued to work in silence as Cecelia monitored from the opposite side of the bed. She took her brother's limp hand.

"Why is he like that?"

Curio couldn't see Galerius's state but imagined his swelling must have worsened.

Kinara did not answer but instead collected her supplies back into the basket. After she shifted away, Curio saw the swelling had not changed, though now his face was smeared with ointments and honey, and wrapped in white bandages. His nose was splinted with what seemed pieces of bone or antler and held down with more cloth.

Yet he knew Cecelia was asking after Galerius's expression, for he stared wild-eyed at the ceiling as his head rocked side-to-side. Curio leaned in closer to see if Galerius recognized him.

"Why does he look like that?"

Kinara stared at Galerius before answering. "I gave him a draught to calm his nerves and ease his pain. Same as I have given to you. It will quiet him for a few hours, and allow him to rest."

Curio gave a knowing smile. Those draughts had placed him in a strange twilight sleep, granting him dreams that were sometimes pleasant and other times horrific. Yet it eased his pain and helped him remain still. It seemed excessive for Galerius's condition, but then he did not know the extent of his injuries.

However, Cecelia sat beside her brother, clutching his hand in her lap and her thin brows drawn together. Her concern could not be so easily assuaged, particularly since she had placed her future in her twin brother's hands. Without him, she would have to return to her father and to the man he had chosen for her husband. A sudden tightness formed in Curio's belly at that thought. She was a caring and gentle woman and did not deserve a man who would mistreat her. Yet it was her father's right to do as he pleased with her. Curio would be wrong to interfere, even though circumstances had made him complicit in her misdeeds. He could not justify further interference.

Still, with her so full of concern and fear, he could not help but remember her sitting patiently beside him throughout the night. After such care, could he send her to a man so abusive that she would rather become a social outcast than become his wife?

He put his hand on her shoulder, and she looked up at him with shimmering eyes, then leaned into his side as she continued to hold Galerius's hand.

"She's...she's...." Galerius stopped rolling his head and fixed on Curio. His voice was slurred like a drunk's. "Trying to kill me."

Kinara laughed as she collected her basket of blood-stained cloth. Curio did as well, but Cecelia took it seriously. She glared at Kinara, who had already seemed to put it all out of her mind. Her back was turned and so did not see Curio gently shaking Cecelia to console her.

"It is only his pain and the effect of the draught. It made me feel like I was outside my body, probably like your brother feels now."

Galerius had already closed his eyes and now had a faint smile, though it might have been from the swelling and the wraps contorting his face.

When Kinara turned, she seemed to pause as if surprised to find Curio seated with Cecelia. Her big eyes flicked between them and Galerius, and she turned back as if remembering something before she left.

"Master Curio, you fell? I should also examine your wound."

Curio searched around for a bed, knowing there was none, and offered an apologetic smile. "There's no place for me to recline. We need Galerius to help lift me off the floor. So, there's no way to do it. Besides, I'm fine. I am tired from all that struggle. But the brute did not attack me."

Yet both Kinara and Cecelia frowned at him and he knew he did not have an excuse. He simply did not want to know if things were worse now. The pain had certainly increased, but he did not have any bleeding. Surely he was fine, he told himself.

"I could get one of my father's assistants," Kinara said. "But the apartment next door is empty. We can use the bed there for a short time. You should rest as well."

Curio looked at Cecelia to spare him, but she nodded in encouragement. He realized he would have to face reality eventually.

"All right, I'll go. But what about payment? Varro and Falco already paid for my care, but not Galerius's. How much will this cost?"

Kinara shrugged as she pointed Curio toward the door. "Your friend doesn't require much ongoing care. He will be awake in a few hours and you will have your bed back. Consider this all part of the fees already paid. It was nothing to set his nose and clean up his cuts."

"I feel I should pay you something. You have consumed medicines and bandages, after all."

"Follow me," was all Kinara said.

"Go on," Cecelia said. "I'll stay with my brother for now. But I'll check on you soon."

So Curio hobbled after Kinara. Her skin and hair were silky and dark, and if she had not identified herself as the doctor's daughter he would never have guessed it. She was a strange but attractive woman. Being so headstrong probably made finding a husband difficult, particularly if the doctor doted on her, which he must certainly do. He would not have taught her medicine otherwise.

Now he was stretched out on a bed in a dark room. The straw in the mattress smelled fresh and prickled his skin through the covers. The opened door provided the only light, and shadows of pedestrians flicked across it, leaving a whirl of conversations and laughter in their wakes.

Her cool hands slipped beneath his tunic, and she began to carefully unfold the wraps around his stomach. Her fingernails dragged across his skin as she worked, and her body pressed on his whenever she had to pull a bandage under his torso. A sweet fragrance wafted up from her, and he had to turn his head away. Her hair brushed against his face, and he was keenly aware of her softness as she worked around him. As much as he resisted, reminding himself this was the doctor's daughter, his crotch stirred. How humiliating would it be to spring to attention while she was trying to work?

But then that awkward moment ended when cool air touched his spear wound. What had felt flirtatious and scandalous now resolved into bright pain as her fingers gently pressed a cloth to his wound. She clicked her tongue.

"After how tightly I bound this, I cannot understand how you got dirt in there."

"I spent a lot of time on my face on the ground," he said with a feeble smile.

"I thought your lover promised to keep these bindings tight."

Curio raised his head from the straw-stuffed mattress.

"My lover? I think you're mistaken. And she has been taking care of the bindings. I rolled around enough that I'd be more surprised to find it clean under there."

Kinara sat back searching for something. "I'll need fresh water from your room. There's still enough to clean you up. Wait here."

He watched her exit, leaving her basket with bandages and containers on his bed. While he waited, his mind turned to what she had said. Was he in love with Cecelia? Everyone seemed to see them as a couple. Everyone except himself. Of course, he only had a few opinions to go by.

If Falco and Varro were here, they would tell him the truth. A chagrined smile came to his lips. Did he need them to tell him what he felt? The funny part was he did, in a way. If he were to marry Cecelia—a wildly improbable chance, he admonished himself—it would have a huge effect on their operation. Certainly, Servus Capax seemed dead now. After what Rufrius had told Varro about killing all the members, there might only be Centurion Ventor, Legate Marcellus, and them left. But it did not matter, since Falco and Varro were better than brothers to him. They would do everything together, or so he believed.

He would not risk anything interfering with their partnership, even delaying marriage until later in life.

Then Kinara reentered with the wooden bowl from Curio's room. She held it against her hip, cinching her stola against the curves of her body. With the bright light framing her from behind, Curio once more reacted to her comely outline.

Immediately he tilted his head back and closed his eyes.

You'd make a fine husband, Curio, he thought. *Cecelia's right next door and all you can think of is the woman in front of you.*

He kept his eyes closed while he listened to Kinara pad across the same scuffed mosaic floor as the one in the other apartment. The water sloshed in the wooden bowl as she set it on a nearby table.

What were Varro and Falco doing, he wondered. They had probably found women to pass a night with in some Greek town along their route. That's what he needed. After all, he hadn't had a break since he could remember. That was why every woman within a dozen yards aroused him, or so he decided. His lack of any female companionship was probably confusing him about Cecelia as well.

Water dribbled into the bowl and a moment later cold pressure beside his wound radiated with electric pain. He shouted, more from being jarred out of his thoughts than the actual shock.

Kinara winced back, raising her lush brows at his reaction.

"I hardly touched you. Do you need the draught for a simple cleaning?"

He stared at her, then swiftly reclined before he held her gaze longer than appropriate. There was something about her eyes that both captivated and frightened him. Right now, he could not meet them.

"Sorry, I was starting to fall asleep while you were gone and that surprised me. I'm fine now."

Following a long pause, he heard Kinara dip the cloth back into the bowl. This time she touched him gingerly, dabbing at the wound. She rested her hand on his lower abdomen as she worked, slowly wiping away the dirt. Even with such a light stroke, he still experienced the sting and burn of the wet cloth.

She shifted on the bed, seeking better angles as she worked. Yet her hand always returned to his lower belly. At first, Curio thought it was just a convenience. But her fingers began to lightly comb across his skin as she cleaned the wound. It was a steady, sensual rhythm.

"It's not as bad as I thought," she said. "The stitches are still firm."

And Curio was also firm. He couldn't ignore Kinara's questing down the length of his body. Her smooth fingers slid over his lower belly, ranging far beyond what was convenient positioning. While he kept his eyes closed, his breath grew hotter and his stomach tighter. The flourishes of pain from the cloth enhanced his anticipation in a way he would never have expected.

"How is he?"

Cecelia's voice was as loud as an onager stone shattering a fortress wall.

Kinara's hand withdrew with calm swiftness, but Curio twisted over his erection until the pain stopped him and he yelped.

"Just some dirt beneath the bandages. You were supposed to keep them tight."

Curio now opened his eyes and found Kinara sitting by his legs and wringing a cloth into the bowl of water. Cecelia paused in the doorway, the same bright afternoon sun creating a golden halo through her pulled-up hair. She had one hand on the base of her neck as if surprised. For a horrific instant, he thought she suspected him.

"I did as best as I could. He got into a fight, after all."

Now Kinara dropped the cloth into her basket and withdrew a ceramic jar.

"Empty that bowl," she said.

Cecelia did as she was asked, wordlessly retrieving the water bowl and taking it outside.

To his relief, all the excitement ebbed out of his body and he could safely lie on his back again. If Kinara had anything to say, she did not use the moment to make an excuse. She did not seem perturbed at all. He wondered if maybe he was imagining too much and had shamed himself with his reaction. She lifted the cover from the jar and the scent of honey salve spread over him.

When Cecelia returned with the emptied bowl, she gave Curio a glowing smile.

"Galerius is snoring now. So I thought I'd check on you."

Kinara went back to work, reapplying the salve that had rubbed off during his struggle on the ground. She used a flexible reed to apply it, the stickiness tugging his flesh as she spread it around his wound.

Cecelia sat on the opposite edge of the small bed from Kinara.

Curio lifted his head and gave a wan smile. The juxtaposition of a good and loving woman against a lascivious temptation was not lost on him. He swiftly set his head back and closed his eyes again.

"What happened to cause you to get into a fight?" Kinara asked. "My father only suggested you walk every day to rebuild your strength but not to wrestle in the streets."

"Well, I mostly wrestled with myself." He mimicked his struggles to get off the ground while Galerius took a beating. Then he described all that had happened in detail. Before he was done, Kinara had redressed his wounds and pulled his tunic tight, giving him a gentle pat on the chest.

Cecelia's expression soured as he described the belligerent Roman, and at last, she sat with both of her pale arms crossed.

"That monster should be made to pay for his crimes." She looked at Kinara. "How can we get justice in this city?"

Kinara tilted her head and drew her full brows together. She seemed to consider the question, but then only had one for Curio.

"Can you give a better description of this Roman?"

"Well, I was on the ground for all of it. I can tell you he had hairy feet. He was a big man, though everyone is big compared to me."

Cecelia put a delicate hand over her mouth and stifled a giggle. Curio smiled at her.

"He had the look of the battle-mad. Like those men who never come back from a war, even though their bodies did. I'd say he has a look somewhere between Varro and Falco, but you probably don't know them."

"I met them during your treatment," Kinara said. "You were not conscious most of that time. Varro is your commander, yes? He has a hard look and the tall one is just hard."

"That's a fair judgment. So it was that sort of look on his face, but that's the only similarity. Falco and Varro are both good men. This man looked like he wouldn't be happy if a day passed without violence. He probably tormented his family dog when he was a boy and beat up the neighborhood children." Then he added under his breath, "Though that does sound like Falco."

Kinara scratched her arms as she seemed to evaluate the description offered.

"Did he have bulging eyes and a red scar on his cheek?"

"I was on the ground. I couldn't see that kind of detail. Maybe he did. I'd have to ask Galerius, but I doubt he saw little more than fists. Do you know who he was?"

Kinara nodded.

"I could be wrong, but I think you met the man we call Taurus. I think his Roman name is Pertinax. He is a Roman expatriate who had been a prisoner during the last war with Macedonia but did not return home when released. He's famous for sending men to see my father."

"So it was nothing personal." Curio laughed and settled back down to recall this beast called Pertinax. "You call him Taurus because he's strong like a bull?"

"I suppose so," Kinara said. "And for his behavior." She began to collect her supplies back into her basket, finally rising from the edge of the bed.

"We should bring charges against him," Cecelia said. "He had no reason to nearly kill my brother."

"He's connected in Athens," Kinara said. "And you are not. For as many who are repulsed by his violence, there are just as many who are drawn to it. You won't get justice easily. You should forget him."

Curio grunted in agreement. "He didn't go back to Rome because there must be a score of people waiting for revenge."

"Actually, he married an Athenian. A good woman from a good family. It was quite the scandal."

Striking the straw mattress with his fist, he cursed. "Isn't that always the situation? So he could use his family connections against us."

"I'm not sure about that," Kinara said brightly. "He beat his wife to death a few years ago and his son died shortly after. Some say the boy died violently, though I'm not sure of the truth."

The statement drove the light out of the room, and Curio looked at Cecelia. She sat back with both hands covering her mouth and her eyes wide. He felt an immediate instinct to comfort her and assure her nothing like that would ever happen to her. Yet he could not sit up from prone without assistance, and so could only offer his best soothing voice.

"You are far away from him here," he said, indicating her jilted groom rather than Pertinax. Of course, Kinara tilted her head with a frown.

"Actually, we see him often on this street. A favorite wine house of his is down the road."

"He meant the monster my father tried to marry me to." Cecelia's small hands now made fists and her shocked expression turned to a determined frown. "My brother and I have escaped, and Curio is protecting me."

"Is that so?" Kinara's lips twisted in a smile. "Master Curio is your defender?"

"Well, before he was wounded," she said, her fists loosening and turning a doting eye to Curio. "When he is well again, I'm certain he will protect me. The gods have told me so."

"Really?" Both Curio and Kinara asked the same question at once, though Curio's was filled with more urgency. He had never heard such a thing from her or Galerius, but she perched on the edge of the bed with a beatific smile.

"Yes, right before Curio and his friends came to my father's home, just when I thought there was no hope left, the gods showed me he would arrive to take me away to safety."

"This sounds like a fascinating story," Kinara said. Her eyes flashed and she set her basket on the bed as if deciding to remain for the tale. But Curio was not ready to hear what strange ideas Cecelia had about their future.

"Actually, I am more exhausted than I was letting on," he said. "I want to rest now. How long can I use this bed, Kinara?"

"Use it for the night," she said. "The young man next door might still be unsteady after taking the draught. You both could use a long rest. But maybe your ward might accompany me. I am curious to hear how the Roman gods speak to their worshipers."

This seemed to delight Cecelia, and she slipped off the bed as if ready to race out the door. "I have nothing else to do with my two men sleeping all day. I would enjoy helping you."

Kinara gave her a cool look, and Curio could not help but feel like she was a hawk circling a mouse.

"I'd welcome the help." She looked once more to Curio. "My father will come to inspect my work later today. Just rest here, and don't go looking for trouble."

Kinara again retrieved her basket and handed it to Cecelia without a word. She took it without protest, and her face seemed to glow with the anticipation of describing her messages from the gods. Curio would have to find out the details from Galerius, who would undoubtedly know the story.

Cecelia looped the basket around her arm and then tilted her head at Kinara.

"Does this Pertinax fellow work with another Roman called Sextus?"

"Sextus? If he does, then I'm not familiar with the name. But that means little. I see more of the men he beats up than those in his employ. However, there are not many Romans in permanent residence in Athens. I do know that he rents his knowledge and contacts in the city to Romans who intend to remain here for a while. Perhaps this Sextus is a client of his come to Athens on some business."

If the description of Pertinax's brutality had driven the light from the room, then this latest revelation sucked all the warmth out of it.

"It's impossible, Cecelia." Yet Curio's voice was cold and disbelieving.

If Varro were here, he'd say the gods were at play again, and he would agree.

4

Curio heard Galerius calling out through the wall after a few hours had passed. His voice was weak and muffled, but the apartment walls were only thin wood. If Curio was a taller man, he might have been able to hang off the edge of his bed and bang the opposite wall to console him. He had awakened from the draught Kinara had fed him and now found himself abandoned. It would be disturbing and perhaps frightening given the violence earlier in the day.

He shouted back, but Galerius's shouting seemed oddly timed to match his own. Curio groaned in frustration and then grabbed his crutch. He poked across the small room, barely grazing the wall. Yet in so doing his twisting pulled at his stitches and caused him to lie still.

However, Galerius fell quiet now and Curio once more shouted.

"I'm in here! Just come over if you want to talk." He dropped the cane and closed his eyes, folding his hands over his chest as he rested on the straw mattress.

He hoped Galerius would want to talk, for he had too many questions. He knew the twins had seized a chance to escape their father when he, along with Varro and Falco, had arrived at their home. Yet he had never once heard about some sort of prediction. If the gods were naming him to strangers, then he wanted to know. However, the skeptic in him said Cecelia's fanciful dreaming might be at the bottom of it all. More than likely, she made up a story to convince her brother they could succeed in an escape. Galerius was a fine lad, but naive and unprepared to live an independent life alone in Rome.

Their entire plan was that of children barely become adults, assembled out of their misconceptions about how life worked. After all, neither of them seemed to have a plan for what the rest of their lives looked like. They were without family and status, at least if they wanted to remain out of their father's grip. He shook his head at the thought of the two of them trying to make it in Rome. How fast would the Suburra scum suck them into a mire of a criminal life or else sell them into slavery? He would give them a week.

The thought of them as slaves tensed his body. The twins had grown on him. He was grateful for their care and companionship through what would have otherwise been a lonely and tedious recovery. He had begun thinking of Galerius as a client and himself as the patron. Although his father, Cilnius, still had complete legal authority over everyone in his family and could even sell Galerius into slavery if he were so cruel. Cilnius had been Curio's enemy, but out of misguided patriotism. He could not see him treating his son so horribly.

Now he considered Cecelia. She would suffer the worst out of all this. Curio wondered if he could legally marry her when she had been promised to another man. Such points of custom and law had never troubled him before, particularly because he had not considered marriage.

Yet Cecelia was a fine woman. If the gods had deemed they should be together, then he could not ask for a better matchmaker. Although the gods' bargains always came with a price.

"What are you dreaming about?"

He screamed at Galerius's voice so close to his face and recoiled into his bed so that the thin straw mattress crushed against the wooden slats beneath it.

Opening his eyes, Galerius's swollen and bruised face hung over his own.

"For fuck's sake, if I had a sword I'd have run you through. Don't sneak up on me like that."

"Sneak? I think you fell asleep again. I came in through the door like a normal person. Where is Cecelia and what are you doing here?"

Curio let out his breath and shifted to make room for Galerius at the edge of the bed. He then explained all that had happened, of course leaving out the strangeness between him and Kinara. When it was done, they sat in silence. Outside the half-opened door, the afternoon sun no longer filled it with light. Curio glimpsed people passing by and heard their conversations. Through the wall behind him, he heard scratching and cooing pigeons.

Galerius drew a long breath when Curio finished. He put his hand to the back of his head as he explained.

"Cecelia was in a panic. Your arrival distracted my father from her betrothal plans. The night you arrived she had a dream of a woman wreathed in golden fire and wearing a silver crown. She promised by morning her husband would come to take her away to a better life. Then that man stepped out of the light. She insists the man in her dreams was you."

Curio rested with both hands folded over his chest as he stared blankly into the darkness of the ceiling. He tried to recall the night he and the others arrived as Cilnius's prisoners. They had been banged up in the fight, and he was uninterested in anything around him. Perhaps Cecelia had been watching and later used his description to convince her brother of her dream's veracity.

Yet she also seemed convinced of her visions. The gods did sometimes speak to people in their dreams or else in disguise. Usually, they communicated through omens and animals. He had never experienced anything like a divine visit, though Varro had back in Iberia. So it was not impossible that Cecelia could be a favorite of a goddess and receive a direct message.

"I don't know what to say." Curio tapped his fingers on his chest as he thought.

"Do you like my sister?" Galerius asked. "She would be good to you and make a happy home for your family."

"It doesn't matter what I want. Your father would never approve of the wedding."

"My father isn't here. Once she is your wife, then there would be little he could do."

They fell into silence and Curio tried to imagine what marriage would be like. He had his mother and father as a model, but they had been poor farmers hardly making enough to sustain themselves and their children. Their marriage was more like a mutual effort to survive until the next sunset than anything else. His older brother had married a short time, but then he died along with everyone else who caught the pox. All of his family had died and left him as the sole heir to their family name and tiny plot of farmland, such as it was. He abandoned it to join the legion.

And that had been his home and family ever since. He could not figure out how to fit a woman into it, particularly one in Cecelia's circumstances.

"Just think about it," Galerius said at length. "Also, you won't send us back to my father. Just so you know, if you decide against my sister, then once you are well again we will go our own ways."

"Of course we will." Curio's voice filled with irritation at the implied threat. "It's not like you two could follow me on my next mission."

He closed his eyes and felt Galerius rise from the bed then heard him close the door as he left. His mind raced with confused imaginings of domestic bliss and the camaraderie of Servus Capax and the legion. A life without the constant threat of violent death would be welcomed. He had served his time, and even if recalled to the legion as an evocatus he would be in the triarii. There couldn't be many more wars left now that Carthage, Macedonia, and Iberia were all settled. After a generation of war, peace was in Rome's future.

He could expand his farm and begin a family, and one day tell his sons about his adventures. But he would have little more than chores to do each day, and a routine that would never vary for the rest of his life.

How long would he be satisfied like that? He had tasted victory in the battle lines of Macedonia, rode free through the deserts of Numidia, walked beside kings in Iberia, and protected the Republic from hidden threats. Could he trade all of that for days of plowing fields and enjoying simple meals in a small garden?

For the rest of the afternoon, he rested. The morning had been too much exertion for him and he needed to recover. It still infuriated him when he thought back to his helplessness and reliance on the crutch. He had thought himself stronger, but then again, he was recuperating from a wound that should have killed him. It would take time to return to full strength.

The sound of Cecelia's voice awakened him with a start. He hadn't realized he had drifted off. She was adjusting the blanket to cover his feet. The door behind her hung open and a rose-colored light filtered inside. No one passed by the opening and the buildings cast long shadows into the empty street. Athens was closing down for the night.

"You were gone all day," he said, pulling up his feet.

"Kinara is a busy woman. I met with Doctor Nisos as well. He will visit you tomorrow since Kinara already examined you today."

"What about Galerius? He had his face punched inside out. I hoped the doctor would look at him today."

Cecelia had also bought a wooden bowl filled with meat in a brown soup, and steam curled up from it. A small cup and jug of wine also sat with it on the bedside stand.

"Kinara said he was fine. Now, sit up so I can feed you."

"I can feed myself."

Yet Cecelia would not allow it, and Curio sat up enough that he could eat the soup without spilling it. It was a savory mix of lamb meat and blood with curious spices and too little salt for his liking. Cecelia thought it disgusting, as her nose wrinkled whenever she held out a spoonful of quivering, fatty meat.

While he felt like a child and would never let Falco or Varro see something like this, he enjoyed Cecelia's attention. She used a cloth and dabbed away any soup that dribbled onto his thin beard.

"You will need to shave soon," she said. "I could help with that, though I'm not sure I know what to do."

He ate in silence, staring at this woman who claimed the gods had placed them together. Whether that was true did not matter. The more time he spent with her, the more he realized he agreed with the gods.

As he ate, he discovered on the table a small vase holding a half-dozen white flowers. He had never seen these before, and they appeared fresh. Cecelia noticed his frowning at them.

"They grow all over the city in fields between houses. I thought they were so pretty and might help cheer up this tiny room. I hope you like them."

"They are pretty flowers," Curio said. "I don't deserve your kindness. I've done nothing to earn it."

"Nonsense," she said, pouring him a cup of wine to wash down the tangy flavors of the soup. "You've protected me and my brother from my father."

"Have I?"

He stopped there. Of course he hadn't. But he did not want to talk about that detail. Instead, he sat up higher and accepted the cup from Cecelia. Rather than drink from it, he set it back down on the table and took her hands in his. Her eyes widened and she inhaled.

"I'm not sure what the future will bring. You say a goddess promised I would protect you. If you were to remain with me, then you would visit many dangerous places before I could find a place to make a home."

Cecelia blinked and bit her lip. She shook her head but seemed unable to speak. Curio squeezed her hands.

"I don't know what I'll do about that, but I know I don't want us to part. You must be brave and be prepared to live in hardship, maybe for years. But I promise I will repay your love and keep you safe."

Tears streaked down her red cheeks, shining in the low light from outside. She pulled his hands to her body and squeezed.

"I will go wherever you take me. You will never regret it."

The rose luminance of twilight lit up the fringes of her hair. For a moment, Curio imagined that she was herself a goddess wreathed in flames. He seemed to be falling toward her, her pink lips parting as he did.

"How long are you going to be in there? I'm so hungry!"

Galerius's nasal shouting coincided with his banging on the shared wall between apartments.

Cecelia nearly flew off the bed in response while Curio fell back onto the mattress.

She smoothed out her stola and slicked back her hair with both hands.

"The soup and wine were meant for both of you. Let me bring him his meal."

Her face was tomato red as she collected the bowl and wine jug. Curio watched her graceful bends and delicate movements. She flashed a smile at him as she backed up to the door.

"There are two rooms you could sleep in tonight," he said, propping up on his elbows. "I would like it if you slept here."

He shuffled aside on the narrow bed to make space. It would be cramped, but neither of them were big people.

She turned her head with a shy smile, then nodded.

So Curio waited patiently, watching the sun fade from the unbarred door and listening to the gentle murmur of brother and sister through the walls. He floated on immense satisfaction, arms folded behind his head and thoughts drifting on a warm breeze of anticipation.

When the city grew quiet and all the day's chores were done, Cecelia came to him.

The door closed behind her, and another kind of door opened in the darkness that followed. No lamps were lit, but the spark between two lovers was light enough.

She found his bed and his embrace, and together they abandoned their pains and fears in pursuit of that singular moment of clarity. When done, breathless and throbbing, they remained wrapped within each other's arms to slumber amid the silent city of Athens.

Curio did not dream. During the night, he sometimes awakened when he tried to move but Cecelia was in the way. He would stare at her outline in the darkness, enjoy her sweet, rhythmical breathing, then pull close to her again.

Then a jolt awakened him.

"It is past dawn, and you are still asleep."

He and Cecelia awakened with a start, and Curio sat up so fast that his wound burned in protest.

Kinara stood at the edge of the bed, a basket of medicines and bandages tucked underarm. She had apparently kicked the bed frame. Her thick brows were pinched in disapproval.

"I hope you did not strain your wound again last night." She set the basket down beside the bed. Cecelia pulled up the blanket to cover her nakedness, her face a shining red beacon in the pale light flowing from the open door.

"Well, nothing worse than I got from the shock of your kicking the bed." Curio shifted more of the blanket to Cecelia, who struggled to reach for her stola on the floor. "You didn't need to be so violent."

Kinara chuckled as she began to unpack her basket.

"Well, that one has to get dressed fast. My father is examining her brother right now and will be here shortly."

Cecelia let out a squeak as she tried to put on her clothes under the sheets.

"Just stand up and do it," Curio said. "I won't look if that bothers you."

She gave him a sheepish smile, and Curio turned his head. Strange that she should be so modest after their night together, but he would not question it.

"Since you two decided to sleep late, my father will see that you've spent the night in another of his apartments. I'm afraid he will have to charge you for it."

"I have the drachmae to pay him."

"It was to be my gift to you." Kinara set out clay jars on the bedside table, then put both hands on her hips as she looked around. As she did, she raised a brow to Curio. "But it seems you've found something more pleasing than a free room."

He did not know how to reply, but Cecelia helped redirect the conversation.

"I'm dressed. Kinara, how is my brother?"

"My father is reviewing him now. I'm sure he slept well. The first few times a person takes that draught, they remain dizzy and tired long after the other effects are gone."

Curio understood what she meant, and now that Cecelia was dressed, he turned to her. He took her small hand and squeezed it.

"Go see to Galerius. I'll be right here."

She swung her hand in his and seemed as if she would bring it to her lips, but then looked to Kinara and blushed. She pulled her hand back and promised to return soon.

Turning around, he found Kinara waiting on the stool beside Curio. She had no expression and appeared bored at the delay. Once Cecelia exited the room, she gestured for Curio to lay flat.

"You had an active day yesterday," she said. "You don't feel any pain?"

"Nothing worse than usual," he said. "I guess I scraped my knees yesterday while groveling. That stings, both my flesh and my pride."

Kinara chuckled and began her cleaning and examination of Curio's wounds. Her smooth fingers prodded and glided across his flesh. But they did not wander as they had yesterday.

Soon the doctor entered, and Cecelia was directly behind him. The apartment was now overcrowded, and Curio could not even see the doorway.

Doctor Nisos was an aging man with deep forehead wrinkles and possessed a bulbous nose with spacious nostrils. Yet he had a look of kindness to him as if his frequent smiles never faded from his face. Curio had trusted his warm and sympathetic voice from the first. He did not resemble his daughter, Kinara, except maybe in their thick eyebrows. His skin was a lighter olive tone than hers.

"Let's have a look, Master Curio. I understand yesterday you were reliving your legionary adventures on the city streets. You might want to wait before trying that again."

With the room crowded, Kinara packed up her basket and excused herself as her father took the stool she vacated. Cecelia remained hovering in the background as the doctor conducted his examination.

His prodding was more forceful and his testing of the stitches binding the small but deep spear wound made Curio clench his teeth. Yet he seemed pleased.

"Youth is the best armor. The shock alone from such a wound would've killed an older man. You're recovering well, Master Curio. The risk of infection is gone so long as you keep it clean and bandaged. Rest, eat well, and get mild exercise. No wrestling in the streets, please. If you are patient and keep the wound clean, you will be able to wrestle again."

"How soon is that?" Curio looked up hopefully.

Doctor Nisos put a finger beside his large nose as he thought.

"Give it a full year to be safe."

Curio's astonishment must have amused the doctor, for a pitying smile broke across his aged face.

Yet before he could comment, Kinara stuck her head through the doorway and called for her father.

"There is trouble. Pertinax is coming and he has his friends with him."

5

At the mention of Pertinax, Curio reached for his cane. Cecelia's skin grew ashen white and she staggered back against the wall.

"Remain still," Doctor Nisos said, barring Curio with his arm. "You are my patient and therefore under my protection."

"If it's the bastard from yesterday, then I don't think he cares what others want." He again stirred but the doctor's arm kept him pressed to the bed.

Doctor Nisos rose from his stool and offered it to Cecelia. All the while, Kinara remained in the doorway, holding her basket over her arm and keeping watch down the street.

The tiny apartment suddenly felt like a prison cell to Curio. When he reached for the cane again, the doctor took it and set it against the wall.

"Be sure he does not get agitated," he told Cecelia. "I will deal with the visitor."

Kinara stepped outside and Doctor Nisos followed. The door shut with a thin puff of air.

Cecelia did not sit but pressed both hands to her chest and stared at the door as if trying to look through it.

"What about Galerius?"

"Warn him through the wall," Varro said. "It's thin enough for him to hear you. And give me my cane."

"No, the doctor said you shouldn't get up. I don't want you going outside and getting in another fight."

Yet that was precisely what Curio wanted. Of course, he realized that he could not even battle a field mouse, never mind a madman twice his height. Yet it wasn't logic ruling his heart now. He had a score to settle with this bastard, not to mention he had promised to defend Cecelia.

She had banged on the wall and warned Galerius of Pertinax's approach. Curio couldn't hear his answer other than muffled curses.

Then the doctor's voice was loud through the door. These apartments were made of mud walls on brick foundations and partitioned with flimsy wood walls and doors. Sound carried through them easily, and the doctor was just outside.

"I'm looking for Centurion Camilus Curio and a boy who was with him. I understand they came here after I ran into them yesterday."

It was the rocky voice of the man who had confronted them yesterday morning. Curio sat up, all his muscles tensing. Cecelia backed against the far wall with a gasp, both hands cupping her face.

At first, he did not know how Pertinax knew his name, and then realization struck. He had named himself and even gave his rank. How foolish, he thought. It must have made tracking them down much easier for Pertinax.

If Sextus was working with him, then he would know Galerius and Cecelia were here. His name and rank plus the coincidence of having a young man in his company would be too tempting to overlook. However, he realized Cecelia herself had not been identified. Some of his tension eased when he understood Pertinax might simply be investigating a lead—or here on an entirely different matter.

"The identity of my patients and their treatments is not a matter of public record." Doctor Nisos's voice was clear and its warmth had changed into defiance.

He heard someone laugh and then Pertinax's stony voice again.

"So that confirms it. They're here. Otherwise, you'd ask me if I was his relative or something rather than try to send me away."

Then he began speaking Greek.

Again, Curio nearly leaped off the bed, stopped by his infirmity and Cecelia's warning hiss.

He hated not knowing what they discussed. So much information was passing within earshot, but none of it made sense. Of course, the doctor would tell him what happened. But it would be a summary filled with the doctor's conclusions versus his own observations. Curio had long ago learned to trust his eyes and ears before those of others.

The exchange between the doctor and Pertinax did not escalate as he imagined it would. Even Cecelia's hands eventually lowered to her side and she finally sat on the stool beside the bed. Both of them listened intently for anything that might indicate an escalation of troubles.

At length, the two men had reached a conclusion. While Curio did not understand Greek, he caught the tone of a concluding conversation. If others were accompanying Pertinax, none of them made any sounds.

Cecelia shared a nervous look with Curio, who sat up on his elbows as far as his injury would allow. He smiled to assure her nothing bad would happen, but her thin brows furrowed and she folded her hands on her lap.

The group was breaking up now. He heard Doctor Nisos saying farewell and could even imagine Pertinax moving off. Somehow the doctor had deflected him, or else Pertinax had unrelated business. Curio, at last, lied down again.

Then the door burst open.

Cecelia shrieked, and Curio bolted upright, caught only by the limits of his injury. Doctor Nisos shouted in protest, but the bulky form of Pertinax had already entered the small apartment. His muscular arm held the doctor away, and the other pressed the door open.

His face was not unhandsome but filled with an ugly belligerence worsened by his self-congratulating smile. He had a thin, curved scar running from beneath his left eye into his high nose.

"Centurion Camillus Curio! As I thought!"

Then, his bulging eyes settled on Cecelia.

She squealed and fell back to the rear wall, picking up the stool and holding the legs forward to defend herself.

Curio railed against his impotence, shouting for his cane and thrashing on the bed.

But Pertinax did not move, nor did he say anything more. He simply stared at Cecelia as if he had unearthed buried treasure. His eyes widened, and his smile faded.

Then a commotion came from outside, and Pertinax's followers shouted and cursed.

Galerius had come to their aid and now spread chaos outside of the apartment.

Yet within, Curio, Cecelia, and Pertinax all remained locked in silence.

The cane was out of his reach, but Curio decided he could leap off the bed and intercept Pertinax before he could get farther into the room. He shimmied to the edge and slowly worked himself upright.

Then the shouting outside gained Pertinax's attention. He turned to face the doorway.

Curio leapt.

He thudded to the mosaic floor and landed on his shoulder, legs still firmly entangled in the bedsheet. His torso bent at an angle that tormented his wound. The sizzling pain shocked him into immobility. Yet he forced himself to fight through it. His hands flailed out, grabbing at nothing. Pertinax had already left.

"What are you doing?"

Cecelia tossed the stool aside and rushed to pull him flat to the floor. He slithered out onto the cold, gritty mosaic stones and straightened out to relieve the pressure on his wound.

"Protecting you, of course."

Cecelia's face hovered over his and she blinked in astonishment. Then the cursing and shouting of her brother drew her away.

"Don't hurt yourself again. Stay still."

He could not abide that command and rolled over to grab his cane which had fallen to the floor in the commotion. Cecelia stood in the doorway, hands on her head and shouting her brother's name. He could hear Doctor Nisos and Kinara likewise shouting amid other voices. Curio thought of the brawl that followed the traffic accident yesterday. The thought of a mob gathering gave Curio the strength to stand.

Bracing the crutch against the wall, he was able to leverage it as well as an offered hand. It took longer than he wanted, but once he was on his feet, he leaned against the wall to rest his agonized side. Being confined to a bed for weeks had weakened him, and now that he needed his former strength, he found himself helpless.

Still, he pulled Cecelia back by the shoulder, intending to enter the fray outside.

"Get back into the room."

She whirled in surprise which turned to instant anger.

"What are you doing? You'll make your wound worse."

Rather than answer, he guided her back from the door. Galerius was once more on his back in the street, and Kinara hovered over him as she gathered cloth from her basket. The doctor stood in the middle of the street, his mild demeanor subsumed into his outrage. He raised his fist in the air and shouted in Greek as Pertinax and a small group of his followers walked down the gently sloping street.

Even more men surrounded the doctor, and others chased off Pertinax's gang, although none of them got too close.

"Is he all right?" Curio asked, hobbling close to Galerius.

"I'm fine!" The nasal reply was rife with humiliation, which Curio understood too well.

"He just fell in the scuffle," Kinara said.

Cecelia pushed past Curio to kneel by her twin brother's side. Yet

Kinara blocked her as she reviewed his face and head. Cecelia strained to see over her shoulder, her voice desperate.

"What did he want? Was Sextus with him?"

Yet Kinara did not answer and continued to work on Galerius, who twitched and complained whenever she prodded his face.

"Come inside," Curio said. "The doctor is coming back and will explain."

He had just hopped back to the bed and Cecelia uprighted the stool when Doctor Nisos entered.

At first, he cursed in Greek, or at least whatever he said sounded like it to Curio. His pleasant face was now creased with outrage and his cheeks reddened. Outside the door, his followers milled around and chatted excitedly in their language. Curio lay back on the bed.

"I fell getting out of bed." He would rather not imagine how he must have looked like a speared fish flopping to the floor.

Doctor Nisos groaned and narrowed his eyes at Curio.

"I told you not to exert yourself. I just examined you. You're fine, and I don't need to do it again."

It seemed he was so disgusted he wanted to leave. Yet he sighed and shrugged before taking the stool beside the bed. He was rougher this time, his anger and impatience coming through his abrupt motions. Yet as he conducted his reexamination, he became more absorbed in his work and he calmed.

Curio endured more painful prodding of his stitches but resolved not to express anything. It felt like the doctor had mistaken his wound for a lyre the way he tugged on them. Yet in the end, he bandaged Curio's torso, leaning close enough for him to smell the doctor's sweat. When he sat back, he sighed again.

"There was some blood this time, but nothing serious. If you keep twisting that area you are going to tear it wide open. If that happens, and no one is around to help you...."

Curio had seen men unspool their guts through puncture wounds no bigger than a thumb. He was lucky that hadn't been his fate the first time. A second time, he might not be so lucky.

"You've got to take care of yourself," Cecelia chided. Her voice was once again silvery smooth but full of genuine worry.

"How's Galerius?" He knew what he had to do, and did not want to think about it anymore. He hated being bedridden.

Doctor Nisos wiped his hands on a cloth.

"He's annoying. Also, he's in your bed. You know this apartment was not yours to take. Fortunately, your companions paid a generous fee for your care. I am honored that they placed so much trust in me. But he does not need the bed anymore. It's just a broken nose, which has been expertly set. He'll be fine if he stops trying to fight Pertinax. What did you tell him to make him leave?"

Curio blinked, then looked to Cecelia leaning against the wall. Had she said or done something to make him retreat? She shrugged.

After explaining Pertinax's reaction, Doctor Nisos furrowed his brows and rubbed his chin.

"He has always been a strange man, prone to wild swings in his mood. Before he entered, he was determined to find you and Galerius. But you say he just looked at her and left?"

He pointed to Cecelia, who nodded in confirmation. The doctor raised his shoulders and sighed.

"When he came out, he just ordered his followers to leave. He gave no reason for his change of heart."

"We won't reject that gift," Curio said with a weak smile.

They all sat in thoughtful silence, listening to Galerius just outside the door complaining to Kinara about her treatment. At last, the doctor stood. His sagging posture told Curio he had more unpleasant things to say.

"Look, your companions paid your fees for months ahead of time. They were not sure when they could return for you."

Curio sat up at the mention of Varro and Falco. They had promised to return soon, which he knew was a platitude.

"I would've been happy to keep you here. But I cannot risk trouble with Pertinax and his ilk. I have other patients and I don't want them harassed or my property damaged when he decides to return. I will refund the unused payment to you. You will be able to find suitable lodging elsewhere with it. You can leave word with me where you are, so your friends can find you upon their return."

Cecelia shrank back against the wall as the doctor spoke and covered her mouth. Curio realized this might be the outcome of today's conflict, but he still felt surprised at the suddenness.

"Pertinax could still trouble you for my location," he said. "He might decide to beat it out of you."

Doctor Nisos's forehead wrinkles scrunched together.

"In that case, don't tell me anything. Just go. Watch for your friends' return. I will have Kinara bring you the unused payment today."

Curio nodded and Cecelia remained pinned to the wall in shock. The doctor's face reddened.

"You are mostly healed, Master Curio. Just rest and keep the wound clean. Get activity every day and you will rebuild your strength. You don't need my constant care now. If you worsen, then come back discreetly."

He sounded like a man convincing himself of his decisions. Yet Curio gave a solemn nod.

"Is there anywhere I can stay that Pertinax won't find me?"

"Athens is a large and old city with many secret places. Of course, I'm not familiar with them, but I know they exist. You might need to find someone who knows one. I think Kinara might have some ideas. I would suggest starting with an inn across the city from here. But keep moving or else Pertinax will eventually catch up. If he intends to find you, his connections will aid him."

"Then I better make connections with someone who hates him." Curio gave a bitter smile and scratched beneath his torso bandage. "It shouldn't be too hard given what I've heard."

"Many hate him specifically because they fear him. Most Athenians would rather avoid trouble with his kind. I don't know what you've done to attract his attention, but you've made a powerful enemy here."

Curio knew why Pertinax was after him, and it was not personal.

Sextus must be employing his services, as improbable as that seemed. He was actually after the twins.

The three stood in silence until the doctor left without another word. Once he was gone, Cecelia rushed to his side.

"What are we going to do now? We don't speak Greek. How are we going to avoid that monster while we are waiting for the others?"

Forgetting the bliss of just the last hour, his shoulders tightened with anger. He wanted to ask what the plan would have been if she and her brother had not attached themselves to him. None of this was his problem, and now his recovery was at risk because of it. If Pertinax decided to work him over, then his injury might become permanent, ending his soldiering career at the least and likely forcing him into the ranks of war veterans begging in the streets of Rome. Suddenly, he wished he hadn't turned his head to so many of them.

Yet Cecelia continued to stare expectantly, and those innocent eyes burned away any anger he felt.

"We won't need to hide long." He took her trembling hand and held it to his side. "Varro and Falco will send word soon, and we'll relocate far from this place."

Cecelia's thin brows remained creased in worry.

"Are you certain? Why did Pertinax want to see you? It must be that Sextus is here on behalf of my father. He is paying that beast to hunt us down so he can drag us back home."

"We don't know that for certain."

"But it seems likely, doesn't it? You said he mentioned a man by the name of Sextus. You heard what Kinara said about Pertinax. It all makes perfect sense."

"But why would Sextus be here in the first place?"

Miffed by this question, Cecelia withdrew her hand. "I'll go check on Galerius."

Curio remained resting on the bed as Cecelia stepped out into the morning sunshine. Originally, he had complaints about the doctor's beds. They lacked depth and the straw stuffing was close to rotting. Changing it when he was bedridden had been impossible, and the smell annoyed him. Yet now he would not be sleeping on the doctor's bed tonight. He would probably be sleeping on the floor of a shared room amid flea-ridden drunks.

Yet he had to remain positive if they were going to last long enough for Varro and Falco to return. More than likely, they would send a message to the doctor, probably summoning Curio to their location. In any case, he had to endure a few weeks until that message arrived. To leave earlier would invite confusion and perhaps separate them permanently.

He flattened out on the bed, enjoying it for the last time before the rest of his stay became a cat-and-mouse chase through Athens.

6

The room Kinara had found them was cheap and smelled of sweat, but larger than the doctor's apartment. Curio got the use of the bed, which was little more than a low table piled with what might have once been a stuffed mattress. Now it was a stained wool pile that barely provided cushion. A small lamp guttered on the tiny round table where both Galerius and Cecelia sat. She was examining Galerius's face for the twentieth time this hour. Curio had counted. He was glad she was no longer peeking under his wrap.

"It has only been a day," Galerius said, patiently staring through the dim light at the cracked plaster wall. "My nose is not healed yet."

"But the swelling is so much better now." Her voice was silvery bright as she tilted her head to inspect her brother's face from a new angle.

Curio smiled and turned to stare at the ceiling. The room was well within their means, and they paid extra for anonymity. He supposed someone could outbid him, and the innkeeper would reveal their hiding place. But Kinara had promised this was a good place to remain unknown.

While brother and sister murmured to each other, Curio's mind drifted. He thought back to last night when they fled by cart from the doctor's apartment. Kinara had gifted him wrappings, salves, and a set of sponges to use for cleaning the wound. She interrogated Cecelia on how she planned to care for his wound since she could not do it herself.

Cecelia passed Kinara's test, and she happily proclaimed, "We are to be married. I will work tirelessly to keep my husband healthy."

Kinara raised her lush brow at the statement but did not say more before putting them in the cart. They had to travel while Pertinax's cronies were not watching. It seemed an unnecessary precaution, given that he had not returned all day nor had anyone else troubled them. Still, Pertinax might be just as able to learn their movements by intimidating the locals.

Just before they left, Kinara checked Curio's bindings one last time while he lay flat in the cart bed. Cecelia and Galerius were seated in the front with the driver. She slipped his cane beside him, then took his hand in hers as she leaned over him.

"It might be wiser to split up. Let them hide in one place and you hide in another. This way, Pertinax does not catch all three of you in one swoop."

"I still need help getting up," Curio said with a weak smile. "I can't be alone just yet."

It had been gloomy in the early evening, with light like the murky amber globe filling the room now. He could not read her expression, but she stared hard at him as if thinking. Then she leaned closer.

"I know a place where you could hide near me. I would remain with you during the day and care for you like always."

"But you've got other patients and your father wouldn't approve."

"I would make the time. We only have four other patients in residence. Most of the day, I'm not even doing medical work. Who do you think prepares your meals and draws water from the well each day? It's women's work."

Now he could see her eyes shining in the dark. She seemed to be congratulating herself on her unassailable logic. Yet Curio sighed.

"Cecelia will have to do that for us now." He stretched his other arm to place it over Kinara's. "I appreciate what you are suggesting. Even though I'm in no shape for it, I am responsible for the twins. They are adults only in name. They still need my guidance, and I can't leave them alone."

"But none of you speak Greek."

"I'll let my hands communicate for me." He lifted his hand pointing at imagined goods and holding up his fingers to indicate what he wanted. "I'm just going to be lying on my back most of the time, anyway."

The driver complained about getting underway, and now Galerius turned around to look. Kinara withdrew from the cart and promised she would come to check his progress periodically.

Now he shifted on the bed and ran his hands over the bandage, the same one Kinara had wrapped yesterday. Given he had spent an intensely boring day in the room on this bed, it was not dirty. The only excitement had been walking in the alley behind the inn. Without crowds to worry him, he could even walk a short distance without his cane.

Cecelia had brought up meals from the inn downstairs and now collected the plates to return them. While she was away, Galerius began to ready their bedrolls for the night.

"Are we really going to hide here until the others send for you?"

Curio listened to the bedrolls spreading out on the floor. Beyond that, he could hear the conversations of other patrons below.

"It's not much different than being in the doctor's apartment."

"Maybe for you. But I was getting to learn the city. Now I'm no better off than you."

"Well, you look worse than me, to be honest."

He sat back on the bedroll, testing his swelling. "Cecelia said it looked better today. Anyway, how did Sextus find us here?"

"I don't think he was specifically looking for you in Athens." Curio now sat up, propping his back against the wall. "He might've been passing through on the way to where he knew we headed. After all, he had seen that map you stole. Your father knew we were heading this way, and sent his hound after you. When he stopped here, he probably learned of Pertinax and contacted him on the off-chance of news of your passing through. Athens is a common stop along the way to Crete. Like a fool, I had just given him my name and rank. He saw you. Now he had something to sell Sextus and we have a problem."

"What luck." Galerius continued to unfold the rolls. "Why do you think he ran off after seeing my sister?"

"Haven't you seen how she looks when she's mad?"

At first, Galerius cocked his head but then laughed as Curio imitated a scratching cat.

"I hope we don't see him again, and Centurion Varro sends his orders soon." Now Galerius leaned on the bed and patted Curio's arm. "Then we'll be brothers. Cecelia is not satisfied unless she is caring for someone who appreciates it. You will be a happy man being married to her."

"I can't believe it," he said, once more flattening out on the bed. "I want to recover as fast as possible and clear up things with your father. I can't have him at war with me for the rest of my life. Then there's the man she is promised to."

"He's a piece of shit," Galerius said. "You can buy him off. My father eventually will see reason, especially once he understands that you're a hero and not what he believes you are. Anyway, Cecelia is worth your trouble."

Curio did not answer but agreed nonetheless. Cecelia returned, oblivious to their conversation.

Soon, they settled for the night and fell asleep. All except Curio, who listened for their breathing to steady and their sleep to deepen.

Whether he was ready for this adventure, he did not know. If things went as he hoped, they would all be able to sleep easier.

Earlier, he had secreted a portion of their drachmae into another pouch. The twins had not concerned themselves with money, a holdover from their easy lives as children of a wealthy merchant. They did not know how much he had been refunded and expected Curio to handle expenses. Now he took the pouch, then quietly drew up his cane as he levered himself upright.

He hadn't been honest with Kinara yesterday. He could sit up, although slowly and with discomfort. When he was sitting on the edge of the flimsy bed, he rested a moment to be sure the twins did not stir.

Moving unseen and silently had been his specialty since childhood. Using this ability coupled with his gregarious curiosity, he had navigated a harsh youth by either evading or befriending his enemies. He just hoped all the downtime had not dulled them, as he needed both tonight.

He wore his cloak, tied his tunic belt, and even secreted a knife behind his back. It was for kitchen work but could serve in a desperate defense. He did it all without a sound, even as he rested on his crutch. The twins remained gently snoring, two lumps spread on the floor by his bed. He stepped between them with exaggerated care.

Then he was downstairs and navigating through the backrooms to where the alley service door was bolted. A slave slept in the far corner of the kitchen but did not raise his head. To Curio, the cane had sounded like a banging drum. But his touch was still light, and now he was ambling down the alleyway with it barely making a tap on the hard earth.

Athens was asleep, but he was absolutely confident that Pertinax and his ilk thrived during this hour. At least his cronies would be searching for him, even if the man himself was otherwise abed.

The moonless, starry night only enhanced the ancient loneliness of this city. Despite how large it loomed in the popular imagination, Athens seemed little better than a sleeping village now. He watched for danger as he waddled down the unpaved streets. He was searching for Pertinax, but other trouble might find him first.

Curio knew they could not evade the man forever. Varro and Falco might still be en route to Senator Flamininus even now. Many more weeks would pass before they sent word to him. He had seen the lie in Varro's eyes when he promised to return soon. Same for Falco. He was like a brother to Curio, a man he understood too well. He didn't even meet his eyes when promising Curio wouldn't be alone for long.

Therefore, he would never evade Pertinax before they came for him.

He had to sue for peace.

While Pertinax had been a drunken brute and had visited unrestrained violence on innocent Galerius, he seemed to have some sense of honor. He had expressed disgust at having knocked over Curio, whom he called a cripple. When his bloodlust had been slaked, he regretted what he did and tried to buy forgiveness from Galerius.

Pertinax was not a model citizen. He wasn't even a good man. Yet Curio believed somehow he could reach an agreement with a fellow Roman and soldier. If anything, he believed a higher bidder could buy out Pertinax.

While he had no idea what his fees were, they must all be negotiated. He was not like a shop owner with established prices for common goods. His value was in connections and information for sale to fellow Romans who lacked both in this tradition-bound city. The price had to be variable. Now, if he understood rich merchants, he guessed Sextus had only been provided the minimum funds needed to complete his task. Of course, this was all for Cilnius's children and he might have been more generous.

But Sextus would've been conditioned to stinginess and probably haggled Pertinax to his lowest rate.

Curio was counting on that. If he had to spend his silver cycling through hiding places, he'd rather spend it to buy out Pertinax instead. It seemed the sort of risk Varro would take in this situation, and so here he was limping down the streets hoping to pick up someone's attention who could lead him to Pertinax.

That person appeared about a dozen streets over from where he had started. By this time, Curio was gasping and dripping sweat despite the cool night air. His muscles ached along the backs of his arms and shoulders. Now a man blocked the street before him and he forgot all his pains.

The lone figure was squat with muscular shoulders that made his head appear to vanish into his torso. He suspected others lurked in the indigo shadows filling the sides of the street. The stars glittered above the figure, appearing over the abrupt line of the Acropolis in the distance.

"I'm looking for Pertinax," he announced. He realized that Latin would be useless among the thieves of Athens and so tried his miserable Greek pronunciation of the nickname, "Taurus."

The man spoke in a threatening voice, none of it making sense, and his chuckle was unfriendly. Others stirred in the shadows to either side of the road. But Curio continued to repeat both Latin and Greek names until it appeared the squat man understood.

Curio found himself led off the main road to where others hid in the shadows of a square, dark building. They allowed him into an unlit room, and Curio hobbled through the opened door. Had they wanted to bash his head open, they did not need to do it in this room. He had provided them a half-dozen opportunities already.

Yet still, his heart raced, and he felt the small knife at his back and the weight of the coins on his hip. The room was utterly black until a lamp flared. An old woman with a massive black wart on her cheek set it on a round table along with a clay mug and wine jug. She then vanished back into the shadows as silently as a ghost.

The squat Greek pointed at the stool and seemed to be instructing him to wait.

He sat for over an hour as sweat trickled down his back and his grip nearly crushed the mug. He felt as if he existed only in the bubble of yellow light. The wine was worse than vinegar, but he sipped from the mug for fear of giving offense. Perhaps someone watched from the darkened corners, but he would have had to be quieter than a mouse. Curio was certain he was alone with the lamp and the vague odor of garbage permeating the room.

At the end of his hour-long wait, the door rattled as a deep voice spoke on the opposite side. Then it opened and Pertinax stood framed in the opening.

At least he was the right size and shape based on Curio's memory. He had mostly ever seen the man from flat on his back. Tonight he would meet him as an equal, though the cane resting against his leg seemed to press him as a reminder of his true condition.

"You're a brave man to come into the streets at night calling my name."

It was Pertinax's voice, and he could hear the smile in it.

"I didn't know how else to find you. There's no sense in running all over this city trying to avoid you."

"The twins?"

Pertinax swept into the room and closed the door behind himself with a dull thump. He stepped into the bubble of yellow light, which cast deep shadows over his muscles and enhanced his ferocious stature.

"They're asleep and have no idea where I am."

He suddenly thought of them awakening and discovering his absence. Cecelia had often checked on him at night in the early days of his recovery. He hoped they both slept through this and did not do something foolish like go searching for him.

"I'd have come sooner if I knew you were waiting here." Pertinax pulled up another stool and sat across from Curio. There was a second mug waiting for him, but he only slid it aside with the back of his strong hand. The scar on his face seemed deeper in the uncertain light.

"But you came." Curio smiled, hoping he sounded as confident as Varro would in the same situation. For a man who held so many doubts about himself, he always seemed assured and confident. If Curio had not spent so much time with him, he would never know otherwise. "Now, it's late and I need to return soon. Let's not waste any more time."

Pertinax's wild eyes narrowed with a smile and he folded his strong arms and tilted his head.

"You don't understand your situation, do you, Centurion Curio?"

"I understand enough. A man from the Mutina area arrived here recently. He calls himself Sextus and has a Second Legion tattoo on his arm and a red scar over his nose." Curio traced the bridge of his nose with his finger. "He wanted news about three Roman centurions escorting two young twins, a boy and a girl. He named the centurions to you, mine included. Despite being as drunk as you were when we met, you remembered my name. Once you gave it to him, he described the twins and it matched what you remembered about the boy. Now Sextus wants you to deliver them to him."

Pertinax leaned back and rubbed his chin, his smirk fading.

"That's a good bit of deduction work, Centurion. Of course, seeing how you kidnapped them, you should know your pursuers."

Now Curio smirked. "That's not the truth. They're fleeing their father. But tell me, do you care about the truth? You're not helping Pertinax because he's a fellow Roman in distress. He paid you. How much?"

"Enough. Anyway, you can't take back what I told him already. The two of us are no longer in business together. He needed information, and I provided it. It's up to him to find and catch you."

Curio's hand lingered over his purse, but it froze in place with this new revelation.

"You mean, you did not come looking for us yesterday to take us away?"

"No, I just needed to confirm the girl is here, too. I told him where to find you, and warned him that snatching two people who are barely adults out of Doctor Nisos's hospital would go badly with the city elders. Of course, for a sum, I could help him with that. So, he's deciding how much he can afford right now."

The light seemed to twist Pertinax's face into a leer, but in a blink, it was again impassive. He stared at Curio with hooded eyes that noted his hand beneath the table. He quickly set it on the board to show he meant no trouble.

"Why did you look at Cecelia like that and then flee? You could've delivered all three of us to Sextus at that moment."

Pertinax withdrew out of the lamp's light, almost as if he had recoiled from the question. He folded his arms and it sounded as if he growled at the thought. Yet it became a thick cough, and at last, he poured wine from the clay jug. After gulping it and grimacing at the taste, he stared at Curio.

"She is beautiful. I can see why her father wants to marry her to a rich man. She can command that kind of husband."

"She's not that beautiful." Curio felt a twinge of shame for denigrating his future wife's appearance. While a good-looking woman, primarily from the glow of a pampered childhood and a kind spirit, she was not one to calm a raging bull with her smile. Yet she had done so to Pertinax.

"Then you have poor taste. I would have her for myself if she wasn't promised to another." His eyes seemed to behold her now, growing out of focus as he rolled the clay mug between his strong hands.

"I don't think she'd have you." Curio straightened up on the chair and strengthened his voice.

"Really? Then she's running off with you, is she? You're the kind of man she wants? Small and unthreatening, just like her mousy brother."

Curio's instincts warned he was headed into a conflict he should avoid. As much as it galled him, he held up both hands in denial.

"Not at all. She's escaping from a marriage she does not want."

"And who cares what she wants?" Pertinax leaned forward, his eyes flashing. "You? All this trouble because you hope a stranger's daughter will enjoy a happy marriage? Do you take me for a fool? You want her for yourself. It's the only reason you're doing this."

Curio found himself stuttering and Pertinax folded his arms in victory. He laughed and then turned his head aside as if brushing off the conversation.

"I'm just teasing you, Centurion. She is a beauty. Looks just like my deceased wife. So much it scared me. Yes, I left you because of that. I'm not ashamed to admit it. But I also fulfilled my contract to locate you for Sextus. I wasn't obligated to bring you to him."

"Then you're currently unemployed?"

Pertinax shrugged. "I suppose so."

"Then I'll hire you to misinform Sextus. Tell him we escaped the city by ship and headed for Crete. Tell him I had been left behind by the others due to my injury and now I am running from him. He'll believe that."

Curio thought Sextus would be expecting them to head toward the location on the map Galerius had stolen. He would not know they had already completed that mission. As Varro often said, you can get a man to accept any lie as long as he is predisposed to believe it.

Pertinax tilted his head and touched his chin in imitation of deep thought. "Well, for a price I could do that. But he might not believe me. I think it will cost you twenty drachmae."

"What? How much money do you think I have?"

"Twenty drachmae, at least. The twins are rich, aren't they? Plus I threw a handful of coins on the boy."

"Those were obols," Curio said. He imitated squeezing an empty pouch with his left hand. "That would leave me with nothing to survive on. I'll give you ten drachmae to ensure Sextus accepts the lie as truth. He won't be hard to convince, I promise."

Pertinax squinted at Curio as if considering, then sighed.

"Ah, you really don't understand your circumstances, do you? Why did it take me so long to get here? Think on it, Centurion Curio."

The two Romans stared at each other in the dim and fluttering light of the clay lamp between them. The clay mugs cast dancing shadows on the table as Curio thought.

Then he raised his eyes to Pertinax's. The lamp flame danced in their reflections as he smirked.

"You went to fetch Sextus. By Jupiter, you brought him with you."

7

The cane pressing on Curio's leg checked his impulse to flee the dim room before Pertinax could seize him. Any struggle or rapid action might worsen his wound on the verge of healing. Yet his heart already thumped as if he had burst into a run, even though he remained seated at the table across from his smug enemy.

Rather than grab at Curio, Pertinax reached for the clay jug and poured himself another mug of wine. Despite the sudden revelation that Sextus and his men waited outside for him, nothing disturbed the placid midnight of Athens. The only change was Curio's panic, and he realized he could achieve nothing in his physical condition. Therefore, he drew a long breath and tried to ease his racing pulse. This drew derisive laughter from Pertinax.

"You understand now, Centurion Curio. I bet it stings worse knowing you set the trap for yourself."

Curio licked his lips and felt the heat on his face.

"I admit, I feel foolish."

This drew real laughter from Pertinax, who paused to gulp the wine. It ran in thin red lines down his rough-shaven chin as he drained the mug. When done, he gasped but refilled the mug again.

"You, Sextus, me, and the twins, all of us are foreigners here. But I'm the only one with any anchors. All of us fine Roman citizens lost in a strange world of the Greeks and their traditions. The funniest thing is that all of you depend on me. The Athenians don't want to be bothered with foreigners, especially Romans. If they offend the wrong one, they could have the legions at their gates tomorrow. So, they're fine to let me deal with Romans, and they only deal with me."

While Pertinax gloated at his self-importance, Curio's mind raced ahead. He wasn't going to outrun anyone. His mind was his only weapon now. He wished Varro were here to talk his way out of this mess. A score of half-formed thoughts flitted through his mind before one caught.

"Sextus won't pay you. You're better off accepting my offer."

Halfway through his third mug of wine, he paused to look over its rim and cock his eyebrow. The mostly empty mug deepened the pitch of his voice.

"He has already paid me."

Curio shook his head. "For the information you provided. But you're charging a fee for delivering me, which will lead him to the twins. Now, I know he has not paid you for apprehending them on his behalf. Because that's exactly what he asked you to do. His master warned him not to make trouble where he does business. Seeing how he is based out of the east coast, he certainly trades with Athens. So, I've already guessed the truth and can guarantee Sextus will short your fees."

Without finishing his mug, Pertinax set it on the table. He drew his bulk together and leaned on his elbows.

"Tell me what you're thinking, Centurion."

"You can turn me over to Sextus. But I'm just a source of information with limited value. When he finds the twins, he'll note Galerius's broken nose and swollen face. A detail I'm sure you omitted in reports to your client. When he sees this, and the twins point their fingers at you, Sextus will cut your fee."

Pertinax stared at him flatly. Curio met his formerly brilliant eyes.

They were now clouded with doubt. His voice was low and threatening.

"He wouldn't do that in my city."

"But it's not your city," Curio said. "You just explained it yourself. You exist at the Athenian's pleasure. They won't care if one Roman kills another Roman. Sextus didn't show up by himself, did he? His master is a wealthy and powerful merchant. He dines with consuls and senators. You have thugs at your command. He has soldiers."

Pertinax gritted his teeth as he imagined the conflict Curio constructed for him.

"Listen, you and I don't need to be enemies. Sextus will promise you more drachmae than me, but you will be lucky to get half of it. He's a merchant's trusted servant. You know those types. They haggle no matter how small the matter. With me, I need your help and will pay you the twenty drachmae you asked for. No need for fighting in the streets."

At last, Pertinax held up his hand.

"Enough. At first, this seemed like an interesting job. But it has become boring to me and I'm losing sleep and drinking piss out of a jug for nothing. I hadn't thought about the son. I could set this up so Sextus can't complain. Though, I'm not sure I like him that much. You're less irritating than him. That's a compliment, too, since I don't care for self-important officers."

Curio did not care for compliments from scum like Pertinax, but he inclined his head nonetheless.

"Let me go, and tell Sextus whatever you want. The story about us fleeing to Crete will still sound convincing to him. So, he goes away and you still profit. I can't see how you lose in this."

Something like conflict passed over his face, but soon he sat back and gave a conspiratorial smile.

"He came with a full crew, but most are still at the port in Piraeus. If he got uptight with me, he might try to bring them ashore. But it's a long walk here, and I have friends at the harbor who could make his life miserable."

Curio could not remember the port and the journey up the long, walled road to Athens. The defended road was unlike anything else in the world. He regretted being only half-conscious when traveling upon it.

Now he set his pouch of drachmae on the table. The leather muffled the clinking of the coins.

"Count them if you don't trust me," he said, then looked over his shoulder. "There must be a back way out of this room."

Pertinax scooped the coins off the table and nodded. "The hag will show you out."

"Then it's agreed? You will accept the coins and get Sextus off our trail?"

"I'll tell him what you said, and if he does not accept the lie then he's still your problem."

Curio's fists tightened under the table. He disliked this man, and if he had not been recovering from a nearly mortal wound he might teach him a lesson about size and strength. Instead, he pursed his lips as if considering options.

"You will also leave us alone?"

Pertinax spread the pouch open to look inside, then stuffed it into his tunic. His predatory eyes examined Curio.

"I want the woman. I'll make a better husband for her than whomever she was running from."

Curio had already taken his cane, expecting to conclude their business with a dismissive grunt. This set him back on his chair, the cane slipping from his hand to slide to the floor. The wooden thump echoed in the stunned silence. Pertinax's deadly expression did not shift.

"She will be happy with me. She'll be safer than staying with you. You've got powerful enemies. They'll eventually run you down."

Snorting with laughter, Curio shook his head. "Safer with you? You beat your wife to death. How can you say that?"

Now Pertinax shot up from the table, the mad rage flushing his face crimson. His eyeballs bulged as he roared into the murky room.

"That whore Kinara slanders me! Who else could have told you such a thing?"

Curio reached behind himself, seeking the small knife he secreted there. Yet Pertinax only stood rigidly before the table. Curio understood why they called him Taurus, the bull. His eyes were wide and jaundiced and his nostrils flared like a wild beast.

"Don't do anything to her. She just answered my questions about you."

He realized how vulnerable he was to Pertinax at this moment. The beast could snap him in half if he wanted or drag him by the hair into the street and then toss him at Sextus's mercy. Curio could not physically match him, but he did not need to act like he realized it. Instead, he summoned his officer's voice.

"Pertinax, we have made our deal. Calm yourself and do your part in it. We will address our other matters later."

The two men stared at each other, giant Pertinax looming over boyish Curio seated on his chair, hand on the hilt of the knife behind his back. Pertinax heaved like his namesake animal, but Curio did not flinch. He simply waited for the rage to ebb, which it did. After long and breathless moments, Pertinax relaxed his posture.

"We have a deal, Centurion. But we're not done yet. Follow the hag, and I'll tell Sextus you slipped me. He might want to chase you. So be wary. I don't want him getting to you before I do."

Curio tilted his head, then bent to search for his fallen cane. Their eyes never unlocked as Curio swept his hand over to the floor, grabbing his cane, then rising slowly to his feet. He left the knife tucked into the belt at his back.

Pertinax then called out in Greek, and the old woman with the massive wart reappeared. After a clipped exchange, she picked up the lamp and then looked at Curio with disinterested, watery eyes.

He followed her out, only to pause long enough to look back at Pertinax watching him. While his rage had subsided, he still radiated threat as he stared after him.

The small home had a single other room where reedy children cowered out of the faint lamp glow passing through their space. The old woman escorted him to a tiny courtyard and chicken coup, then opened a gate into the darkness of Athens. She looked at him expectantly.

Curio exited onto the unpaved street, and the old woman closed the gate door behind him, shooing him off with a tired wave. He had thought she'd escort him into a secret passage or similar. Instead, he had to find his own way back to the tavern, and he wasn't sure of his location.

Had he not been unsteady on his feet, he might have snuck around to the front and confirmed Pertinax delivered the right message to Sextus. However, he would need a head start to avoid potential pursuit. While Sextus might believe he escaped with the twins, he might not believe he had left the city. So he tottered off in the general direction of the inn, using the silhouette of the Acropolis blocking out the stars as a guidepost.

His disorientation led him on a wandering route, which he did not mind as it would foil pursuit. Yet at every corner, he paused to hide and verify he was alone. He always was. Eventually, he reached the inn and carefully retraced his steps, even barring the rear door as he returned to his bed.

He was satisfied to find the twins still asleep despite the length of time that had passed. In a few hours, the cocks would crow and the city would awaken to a new day. Sleep did not find him as he lay restless on the bed. He stared at Cecelia's thin form, remembering the warm softness of her beside him. In the darkness, as he lay on his back, he stretched his hand out toward her.

Pertinax will not threaten you. He did not speak the promise aloud, but it did not lessen the resolve. Both Galerius and Cecelia were under his care, such as it was. And Cecelia would be his wife one day.

That was a strange thought, a decision made with unexpected suddenness. In a perfect life, he would have been matched to another girl in his youth. She would've come from a farming family of his own class. She would've been homely and solid, dependable and safe. She would lack Cecelia's grace and beauty, and all the dangers that came with it. They would work their meager farm, and make a stable living for their family. Curio would've been happy, if bored, in such a life.

Yet his family all died before such arrangements were made. The pain of that loss had never healed. Varro and Falco had become his family now and he felt obligated to get their permission to marry. He smiled to himself at this strange sense of duty.

Stranger still was his unconcern for Cecelia's father. Even with Sextus hunting them, for whatever reason this was less distressing than if Varro or Falco disapproved. He guessed that he could fight Cilnius and whatever he threw at him. But if either Varro or Falco denied him, then Cecelia would have to return home. His family, even if not by blood, came first.

His drifting mind eventually settled and he realized dawn had come. He had fallen asleep but was not refreshed.

Cecelia was first to rise since she would fetch water from the well and deliver their meals from the inn's kitchen. She immediately checked Curio's bandage, and to her credit, she realized something was amiss.

"You had a restless night? These bandages are damp with sweat and looser than they should be."

"Awaken Galerius," he said, groaning as he struggled to rise. Cecelia was quick to help him upright. "I have something to tell you both."

Once both twins were awake and had rolled up their beds, he sat on a stool beside the small table. Cecelia hovered at his side, hands out as if she might need to catch him. But he patted her arm down and asked her to sit on the bed beside Galerius.

"Your face is looking better," he said. "How is your nose?"

He touched the splint that dominated his bruised and puffy face. "It's still here."

Curio milked the nervous laughter before telling them the night's events. He had left out any mention of Pertinax's thoughts on Cecelia. That beast would never get close to her, so he saw no need to cause worry. When he finished, they all sat in silence.

Galerius stared at the floor and Cecelia's face hid behind her fair hair as she kept her head lowered.

"It's good news," Curio said. "Why aren't you happier?"

Neither stirred, and Galerius shrugged at last.

"We don't get excited about anything before we know it's true. Once I confirm Sextus is gone and Pertinax has forgotten us, then I'll feel better."

"Me too," Cecelia said. She extended her thin arm to touch Galerius beside her. "I won't be convinced until we are far away from here."

"Well, that's reasonable," Curio said. Yet anger pinched him for having risked himself to negotiate this truce and not received even a word of thanks. He folded his arms and waited, but both twins remained locked in silence. "Anyway, we just need to hide out a while longer to be sure Sextus has gone. I'm sure Varro and Falco will send a message any day to tell me where to meet them. Then we'll be far away from here."

Cecelia looked up at Curio's quote of her hopes, and she gave him a bright smile.

"Thank you for taking such good care of me and my brother."

The gratitude lifted the fog over Curio's head, and he felt lighter. "We're taking care of each other. For now, it's just the three of us alone in a foreign city."

"Maybe we can go back to Doctor Nisos," Galerius said, his voice hopeful again. "If Pertinax is done with us, there won't be any more trouble. I like it better there. The air does not move in this room."

"He is done with us," Curio said, then lightly rubbed his abdomen. "And we don't need such expensive lodgings now that we're both healing. Once we confirm Sextus is gone, we'll relocate to someplace nicer. But Kinara will still come to check on me and you. In fact, she'll be here today."

With that, they began their day, which entailed nothing for Curio or Galerius to do. Cecelia went to the local well to refill their water, brought them meals, and acquired a needle and thread to repair their clothes. As promised, Kinara visited with her basket of medical supplies later in the day.

With the room as small as it was, Cecelia used the time to visit the kitchens, and once Galerius got his pass from Kinara, he went downstairs to join her. Before he left, he paused in the doorway and adjusted the splint on his nose.

"It's like being caged just sitting in this room all day."

"No, it's far better," Curio said. "I've been on the inside of enough cages to know."

Now he was alone with Kinara, and he stretched out on the bed. As she organized her jars and bandages, he remembered her wandering hands from days before. His stomach grew hot with fear and he immediately looked away from her. So, rather than risk her flirtations, he decided to tell her about Pertinax.

She listened patiently as she unwrapped him. While this brought her body close to his as she worked, she remained professional. Curio chattered away, emphasizing points of his story with hand motions that interfered with Kinara's work. She clicked her tongue at this, but otherwise just listened.

"I can't believe you took such a chance," she said. She had cleaned the wound area and reapplied more of the honey salve. A fly circled as if trying to land in it, but she shooed it away and folded the wraps over him. "Pertinax is unpredictable."

"Maybe," Curio said, staring up at the low ceiling. Light seeped in from a crack, and he hoped it would not rain during his stay here. "But he's predictably vulnerable to money, like all mercenaries. And even though I don't know Sextus, I know the men of his and his master's class. Every denarius has to be pried out of their closed fists, no matter what is at stake. I think I handled this well."

Self-satisfaction warmed his chest. Kinara sat back, her face impassive other than her lush brows raised slightly.

"So Sextus will leave and Pertinax has no more interest in you. But do you think he is serious about Cecelia?"

While riding the wave of his self-congratulatory recounting, he had told Kinara about Pertinax's desire for Cecelia. He figured someone should know, and Kinara was the only other Roman speaker he knew in Athens besides her father, Doctor Nisos. Curio scratched above the line of bandages encompassing his torso.

"He seemed serious last night. Maybe he will forget her after a time."

"Pertinax isn't one to forget what he wants."

Kinara pulled his wrappings tight around his belly, and Curio looked up at the precise moment to glimpse the shadowed promise of her dark skin revealed as her stola collar fell forward. He instantly set his head back to the thin pillow.

"We will hide out here a few more days. The only danger is in sending Cecelia to the well for water. The innkeeper won't do it for us. I can't do it and if Galerius went, it'd attract too much attention. He'd be the only man there, and Pertinax would be sure to learn where we are. I wish I could figure out some other way to get our water."

Shrugging, Kinara collected her jars and dirty bandages into the basket.

"There is no other way. She will just have to be careful. Maybe send her in the evening after everyone has drawn their water. The fewer people she meets, the better her chances of avoiding Pertinax's notice."

"That's a good idea. The water will last overnight for the next day." Curio felt the tension flow out of him, never realizing it had been there as he considered the one weakness in his plan. "Besides, it won't be long before we leave this place forever."

Kinara dropped a jar of unguent, and it thudded to the wood floor. Fortunately, the thick honey prevented it from flowing out before she could scoop it up.

"I suppose you must hate Athens."

"I don't hate it here. It's just not my city. I belong to Rome."

"I would love to see Rome one day. Perhaps, you could take me?"

Curio laughed. "I think your father might have something to say about that."

Kinara smiled, but it seemed tinged with disappointment. She fit the jar into her basket and stood up. She pointed to his wound.

"You were too active last night. The stitches are loose now. Be careful or you will not be able to return to Rome. I should take that cane away from you."

They both looked at the cane against the wall beside his bed. He gathered it closer.

"It might not be a bad idea. I need to walk without it and march again. I need to hold my sword and stand with my brothers in battle."

"Well, then don't rush off. Remain here until you are ready to carry your sword against your enemies again. If you rush, you will regret it."

Kinara was not wrong, but her caution was also not practical.

"We will need a new place to hide soon," Curio said. "Could you help us find another before Pertinax discovers us? I can't be sure what he would do if he found Cecelia."

She nodded, then left without another word.

So the days passed in tedium and idleness. Cecelia began to fetch water by night, and the innkeeper struggled through enough broken Latin to ask when they would leave. Curio still had plenty of coins left to answer adequately.

But Kinara did not return to take them to another location. With no expert medical attention available, Cecelia had to clean the bandages and rotate their use. Curio worried something had befallen Kinara, and considered sending Galerius out to learn what had happened.

"It has only been a week," he said. "We don't need daily attention and I don't want to get caught."

It was growing dark outside and Cecelia was just returning from drawing water. He heard her footfalls on the stairs beyond the door. During their time together, he had learned the pattern of her steps and to read her moods from her looks alone. Though they had not experienced any more intimacy with Galerius constantly between them, they had still grown closer in spirit.

When she entered, Curio did not need his newfound insight to see she was upset.

She balanced the water jug on her head, and Galerius helped set it on the floor. She then stripped off the protective towel and her hair fell forward.

"I met Pertinax."

8

The flurry surrounding Cecelia's news of meeting Pertinax seemed to overwhelm her. Her brother ushered her into the room and Curio leaped up from the bed—something he could now do without aid from his cane—then had her sit on it. He and Galerius barraged her with questions. She put both small hands to her chest and leaned back with wide eyes, though Curio was not certain it was from the shock of encountering Pertinax or their reaction to the news. She did not seem to know who to address.

He called for Galerius to be quiet, then sat beside her and cradled his arm around her shoulders. She leaned into his side, and he could feel her trembling. They all sat still for a moment before Cecelia cleared her throat.

"I turned around after drawing the water, and he was right there."

"Did he attack you?" Galerius blurted out his question and kneeled beside her to check for injuries. His eyes were bright with fear, made brighter still by the dark rings lingering there from his broken nose.

"Of course not," she said. "Look at me. He left me alone."

Curio shared a confused look with Galerius, prompting Cecelia's irritated sigh.

"Even if I'm not hurt, he's still frightening. I had no idea anyone was behind me. It was like he appeared out of the air. No one else was at the well."

She then described how he had greeted her and asked to assist with carrying the water, which she refused.

"How kind," Galerius said. "He thinks you're stupid enough to lead him back here."

"I ignored him and tried to leave. But he wouldn't move. He said Sextus was gone now and I didn't need to hide. He wanted to show me more of Athens now that it was safe to go out. I told him to stay away from us and left. I kept checking behind, but I don't know if he followed me. I didn't see anyone following."

Curio thought back to Pertinax's wild rages, from his brutal attack on Galerius to his explosive temper at their midnight meeting. Worse yet, Kinara's account of him beating his wife to death matched what he had seen of his personality. He hugged Cecelia closer, and she leaned her head on his shoulder. The fragrance of her hair was sharp and clean.

"He will not harm you." He whispered the promise in her ear and she nodded. He stroked her hair, then gently kissed her forehead.

Galerius put his hand on his sister's knee. "Next time I see him, I'll repay him for all the grief we've suffered. Don't think about him anymore."

She smiled and tears brimmed in her eyes. "How can I be afraid with all my brave men protecting me?"

Curio smiled and squeezed her shoulders. However, an honest review of Cecelia's protection left enough gaps to fit a column of war elephants. Galerius was a spirited fighter but lacked training and possessed only average strength. He might prevail in a brawl against a man of his size and ability. Pertinax would rip him up like an old tunic. As for himself, he could stand and walk now with intermittent aid from his cane. As a fighter, he was utterly useless.

"We can't remain here," Curio said, then turned to speak softly to Cecelia. "I know you tried to be sure no one followed, but we must assume someone did. Pertinax has thugs that you wouldn't even know were watching you. My guess is he already knows we are here and that you go to the well for water."

"But I go in the evening when there aren't any other women around. Who could've seen me?"

Her voice rose as if responding to a challenge, but Curio patted her shoulder again.

"Assume you are always being watched. And I don't know if Sextus is gone yet. I've had plenty of time to think about that situation. Pertinax might be delaying until Galerius's injuries are less obvious. It is about time to remove that splint, even if Kinara isn't around to tell you so. I fear he has collected my fee, and then plans to still collect a fee from Sextus."

Galerius sighed and sat on the floor beside his sister on the bed.

"That makes sense, doesn't it? But if he wants Cecelia, then he would be better off sending Sextus away."

"Agreed," Curio said. "Either way, we're still in danger."

Cecelia twisted into Curio's arms, bringing her face nearly to his nose. Her voice was trembling and breathless.

"I did not run from one monster to find another. You are the only man for me."

Rather than answer, Curio gathered her in, uncaring of Galerius sitting close enough that his body touched Curio's leg. He surrendered to her soft lips.

A feminine voice at the door spoke.

"I see you are recovering nicely."

Curio and Cecelia flinched back from each other and discovered Kinara standing in the doorway. She wore a dark gray stola with a gray cloak and hood. She held her basket over her arm.

Galerius sprang to his feet. "How long have you been there?"

They had not closed the door behind Cecelia, and Curio had been so focused on her that he did not see Kinara arrive. Apparently, neither had Galerius.

"Long enough to figure out Pertinax has found you."

She entered and closed the door behind her. Four people

crowded the tiny room, but Galerius sat on the bed as well, making more room for Kinara to set out the contents of her basket.

Curio confirmed what she had guessed, and explained their situation to her.

"Did you notice anyone watching this place?" he asked. "Pertinax could follow you just as easily."

Kinara had already gestured Galerius to the edge of the bed and held his face back with a single hand as she examined his nose.

"I cannot say. But I have other news. Sextus and his Romans have left. That's why I've been so long in returning. I wanted to bring you news when I did."

"Well, you made me worried," Curio said. This raised one of Kinara's lush brows and her dark eyes regarded him a moment as she began prodding Galerius's face.

"You are a poor liar." She then withdrew a small knife from her basket. "Now, this splint is not needed any longer."

Once she had cut away the bindings Galerius raised both arms in victory. He still sounded nasal, but more like his old self.

"Freedom!" Then he paused and gingerly touched his fingers to his nose bridge. "Does it look all right?"

"I do good work," Kinara said. "Protect it and it will remain as straight as the gods made it."

Galerius sighed with relief but Cecelia kicked her feet hanging off the edge of the bed and giggled.

"Do you remember when you walked into the cubiculum door? Don't do that again."

"Let's not talk about that."

Kinara ordered everyone off the bed so she could examine Curio.

"I've washed and changed the bandages every day and kept the wound area clean." Cecelia slid to the floor but stood beside Kinara as she removed the wrap. She only grunted in reply.

Curio remained looking at the ceiling as Kinara worked, feeling nervous about accidentally seeing something he should not. He never realized how intimate it was to care for another person until he had a woman tending him. Before this time, he had only ever been treated by legion doctors and orderlies, all of them men.

The twins backed out of the room to give Kinara space to work but remained just outside the door. Cool air touched Curio's abdomen as the wrap came away.

Kinara sat back and her brows furrowed. He asked after her reaction, but she simply gathered her materials from her basket and called through the opened door.

"Fetch me hot water from the kitchen. Be quick about it."

The order was for Cecelia, but Galerius said he would watch her as she did. Kinara let out another frustrated sigh when they both started down the stairs.

"I feared I was too long in returning. She doesn't know what she's doing."

Curio lifted his head to examine his wound. The motion flexed his stomach enough that the pain and weakness flattened him again. Yet he didn't see anything more than the pressed-down stitches and the glisten of his pale skin. The wound area was like a dark brown mound now.

"It doesn't hurt and I don't have any fever."

"If you don't clean it thoroughly, you risk infection. Look at this mess. Does she really love you?"

"What does that mean?" Curio again flexed his head up, but Kinara was already hovering over him and working on his wound. Her stola sleeve hung open and he thought he glimpsed her breast through it.

What is wrong with me? he thought. *Every time I look at her, does it have to be like this?*

Then a terrible sting radiated out of his wound and he yelped in surprise. Kinara pressed her elbow into his diaphragm to stop his squirming.

"I told you it's not cleaned well. I can't let you get infected now. I was just telling my father that you are the fastest healer I've ever seen. You are an incredible man, Centurion Curio."

He sniffed and twitched as she continued to pat and dab around the wound. Her compliment brought heat to his cheeks.

"Well, it's nothing I control. I guess in my profession, if you don't heal fast, you don't last long."

Kinara chuckled. "I think that is fair to say for anyone suffering a wound like this one."

She sat back then looked toward the door and shook her head.

Curio drew a long breath through his nostrils. "Give them time. I doubt the innkeeper has boiling water at the ready."

She twisted on the bed beside him, placing her warm hand on his chest for balance. Of course, she was just waiting for the twins to return with the water, but it felt strangely intimate. Although it was innocuous, he felt like it meant more. Then he realized she was staring at him intently, and he tilted his head at her. She gave him a hard smile.

"If Pertinax wants her, he will have her one way or the other. Today he tried to be nice. Tomorrow, who knows?"

"I know he's a beast, but would he flagrantly abduct a Roman citizen off the streets? How much power does he have?"

Kinara bit her bottom lip in thought.

"A fair bit of influence. But he is a foreigner after all. The real danger is the elders don't care what foreigners do to each other."

"I understand that." Curio now propped himself up, his freshly cleaned wound stinging as the motion pressed his flesh. "But surely your leaders care about public order. Today he abducts a Roman, tomorrow a fine Athenian girl. They'll want to stop him from becoming bolder with his crimes."

He used one arm to imitate snatching someone by force. Kinara still maintained her skeptical expression.

"I can find you a new hiding place. But the best way to keep them safe is to send them out of Athens." She now looked toward the door, then leaned closer as she dropped her voice. "Send them to a neighboring town. Pertinax has no power beyond the city walls, and he has never stepped out of Athens since he arrived."

"How would you know that?"

"Because it would be the cause of a public holiday if he ever left. At least in his neighborhood. He seldom leaves the city. He has too much to occupy him here. Anyway, get them out of Athens. You would stay with me, and remain in hiding so Pertinax doesn't question you. You're not ready to run off without proper care. Especially after seeing how you look after a week without me."

"I can't do that." He spoke with a finality that startled even himself.

"You can't do what is right?" Kinara raised a single brow in challenge, a crooked smile on her face.

He turned his head toward the mudbrick exterior wall on the other side of his bed. Of course, Kinara was right. Leaving Athens was the proper response to the threat, and the thought had come to him before. He could not bear thinking of abandoning Cecelia, particularly when she and her brother were so vulnerable to other threats besides Pertinax.

"You must stay here, in any case." Kinara's hand remained atop his chest, sliding toward his neck as she adjusted her position. "Your friends would not know where else to contact you."

"Your father could forward their message to me."

"My father is done with your complications. He is a good doctor, and therefore busy. If he became entangled with anyone like Pertinax, his business would suffer."

"So he doesn't know you come to visit us?"

The thin smile was his answer. He heard Galerius's cheerful voice from the bottom of the stairs. Kinara heard it as well, and her hand retreated slowly across his chest.

"Cecelia will be my wife. If she flees Athens, then I must go with her. I'll figure out how to contact Varro and Falco later. Her safety is more important right now."

"Her so-called care will complicate your recovery. If you don't heal properly, you'll never rejoin your friends. You won't be able to do what you used to do." Kinara sat up from the bed as the twin's chatter grew louder up the stairs. "I urge you to reconsider my offer."

Cecelia entered carrying a red clay bowl with steam rising from it.

She held it away from herself and set it on the table where Kinara pointed. Without any more talk of leaving, she dipped a cloth into the water and then began cleaning Curio's torso. The hot water felt good on his skin, and he hoped once his stitches were removed that he could again enjoy a bath. Cecelia had helped sponge him clean in places he could not reach easily. But much of his body still needed a good scrub.

Cecelia tried to watch, but it seemed Kinara blocked her view. She kept stretching and standing on her toes. At last, Curio tapped Kinara's arm.

"Let her see what you're doing, since she'll have to do this when you're unavailable."

Kinara did not answer but shifted on the bed to allow Cecelia in. With the lamplight flickering behind them, Curio felt as if two shadows hovered over him. His exposed skin tingled and he closed his eyes until Kinara had finished with him. She began to wrap him, but Cecelia insisted on finishing it.

When done, Kinara inspected the wrap and cinched it tighter than Curio thought it needed to be.

"I will arrange for you to change locations by tomorrow afternoon. Since Pertinax expects you to only be active in the evening, that's the safest time to make the switch."

She gave Curio a meaningful look. He knew it meant he should agree to her plan. Instead, he croaked his thanks and then faced the ceiling. Kinara lingered in silence, then started to leave.

"We should pay you for your time," Cecelia said.

This brought Curio's head around, and he found Cecelia had taken a single coin from their communal purse. She extended this to Kinara, who looked at it as if she had been presented with a cockroach.

"I do this of my own choice. I don't need to be paid for it."

She left Cecelia with the coin offered toward a blackened doorway.

Galerius tested the side of his nose. "She's weird. But my nose is looking good! So I won't complain."

"You do look much better," Cecelia said, though Varro heard the quiver in her voice. She still clutched the coin in her small fist.

The next morning, Curio settled their bill with the innkeeper who had formerly been upset with their long domination of his private room. He guessed the innkeeper might have rented it out to a prostitute or for other short-term needs. Yet now he tried to convince them to stay, using every bit of pantomime and fractured Latin he knew to communicate the desire.

Curio guessed he was an informant for Pertinax. He was probably paid to watch them and their departure would mean a loss of income. So Curio decided he could use this to his advantage.

"We're leaving Athens today." He then repeated the words and made waving hand motions to demonstrate them traveling away from the city. Once the innkeeper seemed to understand this, he stopped delaying them. But Curio also noted a sly smile. As he and the twins left the inn, he had one of his own.

They took a carriage Kinara sent to drive them farther north into Athens. A young man, perhaps only a few years older than the twins, drove the single-horse carriage while the three of them sat in the back with their meager belongings. Curio of course kept the coins strapped to his side.

They arrived at yet another inn. The twins delighted in this since it seemed to be a more upscale neighborhood based on the freshly plastered buildings and better-dressed pedestrians. However, Curio shook his head as they dismounted the cart with Galerius's aid.

Public inns were not hiding places. He needed a true hideout where Pertinax would never find them. No matter what Kinara said, he was going to rejoin Varro and Falco soon. If he couldn't fight for a while, they would find other work for him to do. This tour of Athenian inns was maddening to him.

He could've learned their destination if he had been more cogent when Varro and Falco left. As it was, he would discover the current location of Flamininus and the Roman delegation. That wouldn't be difficult given Flamininus's fame as a liberator of Greece from the Macedonian yoke. In fact, he decided that after a few more days, he would leave with the twins. Athens was not a viable option anymore.

For now, he admitted he still needed rest and the stitches should be removed by a doctor. He could tolerate a few more days of idling in a private room.

The driver handled their transition to the innkeeper, speaking Greek and gesturing to his three passengers. Curio realized how lucky he was to have Kinara taking care of them. They would probably be driven to hide in rat nests without her bilingual abilities. She knew the city and seemed connected to a variety of useful people. Perhaps working with her father had forged contacts a woman would otherwise not have. Defying her father and society to remain unmarried and practice medicine made her the most independent woman Curio had ever known. There was much to admire in that, even if it also made her the strangest woman he had ever known.

Cecelia took Curio's arm as they entered the inn, smiling warmly as she helped him over the lintel. He still relied on his cane but the assistance was welcomed. The innkeeper spoke enough Latin to demand advance payment. Curio had no idea how long Kinara had arranged for them to stay, but the sum seemed to indicate at least another week.

They settled into their new room, which was both larger and cleaner than the last one, though still only contained one bed and a tiny circular table with a single stool. The biggest upgrade was a white sheet hung across the mudbrick exterior wall to conceal its ugliness.

Curio was amazed at how fast they all adapted to their new routine. He took a short walk each morning on quiet streets that seemed far safer than even Doctor Nisos's neighborhood. The hardpacked dirt led to a grove of trees where children played. He journeyed there and back, using his cane only when he needed extra stability. His strength was returning, at least enough that he could walk unaided. He even dared a light jog for embarrassingly short stretches.

Galerius began to feel emboldened enough to explore the area, at least until Curio feared they were growing lax and curbed their outdoor excursions. He promised more action in the coming days without revealing his intention to follow Varro and Falco. The hint seemed to excite Galerius and he did not complain about remaining indoors.

Cecelia continued to draw water from the well in the evening. She washed Curio's wraps and all their clothes, doing this when he and Galerius were outside the inn. She also fetched their meals from the kitchen and managed their collective treasury. Curio admired her domestic acumen, and she blushed every time he complimented her for it.

"I can't wait to make a proper home for us far away from danger. We will all be so happy."

He agreed though it seemed Galerius was included in her future home. Curio realized he would have no choice, at least until Galerius started his own family one day.

After nearly a week of this routine, the place was beginning to feel like home. Pertinax did not seem to have a presence in this neighborhood. Curio began to feel like they had overestimated his power, probably a bias from his violent introduction. Sextus also never materialized as a true threat. If he was still seeking the twins in Athens, by now he would've found them. He had accepted the misdirection as fact.

So it was one evening Curio and Galerius were awaiting Cecelia to return with their water jug. They both sat on the bed and were rolling dice that Galerius claimed to have found discarded in the street. Curio was currently on a winning streak, but since it was their communal money at stake, they played only to pass the time.

And time passed. Too much time and the sun abandoned the city to deep twilight.

"What's taking her so long?" Curio asked.

Galerius had begun to look sweaty and as if he were having trouble swallowing. He kept rubbing his neck.

"I don't feel good. Something is wrong with her."

"You're just worried." Curio looked toward the door left ajar. "But so am I. Let's go see where she is."

Galerius nodded. His formerly swollen face was now normal and bruises had faded to greenish blotches. Yet now he looked worse than the day he had taken the beating that broke his nose.

Curio led the descent down the stairs and arrived in the main room where a half-dozen patrons surrounded the innkeeper. Their speech was hushed but frantic, and judging from how they had abandoned their wine cups at their tables Curio supposed they had all just learned something terrible.

When the innkeeper noticed them, his eyes widened and he staggered as if to pass out.

Curio's knees weakened and he needed his cane to remain upright. He limped toward the small crowd that flinched away from him as he passed. The innkeeper was a middle-aged man with greasy skin and an ashen face. He stepped back from Curio as if he wanted to run away.

"What's going on? Where's Cecelia?"

The innkeeper spluttered in Greek before realizing Curio did not understand. He looked helplessly at the others, who shouted back at him. Then he put his finger to his throat and ran it ear to ear.

"The girl. She is dead."

9

Curio hunched over his cane, both hands pressing on the heavy shaft to keep himself upright. The crowd of onlookers around him was a blur. He could not focus. His throat burned and he shivered with cold even as sweat from rushing to the well trickled down his back. Voices were like a thick and wooly humming in his ears.

What he saw framed in the light of lamps and candles held aloft by strangers drained all energy from him. Not energy to run or jump, but energy to live. A heaviness threatened to crush him flat to the dirt road.

In his time as a soldier, Curio had witnessed death in its ugliest forms: decapitations, dismemberments, impalements, gaping cuts, exposed bones, burning flesh, crushed skulls, and streams of blood flowing from the tidemark of corpses where enemies clashed. His nightmares were full of these gory scenes, indelibly carved into the tissues of his brain.

But what he saw now horrified him more than all those memories: a twisted body half-hidden in bushes beside the wide enclosure of the public well.

He recognized the pale thin legs and the dainty feet, one still wearing a sandal and another bare. Their water jug was shattered. The spilled water diluted the red streams flowing beneath those exposed legs. Even the hem of her bloodied stola, recently repaired by her own hand, easily marked the body as Cecelia.

Blood was everywhere around the well enclosure. Bright red spray ran down one of its walls, indicating a sudden and violent gash had opened Cecelia's artery. It reached nearly to the roof. More blood glittered on the road and bushes as if she had run a distance while continuing to spray blood.

Someone made to drag the body out of the bushes. Galerius charged at the man who had dared to reach for his sister's exposed leg. Others restrained him and the interloper backed away from the corpse. Curio could not move in response but stood with his eyes fixed on the corpse.

When the bystanders released Galerius, he collapsed to his knees beside the bush where his sister lay dead. He laced both hands behind his head and drooped forward almost to the ground. He did not make a sound.

Curio hobbled beside him, all the strength he rebuilt over the last weeks vanished. His eyes never left Cecelia's legs sticking out from the bushes. People spoke to him in Greek, but he returned a blank stare.

The innkeeper and his patrons had accompanied him to the scene, and from their agitated gesturing and tone seemed to explain the situation to the crowd. They looked sympathetically at Galerius and Curio and backed away.

An impulse to action poked at Curio from beneath the sodden blanket of shock immobilizing him. He couldn't allow Cecelia's corpse to lay in a bloody heap between bushes and the enclosure wall.

"We should cover her," he said hoarsely. He spoke to Galerius, still folded over himself and crouching beside his dead sister. He shook his head.

"This is not real. I'm going to wake up now."

Despite his intentions, Curio found himself unable to act. The bright blood flowing at his feet swirled into the spilled water from the shattered jug. He felt as if he might vomit and looked away.

"Curio!"

The voice was distant and repeated his name two more times. Then a familiar and firm hand grabbed his shoulder and pulled him around.

Kinara's dark eyes were bright in the dim light. She had her basket looped through her left arm, and her clammy right hand gripped his shoulder. Her face gleamed with sweat as she blinked at him.

"Is it true?"

He simply nodded to the legs sticking out from beneath the bushes. Kinara recoiled from him, covering her mouth with her free hand. She let out a low moan and shook her head.

Her presence emboldened the crowd, and they drew closer as they directed their questions at her. Curio remained numbly staring at the corpse of the woman he had promised to protect.

"When did this happen?" Kinara asked. "Did anyone see?"

"I don't know," Curio answered truthfully. He was only now beginning to understand that he had to find these answers. But this brought tears to his eyes.

They streaked slowly down his cheeks into his thin beard. Cecelia had promised to help him shave once they were out of hiding. He rubbed the wetness away and drew a long and deep breath. No matter what he felt, he had to keep his mind from closing down to grief. But it was like fighting against a mountain river current.

Kinara now kneeled beside Galerius. "Do you know what happened?"

"My sister was murdered!" His shout sent Kinara reeling back and drew gasps from the crowd.

However, the shout roused Curio from his sadness. He could hear Falco in his head rebuking him.

"For fuck's sake, Curio, you can't help anyone like this. Tears are for later. You've seen worse. Now, get after the killer before he escapes."

Falco's imagined cursing bounced around his thoughts until they smashed through into action. Curio set his cane carefully on the ground, then he tapped Kinara's shoulder as she comforted Galerius.

"Can you help me pull her out of the bushes and cover her body?"

Kinara stared up at him, her thick brow cocked as if to ask if he was sure. When he nodded, they both approached the bushes.

The prospect of revealing the body both excited and repulsed the crowd. The innkeeper and his patrons had somehow nominated themselves as arbiters of the situation and herded back the overly curious members of the crowd.

The moment he touched Cecelia's leg he thought he would faint. The flesh was cool and bloodless.

"I can manage it alone," Kinara said softly. "Go comfort the brother."

Kinara squatted beside the corpse, digging into the bushes to shove them aside. Curio realized he could not watch her body flop out bloody and lifeless. Kinara was strong for a woman, with well-formed arms and shoulders. He considered how easily she had manipulated him when he was half-conscious and confined to his bed. So he turned away and raised Galerius to his feet. They both stepped around the corner of the well enclosure.

While Kinara worked, he listened to the hushed reactions from the crowd and dreaded what he would find when he turned back. He could not bear to see it, but Falco's irritated voice continued to goad him forward. *"If you don't take charge, who will? Don't you want revenge for your woman?"*

"I will find out who did this and make them pay." He spoke resolutely, but only in a strained whisper. Ostensibly, he was talking to himself but Galerius snorted in disgust.

"What's to find out? It was Pertinax who did it. He surprised her here, and when she rejected him again, he killed her like he did his wife."

Curio drew a sharp breath. It made sense, but he did not have proof. Yet, he had done nothing to find the proof either. That was the galvanizing thought that turned him around to confront what he did not want to see.

Kinara was unfurling a sheet of bandages to cover Cecelia's corpse. She had already draped one white sheet over her face and chest. As she sorted through her basket, a woman from the crowd emerged with a long blanket.

Cecelia was smeared everywhere with blood. She had been stabbed dozens of times. Her thin, pale arm stretched out across the dirt road as if her hand was reaching for him. Then he realized two of her fingers were sliced off, and he turned his head.

Kinara set the sheet over the corpse, and blooms of red formed where it contacted the body. She held something in her hand, wrapped in a bandage. She presented it to Curio.

"This was embedded in her side. I think it went deep enough that the killer could not pull it out again and left it."

He looked down at a pugio of the same kind he carried into battle. Of course, there were no special markings on it. Kinara had wiped the blood from it and offered it to Curio.

"The Scythians will be here soon," she said. "They will have questions for you. If there were witnesses, they'll handle them, too."

The pugio was razor sharp and worn. The blade was nicked, probably in the recent attack on Cecelia. That might have been the cause for it to stick in her flesh. He turned it around in his hand, recognizing that this belonged to someone who knew how to care for his weapon. Someone who had been drilled in its use and whose life might have once depended on its reliability.

"Pertinax."

He whispered the name and met Kinara's dark eyes. Sweat beaded between her lush brows and highlighted her dusky skin. She sighed and lowered her head.

"That seems likely. It is a Roman weapon, isn't it?"

"He ambushed Cecelia. When she would not go with him of her own choice, he tried to force her."

Curio now turned around to examine the scene. The crowd remained a respectful distance. Galerius wrapped his arms about himself and stood with his back to them, facing the well under the enclosure. His eyes roved over the blood splatter on the wall, then down to where the water jug lay in jagged shards.

He could see Pertinax stepping from behind the bushes, confronting Cecelia, and demanding she go with him. "I'll make a better husband than that cripple." He imagined the words and Pertinax towering over her. "I'll never let your father get at you. You'll be safe with me forever."

But Cecelia rejected him and said something that cut open his rage. Probably something about how he had murdered his last wife.

The rest he could not imagine. He did not need to. The bloody outcome was everywhere around him. In his rage, he drew his pugio and delivered a fatal stroke to her throat. The sharp spray of blood had to have been the first wound to splash so high up the wall. The remaining wounds were made out of hatred and frustration, and perhaps to ensure she did not survive to later identify him.

Pertinax might have been in a drunken rage as he had been with Galerius. As a trained soldier and veteran of the war with Macedonia, the wine would not have dulled his strikes. Each one would've been lethal on its own. Curio imagined the blood-splattered brute only coming to his senses when his blade stuck.

He would've stepped back in horror at his crime and then tried to hide Cecelia's body. But when someone approached, he had to drop the corpse half in the bushes and flee.

"There must be bloody footprints." The idea struck him suddenly and Kinara seemed stunned at this deduction. Curio turned toward the bushes, careful not to look down at the white shroud turning dark as wine beneath him.

"They will lead back to his house. That'll prove he did it."

Curio began sorting through the bushes, and Kinara joined him. But he soon realized that there had been too many people here already. He found small prints that might have been Kinara's, and man-sized ones all jumbled together. Someone had discovered the body and jumbled the prints from the beginning. Even moving it had smeared the ground. His hope faded, though he looked beyond the bushes to a small, dark field between two homes that emptied into a nearby street.

"Over there." Curio pointed across the darkness. "He ran that way, and there may be prints to follow on that street."

"He lives across the city," Kinara said. "He could not have stepped in enough blood to leave prints all the way back there."

"I have to check!" he shouted in frustration, knowing she was right but seething at his helplessness. He looked at the pugio wrapped in the bandage. Would this be enough to prove what Pertinax had done? Hundreds of Roman weapons must be in circulation throughout Athens, all scavenged from the battlefields of ten years ago and sold to the Greeks.

"The Scythians are here." Kinara pulled him by the arm. "They will want to see the weapon."

The crowd parted for three burly men carrying long whips. One was feeding the length of his whip through his palm as if preparing to unleash it on the crowd. They obediently fell back from the scene.

Another was clearly in the lead, a square-faced man with thick and curly hair. His nostrils were wide and his face pinched, making him look like a bat. The innkeeper stood beside him, rattling off in Greek and pointing at the shrouded body.

"The Scythians enforce public order," Kinara explained. "We'll tell them what we know and they'll visit Pertinax, I'm certain."

"If he's dumb enough to be found." Curio shook his head, knowing his enemy must have bolt holes everywhere he conducted his illegal business. By now, he was beyond anyone's reach.

The Scythians approached the body and Galerius immediately sprang at the leader.

"Don't touch her! Don't one of you filthy Greeks lay a hand on her!"

The lead Scythian shoved him back with a curse, and his partner with the loosened whip unfurled it with ease. It struck like a cobra, cracking on the ground at Galerius's feet. The impact must have jolted him, for he leaped away with a cry of pain. Even members of the crowd flinched in response.

Curio stepped past the Scythians and seized Galerius by his shoulders, shaking him as he did.

"Keep your head with these men. They're the law right now. Don't give them a reason to go after us. We've got to focus them on Pertinax."

Galerius's red and tear-stained face twisted with pain and hatred, and he gritted his teeth. But Curio held him firm until he at last let out a breath and lowered his head.

Kinara offered him his cane, which he accepted. He did not need it yet, the excitement of the moment carrying him. Yet his legs trembled and his wound ached. He chose to lean on it as he faced the Scythians.

The leader was already growling at Kinara in Greek. Along with the innkeeper, the two explained the situation. The leader kept giving Curio dirty looks, and at last, demanded the pugio from him. With Kinara's prompting, he surrendered the weapon. The leader took it, allowed his companions to glance at it, and then dropped it in a bag slung across his wide torso. The Scythians then began to disperse the crowd. Kinara crossed back to him.

"I've named Pertinax," she said. "They will go to his home and question him. They will find out what he did."

"Then what?" Galerius asked. "I want to see him killed. I want to do it myself."

"He will be tried by the magistrates," Kinara said. "And you two will be present. I'm not sure what the punishment will be. Probably death by crucifixion, since he's a foreigner."

Curio shuddered at the thought, not for Pertinax, but for memories of that horrid form of execution. He had once been hung from a board on the walls of Sparta to die of thirst until Varro rescued him.

How he wished Varro was here now. He would know what to do. This situation made Curio realize he was a follower and not a leader, even if he had reached a centurion's rank. To do that job, he just needed to lead men toward the enemy and make tactical adjustments. A murder was something on an entirely different level, something Varro would have a plan to address. Not only did Curio have to consider justice for Cecelia, but he also had to handle her burial. The thought of this overwhelmed his shaky willpower.

As if the Scythians had read his mind, the leader pointed at the corpse and barked something at Kinara. She excused herself, then lowered her head as the bat-faced man stood over Cecelia's body and gave her instructions. When finished, he shouted at the crowd and two men stepped forward. The Scythian gave them approving nods.

Kinara drew both Curio and Galerius together. "They have volunteered to carry the body to the graveyard district. There is a place to keep the dead who have no home for funeral rites."

Galerius gasped at this, but Kinara continued.

"You should donate to the city for a pyre and burial plot. Due to my work, I know where to hire mourners, grave diggers, and tombstone makers."

Curio sighed. "We only have so much money and we'll need it to bring down Pertinax, I'm sure."

Kinara nodded. "You could also bury her outside the city on your own."

"No! My sister will not lie anywhere near this rotten city. I will take her home."

Kinara pursed her lips. "Then you will still need to build a pyre and prepare an urn."

Galerius seemed on the verge of exploding, and the Scythians were still eyeing them. He held up a hand to Kinara. She was doing no one any good by trying to rush Cecelia into the grave.

"This is too much right now. We will follow her to the graveyard district. Tomorrow, we will handle the other arrangements. We need time to recover from this and rest."

But he looked at Galerius quivering in rage and did not expect to find any rest tonight.

10

Two days later, Curio stood over Cecelia's grave. The sky was cheerfully clear and blue, a bitter contrast to the depression smothering him and Galerius standing by his side. Birds chirped merrily as they wove through the cloudless sky. Were the gods celebrating Cecelia's murder, he wondered. He could not remember a fairer day for such a gloomy undertaking.

The grave district was called Kerameikos and sat between the inner and outer walls of Athens. Kinara used her father's connections, or perhaps her own, to get this small plot to bury Cecelia's ashes. Without her, he could not have survived these past two days. She worked with the innkeeper to spare them from worry for their daily care. Indeed, she seemed to have no other concern than his well-being and hardly left his side the entire time. Curio understood gratitude, but he could not summon any emotion. Later, he would find a way to thank Kinara for handling all of this mess. For now, grief dominated his mind.

Galerius sniffed as he stood over the fresh earth where the plain clay pot containing Cecelia's ashes was now buried. Curio sympathized with his pain, for as Cecelia's brother he had also sworn himself to her protection. It was not lost on either of them that her fleeing an unwanted marriage had led to a worse end and all thanks to their inability to protect her. How many times had Galerius repeated that he should have escorted her to the well? And each time he voiced his regrets, Curio regretted having advised against it in the interest of being inconspicuous.

So they both stood in silent regret over the grave of their beloved. Curio had tried to force himself into some sort of perspective. He had only met her months ago. The situation had made him susceptible to the whims of the heart. They had shared a bed, and more, but nothing was settled.

No one married for love, he told himself. Everything was done by arrangement to maintain or enhance family status in society. What they planned to do was a scandal. The gods had spoken on the matter and punished Cecelia for her brazen flouting of tradition.

Yet all this chatter in his head did not numb the pain in his heart. He would miss her and yearn for the life he imagined they could have built together.

He listened to distant voices and the clattering of potters at work. A shallow river flowed through the Kerameikos and deposited a rich red clay on its banks. Perhaps because of this, potters flourished around the outskirts of the graves. They did a brisk trade in burial urns, and Curio had bought a simple one for Cecelia right here. He also heard Kinara shifting her feet behind them. He roused from his thoughts, at last lifting his head when his neck had grown sore.

Row upon row of tombstones and stelae spread out in every direction. Milky smoke rendered the nearby Acropolis a smudgy outline against the sky. This was as close to it as Curio had come, and he no longer had any interest in exploring more of the city. Nearer to them, a group of women in black stolas and head covers wept over another grave.

"We should go," Curio said. Galerius still kept his head lowered over her grave.

"I will come back," he said. "When I have made things right at home, I will return her to Roman soil. She does not deserve this rotten place."

"That's right." Curio set his hand on the young man's shoulder. "It is only temporary."

He had struggled to contain him over the past two days. First, he had to keep him from doing something rash while the Scythians investigated Pertinax and searched for witnesses. Next, he had to convince him that carrying Cecelia's ashes while so much remained uncertain would risk spilling them. The dead wanted to be buried so they could continue on their journey. Neither of them wanted Cecelia's spirit haunting them for scattering her remains thoughtlessly.

The cremation had been unbearable for Galerius. Even with just themselves present, he had wailed enough that even a hundred other mourners would've been drowned out. During the cremation, Cecelia's corpse bolted upright, showering hot ashes all around. It fell to Curio and an attendant to use rods to press her flat on the small pyre while Galerius collapsed in abject terror. Of course, burning bodies often moved and shifted as muscles shrank and snapped. Yet Curio could not help but see eyes in the rolling flames engulfing her head, furious and accusing eyes. It was as if she had sat up to demand justice for her death.

Now Cecelia was buried and those horrid memories would be added to the catalogue of terrors already filling Curio's nightmares. He hoped time would fade them from his dreams.

They both turned to Kinara, who waited patiently in a black stola. She offered Curio a small smile, then extended his cane to him.

"The footing here is bad. You shouldn't go without it."

"I don't need it for walking anymore," he said. "I'll never recover if I use it all the time."

"Just keep it for rough spots."

"Will this stone be safe?" Galerius remained at his sister's grave. They had purchased the smallest maker with a minimal engraving of Cecelia's name only.

Kinara pulled her lush brows together and tilted her head. "It is too small to rub off your sister's name and replace it with another."

The tombstone engraver had tried to scare them into buying a larger marker, citing the ease of stealing a smaller one. Curio wanted to conserve money, and Galerius intended to return for the ashes. So they had purchased the smallest stone to mark her location when they returned for her.

Galerius kneeled, placed his hand on the marker while whispering, then stood and turned away. They picked a path across the expanse of Kerameikos. Curio did rely on the cane at points where they had to sidestep through narrow avenues among the graves. Once they arrived at the opposite side and crossed back toward the inner wall gate, Curio cleared his throat.

"I've been waiting for a good time to ask," he said to Kinara, who hovered at his side much as Cecelia would have done. "But what have the Scythians discovered? What is to be done about Pertinax?"

Kinara stopped, bringing the others to a halt as well. They were still a distance from the gate where people crisscrossed the opening as they went about their business. The graveyard behind them was empty but for flocks of birds and pockets of mourners.

"When is his execution?" Galerius asked.

"There will be none." Kinara's dark skin shaded darker as she lowered her voice. "They said he never left his home that night, and others attest to it. I'm sorry. But I think he has used his connections to escape justice."

Galerius's wail of rage even turned heads beyond the distant wall gate.

"That's a lie! I will cut his throat, just like he did to my sister!"

Even though he made his threats in Latin, Curio still raced to clamp his hand over his mouth.

"Don't shout threats like that, you fool."

But Galerius wrestled with him, shoving him back so that he stumbled.

"Get off me!"

Curio's heel caught on the uneven ground and he collapsed backward. Kinara shrieked in surprise, dropping her basket and reaching for Curio. But he landed on his posterior, a jolt of pain lancing up his back. Galerius hovered over him, his face red with rage.

"You should've protected her. But a fucking breeze will knock you over! Now she's dead and she's never coming back!"

Kinara covered him as if Galerius were casting stones at him. "What are you saying? He is recovering from a wound that should have killed him."

"No!" Galerius shouted. "The gods said he would protect her. But he was in bed all the time, doing nothing when she was murdered."

"Then blame the gods!" Kinara helped Curio to his feet, putting his cane into his hand.

He endured Galerius's curses, accepting the truth of them. They did hit him like stones. Instead, his irritation manifested against Kinara's fussing with him. As soon as he had his balance back, he pushed her away.

Now he stood before Galerius, whose red face was again streaked with tears. Even if he wore an adult's tunic, he appeared like a scared and saddened child. Curio bore Galerius's continued insults as he called him a fool, a coward, and a cripple.

Curio closed his eyes and used his cane to keep Kinara away. She had the sense to step aside while this inevitable confrontation wore itself out. Finally, Galerius devolved into bitter tears and turned to stomp off toward the gate.

"Where are you going?" Curio followed, easily grabbing him by his sleeve and pulling him short. Galerius yelped and turned around, apparently surprised at his speed. Curio was recovering and regaining his old form.

"Let go of me. I'm going back to the inn."

Yet he did not let go and turned him around. Curio was barely taller than his young friend, but he still looked down on him with a scowl.

"I know how mad you are. I am, too. But don't do something foolish."

He could see the wild resolve in Galerius's eyes. His round features had sharpened and his lips curled in disgust.

"He can't get away with this. He has to pay for what he did."

"He will. But we are foreigners here. We don't have the same protections Pertinax has built for himself. These Scythians are corrupted, it seems. We will find another way. But it's going to take time."

"How long?" Galerius pulled out of Curio's grip, but only because he judged the young man to have calmed enough to listen. "I will not rest until he's dead."

"As long it takes to do it right." Curio lowered his head, hating the platitude even if it fit. "Getting revenge today or tomorrow will not bring your sister back."

Galerius's hard stare softened and his shoulders slumped. He let out a long sigh and nodded.

"What will you do? If Pertinax is paying off the city's leaders, we will have no chance."

"He's not that powerful." He looked hopefully to Kinara, but she did not chime in with encouragement. Her eyes were lost in deep shadows from the cheerful noon sun. So he turned back with a nervous smile. "We'll have to dig into the events of that night. The innkeeper can tell us who else was nearby at that time. Something will reveal itself."

"That doesn't sound like much of a plan."

The smile slipped off Curio's face.

"Well, it's better than confronting Pertinax in the streets with nothing but our fists."

Kinara cleared her throat, stepping closer now that Galerius had calmed.

"Don't start prying into Pertinax and the murder. If he thinks you could reveal him to the elder council, then your lives are in danger. For now, he is happy to let things settle. But he won't hesitate to strike if you start digging."

Galerius huffed and raised both hands overhead. "What are we supposed to do?"

"He's right," Curio said, scratching the back of his head. "The longer we wait, the lower our chances of learning anything useful. We will have to be vigilant for threats, but we have to do something."

"Then stay with me," Kinara said. "I have a hiding place for both of you. Your wound still needs to be cleaned regularly and the stitches removed. You can't go too far from me, no matter what."

"Your father will eventually find out," Curio said. "You've already risked so much to help us."

"Besides," Galerius said, his frown deepening, "by now Pertinax knows you're with us. He'll come for you right away when we disappear."

Curio grunted his agreement. "The best hiding spot is in full view of his spies. We will find a way to investigate without him knowing. In the meantime, we will let him believe we are only recovering and mourning before moving on. He'd be happy to see us go and not risk killing us. That would not only be suspicious but also dangerous. He knows if he succeeds then Varro and Falco are out there to avenge me. It's better if we just left the city."

Kinara seemed chastened at the thought of Pertinax targeting her, but she tilted her head back at Curio's claims.

"You think he will be so easily fooled? Well, maybe, but even if he is not, he would not move against me. My father also has connections, ones Pertinax would not want to offend."

"Then all the more reason not to anger Doctor Nisos by staying with you. We will need his help when we bring down Pertinax." Curio used his cane to point toward the wall gate. "Now, let's go before we become too obvious standing here."

They returned to the inn near the site of Cecelia's murder. Despite the proximity, it did not bother either him or Galerius. This room did not represent her, and her meager belongings had been burned with her. Galerius had retained a memento he refused to reveal, secreting in his small pack. The innkeeper appeared to be a caring man who understood their pain. He sent one of his servants up to them each night with their meals. Of course, he did not reduce their rates. Curio counted their remaining coins after the funerary expenses and other fees. They could live a frugal life for a few more weeks on what remained.

They agreed that rest was of foremost importance. Galerius wanted to search the well enclosure and surroundings, but Curio feared Pertinax or his cronies would still be watching it. Galerius agreed to stay away, but not without his face flushing red.

"Then I don't understand how we are going to prove Pertinax was the killer. Any proof he might have left behind will be gone soon."

"The best proof we had was the pugio, and the Scythians took it. We're not trying to find footprints or something of his at the scene. Unless he left a papyrus with a confession written on it, anything we find will be meaningless. So, we need to find witnesses. Once we have enough people willing to speak against him, then we can bring him to justice."

Galerius stared at him as they both sat in the small, dimly lit room. He heard in his head the unspoken question asking how they would convince those who had been bribed or intimidated to come forward. What did they have to offer over Pertinax? Of course, he didn't have an answer. He hoped a good night's sleep would reveal one in the morning. Because right now, he felt like he wanted to crawl into a hole and never see the sun again.

As he lay on the bed, searching the darkness above for answers, his eyes closed. Only the exhaustion from the ordeal of Cecelia's death and burial led him into slumber. Otherwise, his mind ground away on the problems facing him and trying to think of what Varro would do in this situation Before he drifted to sleep, he considered that justice might have to come from his own hand in the end.

He awakened during the night. The darkness had not lifted. No sounds reached his ears other than the faint snoring from others in adjacent rooms.

And that was what had awakened him.

Galerius was gone.

He had spent most of his life sleeping in tents piled up with seven other men. Their snores were a lullaby to him and when they were absent his sleep grew restless.

Springing upright, feeling a pinch in his wounded abdomen, he cursed as he spoke Galerius's name. In the silence, it was like a shout. As he sat on the bed, he swept his foot into the darkness where Galerius should be. His toes caught on an empty blanket.

"The little shit used my own tricks. And I know where he went, the fool."

He swiped the cane from beside his bed, got to his feet, and then wore his tunic and belt. He fastened the small knife behind his back and wore a cloak. The wrap around his torso was fresh and tight. In better times, he would've leaped to the chase. Now he struggled to prepare. He only took solace in knowing just a week ago even standing without help would have taxed him.

The art of moving silently and unseen was incompatible with using a cane. Fortunately, he could tuck it underarm as he slipped down the wooden stairs, placing his feet so the boards did not squeak. The downstairs was closed and dark, but he knew the back way out and discovered Galerius had left the door open for his return.

Curio would have to walk across town and then hope he remembered where Pertinax was said to live. He was certain Galerius was operating mostly on immature rage and righteousness and had no real plan. Curio guessed he had at least an hour's head start. By now, he might be doing something as stupid as banging on Pertinax's door.

He wouldn't worry about anything until he saw for himself what foolishness Galerius was up to.

Crossing the city at night was less stressful than doing the same in Rome. For all its size and population, Athens was more open and seemed less dangerous at night. Of course, Curio had no idea what neighborhoods were safe or dangerous here. So he had less to fear when everything looked the same to him.

He eventually found the street where they had their fateful encounter with Pertinax. He only needed to follow the slope down, past Doctor Nisos's apartments, and then continue to where Pertinax made his home.

He felt the burn in his thighs from walking for so long but did not need his cane except to probe the darkest areas on the street. He was proud of what he achieved. It seemed he needed pressure to discover his real limits.

Eventually, he came to where Pertinax must make his residence.

The walled enclosures all seemed alike to him. At least Galerius would have the same problem in identifying the right one. The starlight did not reveal much more than silvery roads and rooftops, the buildings and spaces between them remaining impenetrable blackness. A dog barked somewhere, drawing Curio toward it.

He found Galerius crouched beside the wall of a large home. The faint light caught the edges of his cloak as he hunched over something.

Sparks lit up his face with pale light, and then a fire caught, casting his normally boyish features into an evil leer.

Orange fire spread in a line up the wall from where he stood. He intended to burn down the home with Pertinax inside.

And likely consume half of Athens in flames as well.

Curio stifled the impulse to shout and ran toward the fire.

11

Curio forgot his wounds and pain as he rushed toward Galerius across the street. He was so intent on fanning the fire that he did not turn until Curio kicked him flat. With a gasp of shock, he crashed to his side. A clay jug fell from his grasp, spilling viscous dark fluid.

"Are you mad? You'll burn down half the city."

Galerius recoiled from Curio, the orange flames illuminating his hateful face.

"I hope they all burn! They're all corrupt."

The fire spread down a long line of the exterior wall, bringing fearful amber light to the dark alley between walled homes. Curio realized they could do nothing now except warn neighbors of the fire. He remembered the recent horror of escaping a burning apartment in Rome and did not wish such a fate on those whose only crime was being Pertinax's neighbors.

Galerius struggled to his feet, cursing his oil-slicked palms that gleamed in the light. He backed away from the fire.

"We've got to wake up the neighbors. Hurry."

But Galerius's eyes widened in disbelief.

"Now you're acting mad. We'll be caught. Besides, I'm waiting here for Pertinax to come out. I've barricaded his rear gate."

He drew a thin knife out of the recesses of his cloak, its short blade glinting with the burgeoning fire.

Curio's cane struck out with all the force he would use on a wayward recruit. Galerius screamed as it connected with his hand, causing him to drop the kitchen knife and stagger back.

"We're getting out of here and warning the neighbors. Come with me."

The fire now crawled along the top of the wall. Had Galerius not spilled the jug of oil, he might have lobbed it over the wall to help the fire spread to the main building where Pertinax slept. It was a solid plan that Varro and Falco had employed before, but they had never done it in a populated city where thousands of lives were at stake.

Curio snagged Galerius by his wrist, but he dug in his heels and heaved back.

"Let go! He murdered my sister, and he'll pay for it!"

If Curio hadn't been so weakened from his wound and prolonged bedrest, he would have flattened Galerius with a gut punch and carried him off like a sack of barley. Instead, he found himself in a tug of war while standing in front of a growing fire that now climbed up the stucco wall like vines of flame.

He struggled back and forth until he regained his sense. Cursing Galerius's foolishness, he released him, and he shot back to land on his backside.

"You're throwing your life away! Follow me out, or you're on your own!"

"Coward!" Galerius leaped to his feet, wiping his face and smearing it with dirty oil from his palms. "Cecelia was wrong about you!"

However much the accusation stung, Curio knew better than to remain at the scene of an arson. He staggered around, his wounded side aching as he did. But he held his cane more like a weapon than a crutch.

Yet before he had taken a dozen steps, the gate to Pertinax's home slammed open.

Curio whirled to face the thundering voice screaming what had to be an alarm in Greek. He was not Pertinax, but a man equal to his size with a broad naked chest covered in curly black hair. His wide eyes reflected the fire, which he pointed at as he screamed.

Galerius had retrieved the knife and now raised it overhead as he charged at the man.

"For Cecelia!"

The fight was nearly an afterthought for the Greek in the archway. He stepped back in surprise but then caught Galerius's thin wrist in hand, twisting the strike aside and simultaneously slamming Galerius to the wall. He repeated the slam like a man beating out a dusty carpet. The knife fell to the ground, and he threw Galerius into the opened gate as he rushed out toward the fire.

For the moment, no one looked at Curio. His instinct was to rescue Galerius while he was still in view lying on the ground inside the gate. Yet his side ached and his legs were tired. He had only his cane and a small knife no better than the pathetic one Galerius had stolen from the inn. He would be charging toward failure. Besides, the fool had willfully chosen his fate and refused help when it would've done him good. Curio wavered.

Fortuna decided for him, and she was unkind.

A group of men surged down the street, calling out to awaken everyone along their path. While Curio saw some with buckets, he saw one man in the lead with a long whip in hand. A Scythian.

He cursed his ill luck and marveled at the response time of the Scythian peacekeepers. The fire was not even yet a threat to Pertinax's main home and they already had a water brigade ready. Even Rome's night watch slaves were not so swift to respond.

In his condition, he could not outrun them. However, for the moment, he appeared as just another citizen coming to extinguish the fire. So, he started toward it, calling out sounds that he hoped imitated the Greek alarms he heard being shouted from behind. No one would pay much attention to him with an obvious fire so near.

He crossed back to where the bare-chested Greek had retreated into the gate. Galerius was no longer in view, but Curio supposed he might have been hauled off to the side or else gone into hiding. He could at least peer inside to confirm his escape and then flee during the confusion.

Yet before he reached the gate, Pertinax emerged from it.

There was no mistaking his huge frame, now outlined in brilliant yellow from the flames consuming his exterior wall. He was also bare chested, and a ragged red scar ran down his left side to match the curving scar under his eye. The bucket he held sloshed water onto the ground.

They faced each other in stunned silence. It seemed Pertinax did not recognize him.

Curio turned his head and cut to the side, hoping to avoid recognition long enough to flee into the shadows. While he was healed enough to walk without a cane, he could not run like he used to.

"Centurion Curio! You shit-eating rat!"

So much for avoiding recognition. Curio attempted to run, turning hard on his heel to head opposite the oncoming crowd.

But Pertinax started shouting in Greek before switching to Latin.

"Starting a fire is low even for you. You'll be crucified for this!"

His running was no better than a painfully obvious loping motion that marked him as a target.

Something cracked with explosive force beneath his left heel. A bright spark of pain sent him flying face-down into the dirt road. Just as he had done when he first encountered Pertinax, Curio rolled uselessly on the ground. The cane was under him, and it had driven up into his chin, which now throbbed with pain.

Strong hands grabbed him by the legs and arms, effectively binding him in place. As he fought and squirmed, men with breath stinking of garlic and wine crowded him. They thrashed Curio until at last he gave up. Even if he had escaped, they could have brought him down again. He was like a fish bouncing around a dock and hoping to reach water. But the Scythians had landed him for good.

One of them was lost in shadow, but he had shaggy auburn hair that seemed to burn around the fringes as the fire rose higher in the distance. Another held him down while the other bound his hands, muttering curses as he did. He yanked hard on the knot and Curio felt his hands grow cold from reduced circulation. These binds would not be slipped.

Once the Scythian had him in custody, he and his companion hauled him up to face the fire. Now the wall was entirely engulfed in flames, but in this brief time, a long chain of citizens was bringing buckets to douse the fire. Fortunately for Athens, it was a still night and the fire did not spread to the neighboring buildings. Pertinax had vanished, likely gone to save his home.

More Scythians had arrived, distinguishing themselves from the Athenians both in their dress and in the long whips they carried. Most were directing the firefighting efforts, and others aided the residents of Pertinax's home and neighbors. However, Curio settled on the Scythian leading Galerius from the house.

His recently bruised face was now dark with fresh ones. Blood dribbled from the corner of his mouth. As his captor joined with Curio's, he hung his head and kept silent.

The Scythians had a brief discussion, with one leading the others. It seemed Curio and Galerius would discover the wonders of an Athenian prison. They kept pointing between the fire and somewhere toward the Acropolis. They also gave them expectant looks, but neither could understand Greek.

The leader addressed Curio directly, his oily face gleaming with the yellow flames lighting the night. Curio just shook his head.

"I'm a Roman citizen. I don't understand you."

In answer, the Scythian repeated himself, only shouting this time. Curio repeated his statement, matching the volume. They looped in this deadlock until Curio repeatedly shouted the word "Roman."

At last, the Scythians surrounding him seemed to understand and they laughed. The leader stroked Curio's scruffy beard with his gritty palm then slapped his cheek playfully.

"Roman!" Then he nodded to Galerius and repeated his discovery. "Roman!"

Curio sighed and tested the bindings digging into his wrists. Escape was impossible. Of course, he was hemmed in from every side with these Scythian idiots. The leader tugged the thin hairs of Curio's chin, repeating "Roman" and laughing with his companions. These Scythians grew thick beards that they trimmed to neat points. Despite their easy laughter, their faces were weathered and lined from constant scowling.

They were laughing still as half of the gathered Scythians dragged him and Galerius away. Curio took one final glance over his shoulder at the fire before rounding a building. Its intensity diminished as Athenians doused the wall with buckets of water. He had to admire the unbelievable response time to the threat and was glad no one else would become a victim of Galerius's ill-conceived scheme.

The Scythians had relieved him of his cane, which he did not need with a man on either side dragging him across the city. They did not mistreat him or Galerius and instead focused on their mission. Each had the discipline of a soldier, though they must be slaves of the city to be so far from their homeland.

They reached a low and squat building where Curio could finally look behind to where the fire might still be burning. But he did not see anything down the rolling slopes or over the treetops and buildings. The Scythians reported to a sleepy-eyed guard who accepted both him and Galerius into custody. From there, they were led into a black iron latticework cage. The door clanged shut and the two of them had just enough space to sit opposite each other. Their knees would touch and neither could lie down. Sleep would be impossible in this position without first being exhausted.

But Curio knew the Greeks did not keep prisoners long. They would be judged and punished within a few days at most.

So they sat with Galerius's head down. Blood had crusted on his lip and dried where it had pattered to his chest. He did not even shift his position. At last, Curio whispered into the darkness.

"If I didn't know better, I'd think you're dead. Are you hurt?"

Galerius shook his head. Curio stared into the gloom. A foul-smelling torch guttered inside the closed door so that any guard entering would have illumination at hand. There were only a few other empty cages in a stone-walled room without windows.

"There's no one to come to our aid," Curio said, perhaps too cheerfully for the current reality. "I don't think Kinara is that invested in our welfare. But maybe she'll get someone to speak for us."

Galerius shifted at last and turned over his palms.

"I've got oil on my hands and was caught right there. At best, I can try to convince them you are innocent. What do you think the punishment will be?"

"I can only say what would happen in Rome. Probably execution. In a city, there isn't a greater crime than arson. Maybe only starting a rebellion might be worse. But the Athenians are famous for their fairness. If no one was killed, maybe given the circumstances we will get a lesser sentence."

Galerius chuckled without humor. "I don't care about dying now that Cecelia is gone. I just can't stomach that Pertinax lives. If they let you go, promise me you will avenge her."

"Revenge doesn't bring people back to life. Remembering them lets them live on. If we get out of this, then give your sister life by carrying her memory into your old age. Don't throw your life away trying to reach Pertinax. He can't be touched inside Athens, and he doesn't ever leave. The gods will judge him in their time."

At last raising his head, Galerius stared over the tops of his knees. In the gloom, his expression was impossible to read. He did not hold his gaze long and lowered his head without a word, then shifted aside as best he could.

The rest of the night passed in silence. In this windowless room, he was uncertain of the passing of time. Only once did a guard enter with a new torch. After kindling it in the dying flames of the old one, he passed it across Curio's cage. He saw only a shadow obscured in hazy orange light before the guard wordlessly exited the prison.

Eventually, boredom settled him into a half-sleep. Awakening at points, he saw the torch burning down. Galerius remained motionless as if he had willed himself into the stillness of death. Only the warmth of his knees against Curio's indicated he lived. After several cycles, he awakened for good. It must be dawn since he awakened with it every day for his entire life. It was only natural. Yet for Galerius, he snored lightly with his round head resting against the lattice bars. Curio could not help but see his sister in the shape of his head and face.

Eventually, a guard came with bowls of water and hunks of hard black bread he shoved through square gaps in the bars. Galerius had awakened with a groan. He claimed to have no appetite, but Curio forced him to eat.

"You can't be certain if there will be another meal."

"I don't want to die." His voice was small and frightened. "I lied."

"Neither do I. But don't kill yourself with worry before the moment comes. We're alive now."

"How can you be so calm? We're in a cage with no hope at all."

Curio tore into the hard bread, feeling as if he might pull out his teeth to bite off a piece.

"You wouldn't believe how many times I've been in a cage like this. And those were enemies who wanted to kill me. We're just awaiting judgment here. Eat and drink so you'll be ready for what the gods send to you. After you're dead, you have forever to be sad about it. Until then, keep some hope."

Whether he reached Galerius, Curio focused on eating and planning for what might happen. Certainly, arson was a vile crime, and even if he was not directly involved, the Athenians would not care. He was a friend of Galerius and was caught fleeing the scene. Guilt by association assured he would share whatever fate awaited them.

As expected, they did not spend even the full morning in the cell. The guard opened the door and allowed more Scythians inside to unlock their cage. He at least assumed they were Scythians since they did not carry whips or any visible weaponry. Perhaps they thought so little of Curio in his poor condition and Galerius's immature strength that they did not burden themselves with such precautions.

They were led outside to a morning that was a stark contrast to the prior day. The sky had become flat gray and blanketed with wooly clouds. Even Galerius looked up at the glare and shuddered. It was a bad day for the gods to look down on mortals. Their sight was obscured, and Curio's prayers would have to reach higher than those thick clouds.

The guards bound their hands and then put them into a cart. They rolled along streets busy with morning traffic. The two Scythians sat in the cart with them, their strong and hairy arms folded over barrel chests. Along every street, people paused to watch the wagon pass, and Curio felt humiliated. He was a proud Roman citizen, but these people saw him as scum.

They headed up into the Acropolis, and Curio's interest grew even as a cold fear spread in his hands and feet at their judgment. He could not see much of it from the cart, and his gawking drew derisive chuckles from his guards. It was Athen's most famous location, and he regretted seeing it under these circumstances.

A dark thought passed through his mind. He might have a grand view of it when hung up on the walls to die. He shook his head at his terrible humor. Yet how often had he faced death? It was bound to find him one day, and this day seemed more likely every moment.

They came to a place like a large theater. Their guards hauled them out of the carriage and shoved them forward. Again, Curio was impressed at how efficient they were and how they handled their prisoners with dignity. He would have expected to be knocked over, beaten, spit on, and then dragged before the judges. Their guilt was already established, and most guards would add to their captive's suffering in this situation. However, the Scythians did not waste their energy and simply kept Curio and Galerius under firm control.

The guards led them down into the theater, where stone seats for hundreds sat empty. A crowd of men sat at the bottom of the long stone stairs, and white-haired men in clean gray tunics sat at tables where actors would perform for the audience. They had cups of wine and plates of fruits set out, and they picked through these as they watched Curio and Galerius being led down the steps.

Everyone looked at them, and a murmur rippled through the audience. One middle-aged man leaped up from his bench and approached. He first addressed the guards, who stopped him on the stairs, and then looked to Curio.

"I will interpret for you. One of the elders speaks some Latin, but it will be clearer if I do the speaking."

Curio was glad for this thoughtfulness, and it showed a commitment from the Athenians to fairness. He hoped these elders would have mercy in equal measure, even if it was not deserved. He scanned their faces, finding each one stern and humorless. Hope shrank, but it failed utterly when he saw Pertinax seated in the front row. He stared at him up the stairs and then drew his finger across his neck.

The interpreter, his back to Pertinax, did not see this and spoke in his chipper voice.

"Your crimes are serious, but you will get to state your case. Do it well, and you might enjoy mercy today."

But Pertinax's smirk warned Curio otherwise. He swallowed hard and nodded, then the guards led him and Galerius before the council.

12

Curio stood facing the Athenian council of elders, seven in total. Galerius was lined up beside him, and he realized the youth might stand a hair taller than himself. Given the stakes of this trial, it was a vain and stray thought completely out of place. But that was the state of his mind. With everything conducted in Greek, it wandered in strange directions.

Each elder had addressed the audience in turn, and Curio's less-than-helpful interpreter only offered summaries. "He's talking about the danger of fire," or "He wants to hear your claims and then move to sentencing."

Of course, Curio couldn't help himself, even if the trial was in his mother tongue. He was surrounded by several hundred men of every age, and none of them were seemingly pleased with what they heard. They grumbled often, and at other points shouted out when an elder seemed to make a popular remark.

The gray day threatened rain, and a cool breeze swept the bottom of the bowl that formed a theater. Brown and dead leaves rolled past his feet, and Curio could not help but read the omen of his own fate. Galerius remained with his head lowered and face red. Curio had expected him to be all righteous bluster and rage. Perhaps the reality of their plight had stolen it from him.

Finally, the interpreter leaned closer and spoke in a low voice.

"We'll hear from the man whose home you burned. Then you will make your statements and judgment will be passed."

Pertinax stepped forward, nodding to the elders. At least two nodded back, which set a fire of worry in the pit of Curio's stomach. He spoke in what sounded like fluent Greek to Curio's untrained ears. All the while he pointed to his fellow Romans, stabbing his finger like the pugio he had used to kill Cecelia.

His speech was convincing, or so it seemed. Their interpreter forgot to translate until Curio prodded him. "Oh, he is describing how terrified he is of you and how his neighbors blame him for your recklessness."

Curio watched Pertinax deliver an impassioned speech, and even if he did not understand the words, he grasped the dramatic body language. He had expected him to perform only slightly better than his drunken self. Yet here he displayed confidence before the crowd, and he used flourishes of rapid gestures to dramatize his points. Most of the elders sat still, listening with eyebrows raised. The audience likewise had fallen silent.

When it was done, he turned to take his seat and gave Curio a dark smile.

"You're finished," he said to him, his voice only loud enough for them to hear.

The interpreter then instructed them to plead their cases to the elders. Before he led them forward, he leaned in with a whisper.

"I'm no friend of Pertinax, but some of the elders are. The Scythians are here as witnesses, too. Don't try to deny your crime. The elders might be inclined to mercy if you allow a swift end to this proceeding."

Curio nodded his thanks and suddenly found himself looking at Galerius. His face was bright red, and his eyes watered.

"Stand up straight," he said. "Even if what you did was a crime, you're still a Roman citizen. Act like one."

He then turned to the elders and hoped his interpreter would be faithful to his words.

"I did not set the fire, but I take responsibility for it." Without his cane for balance, Curio did not want to dare the dramatic posturing of Pertinax. So he simply set his hand to his chest. "Galerius is under my care. I should have realized he would want revenge after Pertinax's brutal murdering of his twin sister."

The interpreter paused, presumably at the mention of the murder, but completed his interpretation. The elders sat back in surprise, and Pertinax was already protesting. However, the elders waved him down and allowed Curio to continue.

"I know that murder has not been settled, but we know Pertinax did it. Poor Galerius was delirious at the violence of his sister's death. He acted rashly. We are both deeply horrified at what could have happened had the fire spread out of control. We know what we did was wrong, and we ask that you consider our grief and our Roman citizenship when determining our fates. Speaking of which, we are both here on special assignment to Senator Flamininus. I have stayed behind in Athens while recovering from a wound. Whatever our fate, you will need to ensure it is reported to him."

Using the senator's name was his best bet for avoiding execution. He had nothing to prove his claim but hoped the elders were cautious. Athens was a proud city with a strong army of citizen soldiers like Rome's. But they owed Rome much and Flamininus even more. He was Greece's liberator, and invoking his name was like calling on Jupiter himself.

This revelation caused a stir among both the elders and the audience. Even Pertinax now stood, his face shading red as he pointed at Curio.

"You never mentioned anything like that before. It's a lie!"

"You never asked. Anyway, Doctor Nisos and Kinara can attest to it." He looked at his stunned translator and glared at him to continue interpreting. "Send a messenger to Senator Flamininus's camp. He is nearby and will confirm my claim. I was only to remain here long enough for this to heal before joining him."

Curio pulled back his tunic to display the wrap around his torso.

Now the faces of the elder council turned as white as their hair. They argued with each other, and the audience shouted over them. The interpreter looked all around as if unable to pick something to translate. Yet Curio guessed their arguments. Some wanted justice done and not fear Rome, while others wanted caution.

Galerius was invited to speak once the elders regained control of their audience. He gave Curio a pleading stare.

"Admit what you've done. Tell them you serve the senator like me. Nothing else you say will matter to them."

Galerius no longer seemed as tall as he had been moments ago. He did as Curio had instructed, simply admitting his guilt and accepting their judgment.

"I was overcome with grief, and I know Pertinax did it even if haven't found proof yet."

The elder council did not take long to reach their decision and announced it in Greek to the crowd. Pertinax folded his arms and scowled while most of the crowd seemed satisfied if not pleased.

The interpreter raised his voice over the general commotion.

"You are both exiled from the city under pain of death should you return, even in Rome's service. You are also to pay a fine of fifty drachmae each for damages done to properties and the suffering of innocent citizens."

Galerius seemed about to collapse with joy. Yet Curio's legs weakened for another reason.

"But we don't have a hundred drachmae."

The interpreter stared hard at him, and then he called for the elders' attention. Curio felt all their eyes turning to him one after the next and watched their frowns deepen in disgust. Again, they fell to debating until their leader seemed to bring them to a resolution. He cleared his throat and spoke to the crowd, which again applauded.

The interpreter swallowed hard and gave them a sympathetic smile.

"Well, since you cannot pay, then you are to serve a period of slavery to the city until the fine is paid. Then you will be exiled."

"What?" Galerius lost his soggy demeanor and nearly leaped atop the interpreter. "How long is that?"

"It depends on how what kind of slave you are. Latin tutors are paid well. You could join the Scythians. Not all of them are really from Scythia, after all. I'm not sure what they're paid. Hopefully, Senator Flamininus will buy your freedom in any case."

As if in response to the mention, Scythians came forward with chains. Curio stood in stunned silence.

"A hundred drachmae is a ridiculous fine. The entire house couldn't have cost that much, and no one was hurt."

The interpreter shrugged. "Your lives are not worth fifty drachmae each? This is the council's judgment. Be happy. You should've been crucified."

All the while, Pertinax laughed along with those sitting beside him. He was already standing to leave, waving goodbye as he did.

"Maybe I'll buy you," he shouted across the short distance. "I don't need a Latin tutor, though."

The Scythians now came forward to bind them again. The interpreter stepped back, offering his last advice.

"You'll be taken to the slave market today. By tomorrow, you could have new employment. Good luck, and don't give up hope. Maybe Senator Flamininus will buy your freedom."

Galerius wrestled with the Scythians, but Curio simply held out his arms for the manacles they carried.

He was going to become a slave. Only yesterday, he was planning to return to Varro and Falco, and now this. He would have to get a message to them and beg them to come with enough drachmae to pay for his freedom. Whether they would pay for Galerius's remained to be seen. The chains clinked as the Scythian gathered Curio's wrists closer to fit the manacles.

A shout over the general excitement eventually drew enough attention that even Curio snapped out of his fog. The iron manacles were around his wrist, but the Scythian paused at what he heard.

Kinara stood before the elders. She wore a gray cloak and revealed herself from beneath a large hood. Given the threat of foul weather, she was not oddly dressed. Now she held up a sack, the strong swell of her bicep flexing. Her dusky skin shimmered in the flat light as she shouted over the hollering crowd.

"It seems your fines are paid," the translator said, rubbing his chin with a bemused smile. "But how did a woman get into the assembly?"

Curio did not care how Kinara did it and only focused on the sack of coins she set on the elder's table. One of them produced a scale and weights to count out the fine and ensure the coins were acceptable.

"We're saved!" Galerius shouted, still in the grip of the Scythians restraining him. "Thank the gods Kinara arrived in time!"

Pertinax had started to leave but now turned back and rushed toward the elder table. Indeed, other citizens surged forward in protest. It was all beyond Curio, who could only admire Kinara as she stood firm against scores of men arguing against her presence. Yet she seemed to have supporters, including several on the elder council.

In the end, her coins were swept off the table and the sack returned to her much deflated. The elders shouted for peace, which they got in some measure. Curio looked for his interpreter, but he had also lost himself in the arguments. He stood alone with the Scythians, who now held him lightly by his arm.

Kinara scowled at the men surrounding her, pulled up the hood over her head, and then turned from the elders. Only her smile was visible from beneath the shade of her hood.

"Your fine has been paid. You'll add it to the bill you owe my father." Her smile twisted and her voice became playfully mocking. "I'm sure Senator Flamininus will pay it since you're on a special mission for him."

The Scythians had stepped away but still surrounded him. Curio realized slavery was no longer a concern, but his banishment had to be fulfilled. Still, he was tempted to crush Kinara in a hug and thank her. However, propriety and the sudden and sharp remembrance of Cecelia held him back. He simply shook his head in admiration.

"I can't believe you managed this."

"I used my father's name to keep you from slavery," she said. "And I was not going to become one again."

Pertinax suddenly cut into Curio's vision. His face was red and his smile tightly false.

"That's the last favor you'll find here. Begone from Athens, and never return. Or I'll cut your throats myself, and be a hero for doing it."

"Like you did to my sister? I'll kill you first!"

Fortunately, the Scythians still had a grip on Galerius as he struck forward. Pertinax did not flinch but scoffed at the vain attempt to reach him.

"Galerius, calm yourself!" Curio wanted to raise his hand for peace, but his Scythian mistook him for trying to join the fight. He latched onto Curio's wrist and twisted it painfully upside down.

The tussle drew members of the assembly, shouting what sounded like encouragement for a fight. Galerius lashed out at the Scythians while Pertinax egged him on.

"Go ahead, boy. I'll undo all of Kinara's hard work and fix your face for good."

"You killed my sister!"

"I did no such thing!"

"Galerius, calm down!"

But Curio remained pinned in place, and the Scythian curtailed his shouts by twisting his wrist again. Instead, he yelped in pain.

Then Galerius was free and he leaped for Pertinax. His face was scarlet red, his eyes and teeth flashing raw hatred. He drew one hand back for a punch as a Scythian grabbed for him. For his part, Pertinax seemed to lean into it. He made himself a target so that the entire assembly could see Galerius assault him.

Curio jabbed the Scythian holding him in the ribs, striking with more force than he thought he had. The surprise loosened the grip on his arm, and he slipped out to throw himself at Galerius. They collided just before the punch landed.

The two of them collapsed to the ground amid shouts of surprise and delight.

The Scythians had lost their dispassionate demeanors. As Curio struggled to keep Galerius down while he flailed and cursed Pertinax for a killer, one of the Scythians grabbed him by the hair and threw him back.

Before he could orient himself, one delivered a heel kick directly into his wounded side.

The pain curled him up and shot bolts of lightning through his vision. He felt as if his stomach slammed into the base of his throat. He gasped and folded over to protect himself from another kick.

The struggle continued over his body, but he was too numb with pain to care. He focused on how much of his recovery had just been kicked away. The staggering pain rolled back and forth over his side like waves in a reflecting pool. When at last he came around, one of the Scythians dragged him upright.

Kinara pressed beside him, her dusky face now white, and tried to reach Curio's wound. Galerius spit and cursed as he wrestled with his opponent. Dozens of angry, bearded faces crowded around and cursed while the Scythians hauled Curio out of the throng. He was aware of his feet clapping against the stone stairs of the amphitheater, and one of his sandals broke away.

The cursing receded as they reached the top stairs. He had regained enough of his wits to realize Kinara was chattering away in Greek to the Scythians. Every time she reached out for Curio, they shoved her back. At last, one unfurled a whip and Kinara retreated.

"I'll find you," she shouted as they herded Curio into the street toward the waiting cart. Others came with Galerius slumped between them like a snared rabbit. This time, the Scythians hurled both of them into the bed before pulling themselves aboard. At least two of the six men in the cart bed with them had curving daggers at their hips. Their strong, gnarled hands rested on the pommels.

Curio closed his eyes, listening to Galerius sniveling and their guards muttering curses. The wagon shook as the driver mounted it, and then jerked forward.

The pain sloshing over his sides demanded his full concentration. Though he remained doubled over and cradling the wound, he feared touching it and discovering a warm dampness. Yet the stitches were overdue to be removed, and the skin healed. Perhaps nothing had torn. At least nothing externally.

The cart rumbled through the unpaved streets of Athens. They were not being given any chance at farewells, collecting their belongings, or any last look at the city. Banishment was instant is it was irrevocable. From the moment the elder council and its magistrates ratified their judgment, he and Galerius were now vermin in the eyes of Athens—something to be driven out or exterminated.

The longer the cart rolled and swayed through the streets, foreign voices rising and falling as they passed, the more Curio recovered from the stunning kick. Eventually, he opened his eyes and raised his head. The frizzy hair of his guards formed a dark ring around a flat gray sky. A cold pinpoint hit his cheek, the first spray of promised rain. A few guards also looked up, and one said something to make the rest laugh.

Galerius was folded into a corner, with manacles locking his wrists together. His red face hung to his chest, and fresh blood stains dried on the tunic beneath his chin. Curio considered that time in Athens was making his friend uglier by the day. The thought would have made him laugh if he had not been so uncomfortable.

They reached a gate Curio had never seen. Judging from the sun's position, he guessed it was the northwest wall. It would be a favorable start to reaching Senator Flamininus. Although he didn't know his exact location, a Roman senator on official business with his escort centuries would be hard to miss in Greece. Someone would know.

The cart rolled to a stop, and their guards dragged them out of the cart bed. Curio tried to stand on his own but could not avoid the iron grasp of the Scythian dragging him to the ground. He crashed on his hip, jolting him with crippling pain both from this old wound and impact with the hard road. They kicked him again, fortunately not on his wounded side, and raised him to his feet. Conversely, Galerius jumped down from the bed without issue. He had time to stand before they could drag him.

The Scythians growled commands and curses that neither of them understood. Curio folded over his side and limped painfully through the gate with the Scythians on both sides. When they reached the shadowed end of the tunnel, they pointed toward the blue hills in the distance.

"As if I'd ever want to come back," Curio said, his voice weak. "I hope a plague kills all of you."

The language barrier worked both ways, for the Scythians simply blinked at him.

Galerius had cruder words, and his tone hinted at their meaning. Yet rather than rile the guards, they laughed as they formed a line across the tunnel. Citizens had paused to watch but soon tired of the standoff and continued on their business.

"We have nothing," Galerius said. "Not even our coins."

"Help me walk," Curio said, limping toward him. "And stop complaining."

Looping his arm around Galerius's shoulder they started the long walk into the Greek countryside. Neither spoke as they left Athens behind. Curio remembered Kinara's promise to find them. He wondered if she would bother, and why. He thought back to her drifting hand and how she seemed to be tempting him. It made no sense and might have been his confused imagination at play. Whatever her reason, he'd welcome any help she could provide.

After a long and painful walk to the intersection leading into unknown parts, Curio stopped.

"We'll see if Kinara shows up."

"Do we really need her now?"

He shot Galerius a deadly look.

"Have you so little idea of the world? We're two weak and unarmed men lost in the countryside. We only avoided slavery to the city of Athens. Out here, we'll be picked up by brigands and either sold into a worse slavery or enslaved to them."

Galerius straightened his back and looked around as if the brigands were hiding over the hills in the distance. It was only midday with gray skies that would erupt into rain by nightfall. The brooding atmosphere seemed to hide threats over every rise.

"I hope Kinara brings us weapons and supplies, plus our coins."

"We already owe her father enough," Curio said. "But I fear we'll have to lean on their generosity one more time."

Galerius whistled through his teeth. "If we had gone to any other doctor, I can't imagine what would happen to us. At first, I thought Kinara was cold, but she's a fine woman. Without her, we would be miserable."

"I hope she brings her basket of supplies and my cane. Thanks to you, I've reinjured myself."

"Thanks to me?" Galerius held Curio back and frowned. "I didn't do anything."

"You started a brawl and I paid the price for it. You only got a few bruises and a bloody lip. Fortune favors the fool, my father used to say."

"You're not that bad. You can still walk."

"That's true. But I don't feel good. Like something pressing on my stomach all the time." He used his free hand to press the air in demonstration. "And breathing is hard."

"You're just flustered. We'll find a town with a doctor, and you'll be fine."

"Such optimism."

"You just told me not to complain."

Curio accepted the implied rebuke, and the two found a place to sit beside the intersection. His hip shuddered with pain as he lowered to the grass. The fall out of the cart had shaken him worse than he wanted to admit. His breathing remained labored and his side and back ached. He wanted to lie back and close his eyes, but feared he might not awaken.

He said nothing of this to Galerius. They sat for an hour or so, watching the occasional traveling group leaving or entering the city. No one paid them any attention. At last, Galerius sprang to his feet.

"There's Kinara, and she has her basket."

"That's good. I need that pain potion of hers." Curio struggled to stand, spotting Kinara waving at them down the road.

Then a wave of nausea overcame him and his sight faded to brown before plunging into black.

Curio knew no more.

13

Curio traversed a cold and gray landscape, though he did not know by what means. His legs did not move, and he did not feel the road under his feet. He had lost a sandal, he remembered, and every rock had gouged his callused sole as he limped away from the city. But where was he now?

Voices argued over him. He could not keep his eyes open for long before an inexplicable weight slammed them closed like the gates of Athens. Glimpses of figures hovering around him, their faces turned toward a guttering light source, were all he saw. Their voices sounded as if they echoed from another world.

He did not feel pain, only cold wetness. Rather than struggle to the surface of consciousness, he let himself slip down into the dark. He might have drifted within the dark for minutes or days and time had stopped in this numb place. Then warmth flooded into his extremities and his frozen mind stirred.

Awakening again, he discovered a sudden clarity. The gauzy world had been swept aside and replaced with a scene of stark orange light and black shadow that danced across mudbrick walls.

He reclined on a bed in a small room beside a hearth. Wet tunics, cloaks, and sandals were set before it. Galerius sat on a hard dirt floor with his knees pulled up to his chin and arms wrapped around them. The hearth light flickered in his unblinking eyes.

Curio propped himself on his elbows, and his vision swam momentarily.

"You're awake."

Kinara sat on the edge of the wood-frame bed and shifted closer. Her warm hand slid up to a fresh wrap on Curio's side, grazing his skin. He recoiled in surprise, realizing he was naked and covered only at the waist with a thin sheet.

"Is this your father's apartment?"

Kinara's lush brows drew together as she smiled. "Of course not. You are banished from Athens. I carried you to this village to shelter from the storm."

Her hand now gently pressed his chest, and he set his head back on a thin pillow. She kept it there as she slid closer to him.

"The draught still clings to you. Don't move about too fast."

He nodded understanding, then looked at Galerius. If he had noticed his awakening, then he gave no sign. The hearth fire seemed to dominate his attention.

"I removed your stitches while you slept," Kinara said, shifting so she blocked Galerius from view. "The flesh is healed, and you'll carry the scar for life. I am not expert enough to say whether you have suffered internal damage. Even under the draught, you winced when I pressed the wound."

Curio's mouth was exceptionally dry, as it always was after taking Kinara's draught. "What is that potion? I have never heard of its sort before."

Kinara tilted her head and smiled. "You are a medicine expert? Would my explanation mean anything to you?"

"No, but that draught would be of great use to the legions. It would ease the suffering of the wounded."

"Aren't you more interested in where we are?" Kinara leaned over him, her smile bright in the low light. Her stola was damp and clung to her full body. Curio averted his eyes, remembering Cecelia, and shame warmed his face.

"We must be in a nearby town. Have we rented a room?"

"Yes, but not an inn," Kinara said. "A poor woman recently widowed was glad for anyone's company. This is her home, and she is sleeping in the storage room now. She saw your condition and took pity on you. Your innocent face is very persuasive, even when asleep."

She giggled and gently stroked his beard. He smiled but pushed away from her touch. Again, he thought of how Cecelia wanted to help him shave. Kinara seemed to sense his discomfort and withdrew abruptly. She stood from the bed and turned to Galerius.

"Warm the broth for him," she said. "He must be as hungry as you were, and thirstier."

Curio shifted to watch Galerius move. He seemed sluggish and distracted as he fumbled with a ladle that evaded him in a black iron cooking pot. It scraped around the rim before he grasped it, then he scooped out steaming water to add to a clay bowl of light brown soup. He stirred it in, and Kinara threw a pinch of something into it as he did. It might have been salt to help improve the taste of watered-down soup.

"You need food," she said, offering it to him. "The old woman made it for us when we arrived, but I wanted you to rest first."

He sat up and accepted the warm bowl. The taste was salty with fatty meat. His mouth filled with onions and other vegetables, and he enjoyed the salty flavors. While he ate, Galerius spoke.

"Now that you are awake, we should plan how to get Pertinax out of Athens."

Curio paused as he drank from the bowl. He looked over the rim of it at Kinara, who raised her brows and averted her eyes.

"Get him out of Athens? What do you mean?"

"Exactly that. We can't get back in there. So he has to come out here if we're to kill him."

Curio finished the last of the soup and then passed the emptied bowl to Kinara. She smiled nervously.

"I'll wash this outside. I won't be long."

When she left by the room's single door, Curio struggled to sit up.

He found his cane resting on the edge of the wood frame, and he reached for it if only to occupy his nervous hands.

"Galerius, we have been defeated. Cecelia would not want us to throw our lives away trying to get revenge."

"How would you know what she wanted?" His unfocused eyes suddenly filled with anger, snapping onto Curio's. "You hardly knew her. She would avenge me if I had been murdered. I thought you were fearless. Some sort of elite soldier serving the Senate. But at every turn, you prove you're a coward."

"And you prove you are a hotheaded fool." Curio gripped his cane in white-knuckled fists. "Bravery is not judged by how willing you are to toss your life away. That's a measure of stupidity. Take a good look at both of us. You have no fighting skill beyond flailing around like a spoiled brat. I'm hobbled with an injury that needs time to heal. We've made ourselves enemies of the city. Or should I give you all the credit for that problem? Pertinax is entrenched in his little stronghold. You can't dig him out, even if you could get back inside the city. So, what is your honest assessment of success?"

Galerius stood up, looking bigger for the small room and the twisting shadows cast by the hearth.

"That's why we have to lure him out here. Then we'll skin him alive for what he did to my sister."

Curio gave an exaggerated sigh and slumped his shoulders.

"Ignoring all the other problems with your plan, how will we skin him alive when he gets here? He's a strong fighter. Will you challenge him with that kitchen knife of yours?" Curio mimicked the feeble thrust of a small knife. "Or will I beat him with my cane, hoping I don't fall over in the process? Do you think he'll come alone? His companions will be too awed by our overwhelming force to defend him?"

Galerius's face reddened and he bit his lip. For a moment, Curio thought he might cry. Instead, he closed his eyes and sat back.

"Cecelia could not have been more wrong about you. You are useless."

"I'm practical. You are a childish fool. If you hadn't met me and the two of you ran away to Rome as planned, what would you have done? How would you have survived? You don't think ahead to the consequences. You're just the spoiled son of a rich man. Go home, Galerius. Face your mistakes and forget about taking revenge. Let your father use his wealth to do that instead. If anyone should take revenge for Cecelia's murder, it must be him."

"I swore to protect my sister," he said, his voice low and trembling. He kept his eyes squeezed shut. "She convinced me to believe that you would save her. But you led her to death. You wanted her to act natural and go to the well alone like other women. She died because of your stupid plan. I should have protected her myself. So, revenge is mine to take. No one else's. Don't worry, Curio, you will not have to take any risks now. I see what must be done."

Curio felt a blanket of weariness envelop him, and his hands loosened on the cane. He could not accept Galerius's insults, but his gut roiled and his arms trembled with weakness. Instead of the fiery response he imagined, he shifted onto his back atop the bed.

"We'll discuss this in the morning. I'm tired now."

Kinara entered, her stola dappled with raindrops. Her dusky skin gleamed with orange hearth light as she set the bowl aside and rushed to Curio's side. She set a cold hand on his forehead.

"You are feverish. You need rest." She then glared at Galerius, who shuffled over to the opposite wall and turned his back. The room was not big enough for him to escape elsewhere.

Curio stared up at the shadowed ceiling, fighting to keep his eyes open while Kinara pulled the thin sheet over him.

The urge to sleep was overwhelming. Moments ago, he had pulled out from a dark dream, and now those numbing hands were reaching out to him again. Perhaps he did have a fever and this clarity was only a gap in the nightmares fever produced.

"I am not a coward," he mumbled as the world faded. Kinara, who had slipped out of his closing vision, now appeared over him. Her head was tilted with a confused smile. She set her finger over his mouth and hushed him.

He tried to turn his head and hoped the words he intended crossed his lips.

"Don't let him do something stupid."

But then the wintry grasp of dark dreaming clawed him into black sleep.

This time he swirled through a strangled landscape of cold rain and dark, leafless trees. Wolves stalked between them, the fog of their breath forming white clouds in the blue light of an unseen moon. No matter which way he turned, he could not escape them. He stumbled as he ran, clawing the cold earth to regain his footing and continue a mindless, fearful plunge forward.

When he awakened again, he screamed.

He was staring at the ceiling, heaving as if he had been running all night. A mellow light filled the room now, revealing the old rafters that the night had hidden. Bunches of drying vegetables and plants hung from them, interspersed with other small sacks and bundles. The crowded room was warm, though he heard the delicate tapping of rain on the mudbrick wall beside the small bed.

Kinara stood at the foot, casting a wary eye over him. His sudden awakening did not seem to have surprised her. His eyes were wide and unblinking enough that he felt the stinging coolness of the air on them until they watered.

"I am so thirsty. There was too much salt in that soup."

Kinara laughed. "That was a day ago. You have not kept anything down since that night."

Now he sat up, touching his abdomen and surprised that his stitches were gone. Yet there was still pain tugging at the tender muscles there and he winced.

"Where's Galerius?"

Curio's tunic hung from the rafters by a hook, and his sandal with a fresh replacement to match it was set beneath it. But nothing indicated Galerius was still here. The pain in his gut became a low burn as he realized what had happened. He turned pleadingly to Kinara.

"I could not keep him." She put whatever small item she held back into her basket on a corner table. Her smile was feeble as she sat on the bed with him. "You remember his determination? He is begging the gods for revenge. But I fear he is really begging them to destroy him."

Balling his fists, Curio squeezed his eyes shut in frustration and shook his head.

"He's returning to Athens. How does he even plan to get back inside? That fool!"

"He is a fool." Kinara's voice was a smooth whisper, and he felt her slide closer on the bed. "His sister tamed his madness, but without her, he is now beyond anyone's help. You must let him face his destiny. You could not have stopped him."

He opened his eyes, finding Kinara leaning closer than he thought. Her eyes were glittering and dark, full of promise and hope. Somehow, Curio felt revolted. Galerius was throwing his life away exactly as Curio warned him against doing. This was a disaster. He could not keep the blame out of his voice as he backed away from her.

"Why did you not awaken me? You just let him leave?"

"You are fighting an infection," she said, her tempting expression flipping easily to irritation. She likewise backed away but did not rise from the edge of the bed. "I was not going to awaken you to deal with his stupidity. He wanted to die seeking revenge. What should I have done?"

"You should have awakened me." Curio slammed both balled fists into the bed with a soft thump. "He is under my protection."

"He is a man who makes his own choices. He's not yours to mind, Curio. Hasn't he brought you enough suffering?"

"A man in name only. He thinks he must take on Pertinax alone. What a fool!"

"Exactly." Kinara's voice refilled with hope, and she set her hand atop the blanket draped over Curio's leg. "Do not follow him into death. Your life is worth more than a fool's."

The touch on his leg seemed innocent, yet she gave his calf a squeeze that seemed to suggest more. Yet Curio could not understand what more there was to offer. He sat up, carefully pulling his leg from beneath her hand. Now he regarded her with hooded eyes. Even if his throat burned with thirst and his stomach growled with hunger, he had questions he needed answered.

"Why are you still here? If I've been down for days, your father will be frantic looking for you. Did you tell him you came after us?"

Kinara pulled both hands to her chest, pressing her stola tight over the swell of her breasts. Curio had to look away, again cursing his eyes for seeing everything he should avoid in this woman. Yet her dusky skin darkened in a blush and her glossy eyes unfocused. She leaned back, her lips parted as if she were still seeking an answer to the simple question.

"Curio, my father is a great doctor and has indulged me in many things. But you must understand, as a prominent man in society, I bring him shame."

"Shame? I haven't seen anything from him to indicate that. If he did not want your assistance, then he would have forbidden you from his service long ago."

Kinara gave a bitter smile, then turned hopefully to him.

"Curio, take me to Rome. I don't want to live here anymore. Athens is a fine city for some, but not for me. I long for a modern city, one whose light shines upon all the world. I know the language and culture. I could fit into society without any problems."

She shifted closer on the bed, setting both hands over his legs as she did. They pressed on his thighs as she leaned forward.

"I'm begging you. There is no better time than now. We've both escaped Athens and there is nothing there to return to."

Curio's mouth hung open and his sleep-fogged mind churned to generate a response. At first, he was not sure if she mocked him. However, he had never seen her so animated before. Her stare bordered on madness with her dark eyes bulging. She dug her fingers into his thighs like a cat crawling up his legs.

"What are you talking about? You live in Athens. Galerius has gone back to seek revenge, and he is too careless to avoid trouble."

"It doesn't matter," Kinara said with a false smile. "Forget that fool. You had to tolerate him for his sister's sake, but now you owe him nothing. We can rest here until you are healed. No one will find us. Then when your strength is back, we will go to Rome and start a new life."

Curio shrank back and his horror had to have shown on his face, for Kinara withdrew from him and her blush deepened.

"I'm not going to Rome," he said in a hoarse whisper. "I'm rejoining my friends for our next mission. You can't follow me."

Kinara's head snapped up, her eyes flashing with rage. Even though she schooled herself, bitterness tainted her voice.

"You would've let her follow you. I am no different." Now, her eyes faltered, and she began to cry as she turned her head. "I have remained independent all this time. But soon I will be forced to give up everything and become another man's wife. I, the one who healed you and cared for you, will never be allowed to do that again. My father will give me to a stranger. Why can't I be spared from this fate like her?"

Curio did not know how to answer. Kinara slipped back to the edge of the bed and hid her face in her hands. Now he understood her referring to an escape. Like Cecelia, she did not want to be forced to marry anyone, no matter who he might be. She valued freedom, and Curio realized he had benefited from that. Doctor Nisos would never have done half of what Kinara had done for him.

He stumbled trying to find the right words.

"Well, I don't want to make you sad. You've been so good to me, and Galerius. But I am not going to Rome. I suppose you can follow me, and I can help you find passage to Rome. But life won't be easier for you there. I think it would be much harder."

Kinara had stopped sobbing and peeked at him through her fingers.

"I don't want to go to Rome alone. I want you to go with me. We will take care of each other."

"Well, I don't think that will work out. I have no place of my own in Rome. I'm so often overseas on missions of all sorts. I've almost lost all my roots there. If you want to try living in Rome on your own, I can help. But otherwise, you must take care of yourself."

She remained with her hands covering her face. She grew cold and silent, making Curio eager to change the topic.

"In any case, I cannot leave Galerius to die. I wasn't just tolerating him for Cecelia's benefit. He's a good man. Well, boy is a better word to describe him. Anyway, he might be beyond my help now. Even so, I at least have to discover what befell him."

Kinara turned her back to Curio and let her hands fall from her face. She sat at the edge of the bed with her head lowered. Only the drizzle of rain on the small house made any sound. Curio thought he could hear his heart beating.

Her shoulders slumped and she let out a long sigh.

"You are determined to follow him, then?"

Curio let silence be his answer. He had already made his intentions clear. She sighed again.

"You are hardly well enough to do anything for him. If you approach the city, you will be caught and killed. You've not been gone long enough to be forgotten."

"I have my ways to move unseen in and out of walled cities." Curio allowed a smug smile, even though he lacked any tools for the job and had no strength for the task. Still, he allowed a note of pride in his voice.

"And what will you do inside Athens?"

"I will plan according to what I learn."

Again, Kinara fell into a long silence and the rain continued to tap on the walls and roof. She brushed her dark hair over her shoulder, still facing away from him. Then she reached for her basket sitting on the corner table, just within reach. She moved it to her lap, and then began to sort through it. He could not see what she searched for, but heard the clay jars clinking together. It seemed she dug to the bottom, and never found what she wanted. She set the basket down again, and gave a sharp sigh.

"If I help you back into the city, then will you swear to take me to Rome? You're not strong enough to do this without help."

Curio stared at her strong back. As much as he hated to admit it, given all his bedrest and injuries she was probably the stronger one.

Saving Galerius might not take muscle, but probably would need more than himself to succeed. He swallowed.

"If you will help me, then I will take you to Rome. I'm not promising I will stay with you, or when I can do it."

She turned her head slightly and nodded. Curio thought he saw a satisfied smile in her profile, but then she turned away again.

"We should hurry. If we delay, Galerius will probably be dead before we can reach him."

14

By the early afternoon, Kinara returned to the room where Curio sat on the bed after putting on his tunic. He was trying on the new sandal, whose brighter and newer leather contrasted with the weathered black of his own. The door opened to reveal a stale gray sky and the smudges of the outside world. She stood framed in the glare.

"I've used some of your coins to buy a cart from the old woman. She has no use for it now that her husband is gone."

Curio nodded, more concerned with tying his sandals. After the terrible kick to his side, he was not sure if he should risk bending over to do it. Besides, his left hip still ached from falling out of the cart. He drew a sharp breath at all his infirmities.

"I hope you paid her a fair price."

Kinara did not answer, but instead entered to help him.

"You're going to rescue that fool but you can't wear your own sandals."

"There's no one else to help him. I feel so much better now that I'm sitting up. I'm sure that getting the air again and a little rain on my face will improve me even more."

He tilted his head back as if enjoying the sun on it while Kinara pulled his laces tight.

Without anything to pack beyond what Kinara carried in her basket, they exited the house.

The air was cool and damp, but Curio relished its freshness. This was his first time outside since passing out at the crossroads. He had guessed from the lack of external noises that they were in a small village and people and animals remained indoors due to the weather. Yet now that he stood outside the house, he realized it was a lone home set within sparse woods. They had slept in the main house of mudbrick and red tile roof. These were in good repair, indicating the widow's husband had maintained the place. The shutters on the opposite building were closed.

Kinara had moved the cart and mule to the open courtyard. The bony animal looked tired and flicked its tail at Curio's appraisal.

"You left the barn door open," Curio said, pointing across the small clearing.

Kinara's movements were jerky and quick. She looked to the barn and shook her head. Her dusky skin seemed paler in the flat afternoon light. She set her basket on the driver's seat and then reached into the cart to lift away a cover.

"The widow will close it later. We can't waste time. The fool has had a full day to get himself into trouble. Do you need help up to the bench?"

The plan to get back into Athens was simple. They would pose as a countryside couple come to resupply in the city. Curio's face was not famous and the death penalty for banishment could only be enforced if he was caught for another reason—such as Galerius would be when he attempted to kill Pertinax. If the gate guards spoke to Curio, he would feign losing his voice and Kinara would speak for him. The trick would be evading trouble once inside Athens.

"I'm fine. But I want to thank the old woman before we leave."

Kinara looked up sharply, her lush brows a flat line over her eyes.

"She's resting now. I've thanked her already. Come on, I'll help you up."

Before he could protest, Kinara encircled his torso with her strong arms and nearly threw him onto the cart. He had to wrestle with her just to get on the bench with any dignity.

"Now you're in a rush to help Galerius. I don't understand you." He adjusted his tunic and Kinara handed up his cane. The mule craned his head back with an expression that seemed like he suffered the antics of two idiots.

"If we don't save him then you're likely to do something equally stupid. So let's hurry."

They had some dried roots and vegetables that Kinara took from the house, along with a skin of wine. She had packed these in the cart bed. For the time being, Kinara would drive the cart but they would switch roles once on the main road. She flicked the reins and the mule responded. Curio never had much luck with these beasts, and was glad to see this one cooperated with strangers.

The cart rolled away from the small home in the woods. Curio wondered at how the widow would support herself and who would protect her home. It was a strange arrangement, but there was no denying the house was in fine condition. So the widow had somehow made a safe and comfortable living here. Perhaps there were other nearby homes obscured by the gray trees.

He twisted on the bench to watch it recede as Kinara guided the cart down the path. That opened barn door aggravated him. Where was all the livestock, in any case? Giving up on the mystery of this place, he was about to turn around when he spotted a dog.

It rested in the grass behind the house. While Curio could not see a chain or rope, it certainly must have one or else it would've come investigate them. It was a lump of white and brown fur, and Curio expected it to leap up at the squeal of the cart leaving. Yet it did not move. Kinara guided them around a corner and the scene vanished behind a tree.

"She has a dog? How come I never heard it bark?"

"Because you were asleep most of the time. Did you see him just now?"

"He was in the grass behind the house. Strange that he didn't even stir."

Kinara tilted her head and laughed. "That is strange. He is probably just too happy to be outside now that the rain has stopped."

"He's not a very good watchdog." Curio straightened on the cart and enjoyed the refreshing air.

It was a shoddy cart on a rocky road. Each time they struck a stone the whole cart shuddered like it would fly apart. Curio's back was sore to begin with, and the hard bench and merciless path worsened everything.

Still, the farther they were from the house, the more animated Kinara became. Despite her pleas to leave Athens, she seemed excited to return.

"I will need to visit my father one final time before we leave. I have some things to take with me."

"He's not going to restrain you?" Curio asked. They were now out of the woods and on a main road. The rain had created mud but so far their light cart glided over it. Ahead, he could see heavier wagons mired. "He's not going to wonder where you've been?"

"I will handle my father. Don't worry."

They arrived in Athens later in the afternoon and had no issues passing through the same gate the Scythians had used to banish him. The guards had searched their meager cart and asked perfunctory questions that Kinara answered.

"I suppose Galerius had the same luck," Curio said after they absorbed into the spread of the city. He craned his neck to look over the heads of pedestrians as if he might catch Galerius waiting for him on a corner. Of course, every face looked the same to him. The colors of city life were bright everywhere, and the clouds that had hung over the city for days had yielded to sunshine.

They stabled the mule and cart. Curio's purse was now more air than coin, and he realized he couldn't last long in the city. They also secured a room in a rundown inn where the proprietor was eager to have any guests. Curio was now able to distinguish a bad part of

Athens from the better neighborhoods. They were clearly in a less favorable area.

"So, how do we find Galerius?" Kinara set her basket beside the brick ledge that ran along the wall. Curio supposed that was the bed. An unlit clay lamp was the room's only other adornment besides debris accumulated in the corner.

"By watching Pertinax's home. It's his only reason to be here. He'll try to ambush him or something like that. The gods know he has no other advantage."

However, they did not have to cross the city to find Pertinax's home. The path took them through the agora where Kinara asked around at Curio's prompting. They learned Galerius had been caught and had been sent before the elder council again.

They sat on a stone bench in the shade of decorative trees as they watched Athenians rushing everywhere across the busy agora. Curio rubbed his sore side as he held his cane between his knees, looking down a long colonnade to the right. Groups of friends stood in conversation or else rested against the majestic columns. He shook his head.

"Our cells were not far from here. Is that where he is being held?"

Kinara sat beside him, perhaps too close for his liking but it fit their pretext of a married couple.

"From what I learned, his appearance before the magistrates was less than a minute. He is to be executed."

Curio squinted over the splendid red-tiled roofs, so reminiscent of Rome, and tried to imagine which wall he would be hung from.

"I don't know how I'll get him down alive from there. When Varro rescued me in Sparta, he had others to help him."

Kinara followed his eyes, then set her hand on his knee.

"That was Sparta. Here in Athens, we consider crucifixion barbaric. No one has died that way since ancient times. He will be made to drink hemlock."

Curio's heart flipped. "Right away?"

Kinara nodded. "You'll probably need to search for a gravedigger taking his body out of the city. If he went to the magistrate this morning, then he is dead by now. They'll have prepared the hemlock for him. I'm sorry, Curio."

She squeezed his knee, but he pulled away and shot to his feet. The rage he felt banished all the pain in his side. Anger-driven strength filled his muscles preparing to clash with an unseen enemy.

"Are you sure? I won't believe it until I confirm it with my own eyes."

Kinara's face darkened and she stood beside him.

"Don't raise your voice. You'll draw attention by speaking Latin like that. Do you want to end up on the same cart with that fool?"

Though rage seethed through his veins, he realized passersby were already looking at him. While speaking Latin was not a crime, it might make him suspicious. He was sure Galerius confirmed he acted alone, but the elders knew Curio was his accomplice. He also wondered if Pertinax might somehow involve himself as well. So he settled on the bench and lowered his voice.

"Can we confirm this somehow? Are such executions public?"

Kinara shrugged. "It depends on the crime and how famous the executed person is. I think that fool would've been handled right away. He has no relatives or friends here, no cause for spectacle."

"His name is Galerius." Curio gritted his teeth as he spoke. "Use it, please. I know he made mistakes and brought this on himself. But he did not deserve death."

Kinara looked at him cooly, then lowered her head.

"I'm sorry. I'm not as sensitive as I should be. We can go speak to someone at the holding cells. They will know what happened."

The weakness in his limbs struck halfway across the agora as Curio accepted that both of the twins were dead. It was all his fault. He was too weak and too dependent on others. As he bounced between street traffic, following Kinara's confident stride, he felt like lying down and letting himself be trampled to death. How had he led them to this end?

As promised, Kinara approached the guards at the squat, unadorned building where Curio had once been held. She chatted with the guards who pointed toward the amphitheater as they spoke.

Curio remained a long distance away for fear of being recognized. Even before Kinara crossed back to where he ostensibly looked over small carpets set out for sale, he knew what she would report. The bright sun cast a deep shadow over the serious lines of her face.

"It is as I expected. We might find his body prepared for burial outside the city walls. But I don't know where to start. Is it worth the risk to search for him?"

Curio lowered his head. "No. I am tired now. Take me back to the inn."

He must have walked in a daze since he did not remember returning to the tiny room that seemed little better than a jail cell. There were two other rooms, and a prostitute and her customer occupied one. Their moaning turned Curio's stomach.

They settled in awkward silence, Curio taking the bed. Kinara was in and out of the room, fussing with things in her basket each time. He did not care what she did. She seemed happy to be done with this adventure. All he could think of was Cecelia and Galerius.

Only a few months ago he had never heard of these two. Even after meeting them, he had paid them scant attention. Of course, he had realized Cecelia was smitten with him from the start. Even Falco had teased him about it before he consciously noticed it. He hadn't thought much about it then. Yet spending so much time confined with them, he had grown fond of both. Indeed, he had convinced himself to marry Cecelia.

Now they were dead. He had accepted the death of friends as part of life. Yet the twins' deaths were especially cruel to his conscience. If he had been more thoughtful of Cecelia's safety, Pertanix would not have killed her. Had he been able to restrain Galerius long enough for his impulses to fade, he would not have drunk hemlock this morning.

He rested with his arm across his eyes to block the light from the opened door. Eventually, he shifted to his side on the uncomfortable brick bed. The mortar had broken away, and the bricks were loose. He fiddled with one, idly rocking it back and forth as he listened to Kinara speaking outside the room to another woman. Given the moaning had stopped, maybe it was the prostitute. Hopefully, Kinara would ask for some peace.

When the sky turned orange and the sounds of traffic dwindled beyond the walls of Curio's room, Kinara entered with a steaming bowl and jug of wine. There was no place to sit, so Curio sat up on the bed as Kinara placed the stew beside him.

Calling it a stew was generous, as it was more like a greasy brown fluid with fatty meat and sparse, limp vegetables floating in it. He sipped from it, and his lips puckered at the unpleasant medley of salt and spice.

"More salt than broth. The cook is hiding something from me."

Kinara laughed as she prepared her basket. Her mood had steadily brightened throughout the day.

"I will return to my father's home tonight. I don't want to be seen. You should remain here. Once I have what I need, we can leave. How do you feel?"

"Guilty."

"I meant your wound. You have recovered well from that kick, but I want to be sure you're fully healed. We have a long road ahead." She poured wine from the jug into a small clay cup, then produced a jar from her basket. She pinched something out of it and dropped it into the wine. "This will help you sleep deeply. I'm afraid thoughts of your friend will keep you up."

She offered him the cup, her eyes sparkling.

Curio stared at the wine. He had been in this position before, a cup of drugged wine hovering under his nose. It was a nightmare from Iberia and the horrors of that place. Although Kinara was fairer to look at than the Iberian barbarians, a feeling of dread overcame him like the old gods of Iberia reaching across the world to claw at his soul.

"I don't need it."

"Yes, you do. It's not the draught." Her laughter was a light chime. "It's just a pinch of something to aid your sleep. You will need strength tomorrow when we start our journey."

A voice came from outside the door, the woman who had spoken to Kinara earlier. She set the wine down and replied to the voice, then pointed to the cup.

"Take the medicine. Sleep well while I'm gone."

Kinara stepped outside and partially closed the door.

And Curio decided he no longer needed medical attention.

His wound had healed, and his strength was hobbled only due to his inactivity. The Scythians had indeed hurt him, but not permanently as he had feared. It was time he stood with his own strength and regained his clarity of thought. Until today, the first day without draughts or other medicines, he had not realized how clouded his mind had been.

So he drained the wine into the gap in the brick bed he had toyed with earlier, then refilled the cup. He barely sat back in place when Kinara reentered. She glared at the full cup.

"All right, I'll take it." He quaffed down the wine in one hard gulp and did not have to fake his disgust at the vinegary taste. Again, Kinara laughed and then collected the bowl and cup.

"Sleep well. Tomorrow, we will leave this place forever."

Resting on the bed, he let Kinara make her preparations, which included taking her basket. Again, she spoke a final time to the prostitute outside the door and then left.

At least an hour passed, and the sun abandoned the world to the night. With his eyes closed, he listened to the sounds around him. Athens felt incredibly small now, becoming all darkness and the echoes of barking of dogs. Indistinct voices faded from the inn and the areas around it. The prostitute moved quietly about her room, entertaining no guests this evening.

Of course, he expected that. He was certain Kinara had arranged for her to ensure he remained asleep. If he awakened, then she was to occupy him.

Kinara did not want him to follow. Which of course demanded that he must.

Besides, he also wanted to hunt for Galerius's body. He would take the body outside the walls, and bury him someplace out of the way before striking for Varro and Falco.

He would be breaking a promise to Kinara, but he could hardly feel bad about leaving her in Athens. Certainly, she might have trouble with her father for her foolishness, but Doctor Nisos hardly seemed the type to beat her. Given Kinara's strength, he might be risking his health if he tried.

So after the prostitute checked him for the second time—he knew one check would be insufficient to convince her—he collected his meager possessions, tucked his cane underarm like a fighting staff, and slipped out of the inn and into the night-shrouded, unpaved streets of Athens.

15

Despite everything, each step deeper into the city filled Curio with strength. He did not rely on his cane as he slipped from shadow to shadow. Keeping a low profile, pressing to walls as he searched for the next waypoint, he felt like his old self. The night air was bracing, and he drew deep breaths to clear his lungs. Every exhalation blew away the thick blanket that clung to his head ever since he had awakened in Athens. The medicines he needed to manage his pain had weakened his mind. It had been insidious, the fog never recognizable except when it was absent.

The halfmoon shined through thin clouds, a yellow light in the deep blue of early night. It provided enough illumination to inform Curio's path and created enough shadow to conceal him. After dark, the agora was mostly empty space. Compared to the bustling majesty of the place by daylight, by night it seemed forlorn, even dangerous. The buildings and colonnades provided him ample cover from the patrols watching the streets for danger. He assumed these were Scythians, but he stayed far enough that they remained as mute shadows against the light.

He did not know his exact path across the city and only that he should keep the Acropolis to the left and rear. His room had been at the bottom of a gentle hill, one that would have felt like a mountain to him only a few weeks ago. Still, his legs needed rest, and he paused amid the favorable terrain of the agora to catch his breath.

First, he would look for Kinara. He did not remember Doctor Nisos's house. The draught Kinara fed him ensured he would never recall the specifics. However, he knew the street where he had twice encountered Pertinax. He planned to orient himself there, maybe even finding his old apartment. From there, he could estimate where Kinara might be.

Smiling to himself, he moved out after catching his breath. She had no idea of his capabilities, thinking he would be unable to follow her. Certainly, the city was unfamiliar, and yet it had a logic that all large cities seemed to follow. Perhaps also because Rome had taken so much inspiration from Greece—which Senator Flamininus never failed to point out—there was an internal sense to it he could follow. Every road he selected led him closer to his goal.

The specifics of the goal remained vague. He supposed everything depended on what he learned about Kinara. He guessed she wanted to slip into her father's home to gather forgotten belongings and get money for her new life in Rome. She seemed too direct for such subterfuge. Yet what else would require her to sneak out all night?

The unpaved streets rolled away into the dark, and Curio followed them with all the caution of a man who would be executed for just being present. Galerius had thrown his life away, something Curio still could not accept. He determined not to follow him. After learning what he could of Kinara, he would circle to the outer wall and the Kerameikos, where the dead were buried. Galerius's corpse might be held there overnight in case mourners or other family came forward. The city would have its policies regarding how long it would hold the corpse of a condemned man. Tomorrow at the latest, Galerius would be cremated and buried outside the city beside other criminal graves. Curio intended to give him a better burial.

If he could, he would disinter Cecelia's ashes and bury her beside her brother. However, that might be too much for one night's work.

He needed to escape the city at first light before Kinara could track him down. His location would be too easy to guess, given his goal of saving Galerius from burial among criminals. Yet he could not see any other way to arrange it.

He came to more familiar streets, and after searching, he located the one where he and Galerius had first run into Pertinax. Now that he stood at the top of the slope, he wondered how he had considered it a challenge. It just proved how far he had recovered since that day. While he was still out of fighting form, he could at least walk and even sprint if he needed to. Long marches and arduous climbing were for another day yet.

So he threaded the dark strip of road, passing the intersection where a cart accident had gathered a crowd and then the alley where Pertinax had beaten Galerius. He rubbed his side, which was sore but no longer debilitating. It was smooth under his tunic, with no bandages or stitches brushing his palm. He would carry a lifelong scar, but Doctor Nisos's expert stitches and Kinara's attentive care ensured it healed as good as his old skin.

He passed the apartments where Varro and Falco had left him. Oddly, he could not remember which had been his. They were all closed and dark, and if any patients were housed inside, they gave no sign. He was close now, both to Pertinax and Doctor Nisos. So he clung to the shadows on the opposite side of the street where the moonlight did not reach. The apartments were cast in silver light with shadow edges sharp enough to cut cloth.

Hunkering in the darkness, he took stock of the street and where he should hide. All across the city, he had easily slipped the sentries on patrol. Remembering the response time when Galerius had tried to burn down Pertinax's house, he did not want to reveal himself in this area. It seemed Pertinax kept his territory on alert.

Given he was not sure of Doctor Nisos's location, and therefore Kinara's, he decided he could use Pertinax's home as an anchor point. He would probe from there, then return if he did not locate Kinara. It was a convenient landmark in the doctor's neighborhood and would help prevent him from getting disoriented in the dark and unfamiliar area.

He shifted out of the shadows, hewing to the closed doors and stuccoed walls of the buildings lining the street. Flowing down the slope, he came to where Pertinax made his home.

As he crouched behind a wall corner, rough stucco scraping his cheek, he watched the house for lookouts. Being the home of a wealthy man, he expected sentinels on walls or at the gates. Yet the home appeared at rest. The burned wall had been torn down, and masons had already erected the core of a new one. Scaffolding and frames remained in place, but the unfinished wall would hold against unauthorized entry.

Then Curio noted he was not alone in studying the house.

Another figure crouched in the shadow of a wide intersection. His first thought was Kinara, but the figure was male, and the exposed flesh glowed too white under the moon to be her. The figure fixed his gaze on Pertinax's home. He reminded Curio of a cat stalking a bird in a garden.

Any enemy of Pertinax's might be an ally of his. So he pulled his cane beneath his cloak and gathered it close as he backtracked. He then circled the figure to approach from behind, leaving himself an escape route.

Curio slid from building to building, molding himself to the walls and corners as he glided closer to the watcher. From his position, the watcher left his back completely exposed. Whoever he was, Curio decided he was not a professional.

Then, as he stepped closer, he realized he was looking at Galerius.

All of his own professionalism evaporated into cold fear. Was he looking at the shade of his friend who died with hatred for Pertinax in his heart? Was he now forever watching his enemy, looking for a chance to torment him?

Then Galerius shifted his stance, and his heels ground against the dirt. This basic, too-human sound banished the image of a shade and returned it to the flesh and blood human.

The coldness in Curio's hands melted away to hot anger.

"Galerius," he hissed across the small gap between buildings. "It's me."

Galerius fell against the wall where he crouched. He spun around, the moonlight gleaming in his eyes and his mouth a tight line in the washed-out brightness.

Curio swept up to him, regaining his composure, and slipped his hand over Galerius's mouth. They stared at each other, both shocked by the other's miraculous appearance.

"You're supposed to have taken hemlock this morning. Am I holding a shade?"

Galerius blinked and did not answer. So Curio dragged him out of the light and out of sight from Pertinax's home. At last, he seemed to realize he was in no danger and began to squirm. Curio removed his hand, and could not help but give him a playful slap on the cheek.

"I'm glad to see you. After this, I was going to look for your body."

"You nearly frightened me out of it," Galerius said, relaxing against the wall. Enough light bounced into the gap between buildings that his frown was obvious. "What do you mean I took hemlock? Isn't that what they use to kill philosophers?"

"Philosophers and those banished under pain of death." Curio paused to glance down the dark alley to the moonlit opposite end and remembered to lower his excited voice. "I don't understand. Kinara checked with multiple people, even the Scythians. They all...."

Then he did understand. For a moment, his mind turned away from Galerius staring at him from against the alley wall. Instead, he saw Kinara briefly chatting with various Athenians. Now it was obvious to him. She might not have even been speaking to them about Galerius.

"Fuck me," he whispered. "She lied. She wants me to take her to Rome, and not spend another moment here."

Galerius shook free, his frown deepening.

"I don't know what you mean about Rome. What did she say about me?"

Checking the alley once more, he drew Galerius closer and whispered the details. His frown shifted from one of irritation to confusion. When finished, he shook his head.

"Well, she knows how to tell a story. She didn't try to stop me from coming here. Actually, she seemed to think I should take revenge. She even told me how I could do it."

"What?" Curio ducked his head down against his voice. Even Galerius now searched around as if fearing they would be caught. "I thought you went off on your own because I was against the idea."

"I did. But I talked about it with her after you fell asleep. She encouraged me, and even gave me poison to kill Pertinax." He fished inside a small bag he wore across his body. Curio had not seen it until now. "Here it is."

It was a small thigh bone of an animal, with an end cut to form a cap held by a string. The shallow moonlight caused it to glow menacingly.

"She carries poison in her healing basket?" Curio touched the bone set across Galerius's palm. It felt cool and light, but not especially dangerous.

"She says she puts it into that draught she's always giving you. A little can numb you and make you dream, but too much will stop your breathing. I've been here a few days, trying to figure out how to get through that wall I burned down. If I could mix this into his wine, he'd die before anyone could give him an antidote."

Curio blinked at the bone tube, then snatched it out of Galerius's palm. He shouted in protest, but Curio hid it behind his back and drove his finger into Galerius's chest.

"If you plan to kill a man, even a treacherous shit like Pertinax, then you look him in the eye and drive your knife through his heart. You don't poison him like a snake."

Galerius blinked in astonishment.

"Why? You know I can't face him on equal terms. How is poisoning him different from cutting his throat while he sleeps?"

"Don't argue." Curio of course had no logical answer. He again recalled Iberia and the horrible results of poisoning done to both

Roman treasury guards and Iberian wildmen. Yet as he stared at Galerius, he held the bone tube out again.

"If you take this, then you'll do it alone. But if you let me keep it, then I will help you."

Galerius's hand reached out but recoiled when he heard the offer. His young face brightened in the dark.

"You've changed your mind? You will help get revenge for Cecelia's murder?"

Stuffing the tube into his belt, Curio shook his head.

"I still think this puts us in unnecessary danger. Cecelia won't return to us because we killed Pertinax. But you're not going to be persuaded otherwise. So, I feel obligated to save you from yourself."

"How are we going to do it?" Galerius now turned to peek around the corner again.

"I don't know yet. We don't have weapons other than these knives. They'll serve if we can get close." He felt heat come to his face. "I suppose we could cut his throat while he sleeps or else poison him."

The irony seemed lost on Galerius, who crouched lower as he hugged the corner.

"The wall is under construction, and they work on it all day. There has to be a way through it, but it's guarded on the inside. He has a dog that barks at anyone who gets close. That will wake up everyone in the house."

"Poison the dog," Curio said. "Then we slip inside and find Pertinax. He'll be on the top floor. There won't be time for long speeches. Just finish him and escape. After that, we are leaving Athens and never returning. If you want to move Ceclia's ashes, you'll have to send someone to do it."

"That's a great plan!" Galerius stood up and punched his fist into his palm. "I didn't think to poison the dog. But how will we do that? I haven't eaten much since leaving you. If I got some meat, I'd rather have it for myself."

"You'll be sharper on an empty stomach. My first centurion used to tell me that. So, tomorrow we get some meat, then we'll return here at night to carry out the attack. We wouldn't go over that wall, anyway. It's the one everyone will be watching since it seems most vulnerable. We'll need ropes and a hook to scale a different wall. I might have enough coin for those."

"I can show you where I've been sleeping. There's an abandoned home, not close but it will do. Not much protection from the rain, either, as I found out."

Then Curio heard a thump down the alleyway, like something sliding along the wall then collapsing to the dirt.

With his mind unburdened by draughts or medicines, he recognized the approaching danger. It was an itching sensation at the back of his neck as if he expected a dagger to plunge into that very spot. He threw himself against the alley wall and pulled Galerius beside him.

Before he could protest, Curio elbowed him into silence and nodded down the alley.

Something protruded from the shadows, its irregular outline contrasting against the straight walls. He saw a nose and chin and a belly that rose and fell sharply.

"Maybe he's a beggar," Galerius whispered.

Curio withdrew his small knife and shook his head. He pressed deeper into the wall, waiting for the figure to resume moving. The shadowy man knew he had revealed himself. Since he didn't act, Curio realized he had others waiting to join a coordinated attack.

"Run, and don't lead them back to your hideout. We'll go separate ways. If we escape, I'll wait for you on the south side of the Acropolis. Do you understand?"

Galerius's eyes were bright in the weak moonlight as he nodded.

He shoved Galerius out of the alley and turned to run down it toward the man hiding at the end.

No sooner had Galerius stepped outside than Curio heard shouting.

Racing down the alley, the man in the shadows did not seem to understand the moment. He delayed and it was all the time Curio needed.

He closed the distance, raising his cane like a spear and keeping his knife ready. The man against the wall sprang forward and shouted in Greek. Yet Curio drove the butt of his cane into the shadow's face and caught it in his mouth. The shout turned to a garbled curse, and Curio pressed in to stab up with his knife.

The man groaned and convulsed, then slumped forward as hot blood rushed over Curio's hand. Something metallic clattered to the ground as the body collapsed.

Glancing back toward the end of the alley, he saw shapes flitting across the entrance in pursuit of Galerius. He knelt and felt for the weapon at his feet, hand latching onto a larger knife that he yanked from beneath the body.

Two more men filled the alley exit. Curio heard groggy shouts through the walls to his side. It seemed a door was nearby and someone was about to open it.

The two men rushed into the alley, and Curio backed up. He was in no shape to take on two men now. The door in the alley wall opened. He saw the flicker of a candle and heard someone cursing. Diving straight at it, he collided with the door and the man behind it. He plowed through, driving his cane ahead of him. The man dropped the candle, and it snuffed out upon hitting the ground.

He was inside a small courtyard, apparently beside a hovel where a slave slept outside the main home. That slave now rolled in the doorway as Curio's pursuers tried to enter and tripped on his body.

Keeping the longer dagger and cane ready, he raced for the rear gate. He had to cut across his pursuers, and they shouted as he slipped their grasp. Such was his panic that he rebounded off the door as he tried to exit. The bar remained in place.

Staggering around, his pursuers were atop him now. They were cursing him in Greek. The rest of the small house was coming awake behind them as golden light shined through shuttered windows on the second floor.

Using his cane like a whip, he slashed at the sword arm of the first attacker, scoring his flesh and causing him to fall back. This left him an opening to sidestep the second attacker.

Rather than try to defeat both men, he instead flipped off the interior bar from the gate door. It was a small bar, sturdy enough to keep honest men from entering. It thudded to the ground, and Curio leaped into the door.

Now it flew open and he passed through as one of his attackers cut his flowing cloak.

Spilling into the street, he slammed the door behind him and then threw himself against it. His breath was ragged and raspy, but his body flooded with power that came from life-or-death panic. He held the door shut as they pushed. Even at his peak, Curio couldn't hold the door against their bulk. He only did this long enough to angle his knife through the opening.

The blade plunged in and one of them screamed. The pressure against the door slackened and Curio shoved it closed before fleeing.

He dashed into the dark, holding back laughter as he did. It felt good to be fighting again.

Pertinax's thugs spilled out of the door, but Curio was already gone. He had raced across the street into one of several dark alleys. The thugs picked the wrong one, and he heard them calling out for reinforcements as they chased after his shadow.

Curio ran a short distance before his burning and aching muscles begged him to stop. He was still too close to Pertinax's house, but he could not continue. His side ached and doubled him over. He was a long way from his old form, but the blood on his hands confirmed he could still take care of himself.

He heard distant shouting and realized he could understand the words. He crept down the alley to hear better. Local inhabitants were awakening now, lights flickering behind shuttered windows and doors cracking open with fearful eyeballs set behind them.

The voice was speaking Latin and was Pertinax.

"Centurion Camilus Curio! I know you and that pest are hiding out there. You'll never escape the city alive now. I'll be sure every gate knows you'll try to pass through. You're as good as dead!"

Then Pertinax laughed and Curio looked toward the moonlit outline of the Acropolis. He had to meet Galerius there and escape tonight. They had no other choice now.

16

Once the thrill of combat and pursuit wore off, Curio's muscles stiffened and ached. The long walk to the southern side of the Acropolis now felt impossible. He had put enough distance between himself and Pertinax that he took frequent rests. Regrettably, he also leaned on his cane. While he did not require this, he could ease his wounded side as he walked.

Yet Fortuna must have taken pity on him, for clouds drifted before the half-moon. Shadows grew deeper with the reduced light. The city patrols were alert now, at least in his area. No one had sounded an alarm, probably to prevent panicking the neighborhood. However, the patrols he did spot shined their torches into dark places and studied the alleyways as they passed. They were looking for him and Galerius.

While he trusted himself to evade capture, he wondered about Galerius. They shared a similar build, so both had an aptitude for hiding in small spaces. Yet Curio had honed his abilities since youth and through years of clandestine legion missions. Galerius was a spoiled son of a rich merchant who probably only ever hid from responsibility.

Curio was glad he still lived. He had barely time to process

Cecelia's sudden death. Counting Galerius alongside her was too much.

He kept his thoughts in check, always looking to his surroundings for threats. Of course, some of this caution was an excuse to rest his aching muscles. It took longer to reach the massive block of the Acropolis than he expected, but when he did he could not sit down.

Instead, he worked his way up and down its length, searching the dark for Galerius. Occasionally, he looked up at the huge rock formation and marveled at its power. He had never been so close to such a historic place, yet he could see nothing of it besides silver clouds curling over the half-moon.

At last, he picked a spot among the rocks and waited. It took close to an hour, and at points, he dozed while folded into his cloak. However, Galerius appeared scurrying from one rock outcropping to the next. As expected, his motions were inexpert and clunky, but still being the deep night no one witnessed this.

Curio whistled for his attention and stepped out to wave Galerius forward. They both reunited in the fold of rock where Curio hid. Galerius's face shined with excitement.

"We got away!" He spoke in an animated whisper. "Did you hear Pertinax cursing us?"

"I did. But I don't know why you're so happy about it. Did you hear what he said?"

"He'll be dead before he can get word to all the gates. Tomorrow, we'll cut his neck while he sleeps."

"I think the time for that plan has passed." Curio looked at the half-moon as if it had a suggestion, then lowered his eyes. "How good is your hideout? We can't remain here and I don't want to return to the inn. Kinara has probably discovered I'm gone now."

"What is going on with her?" Galerius hugged his shoulders. "Why did she say I was dead?"

"She has mentioned wanting to start a new life in Rome several times. She wants me to take her there. If I got captured trying to rescue you, then her dreams would die. So she convinced me you were dead and that we should leave Athens immediately. We were set to go tomorrow."

Galerius cocked his head. "But why? She seems to have a great life here."

"I supposed it's not as great as it seems to us. She doesn't want her father to marry her off."

He stared at Galerius, who seemed to reach the same conclusion he did.

"You mean, just like my sister? She wants you to save her from an unwanted marriage?"

"That's quite a coincidence," Curio said, rubbing his neck. "I guess it is a similar situation, but not an uncommon one for a woman. What bothers me most is that she encouraged you to go alone. She wanted you out of the way, but must not have counted on me going after you."

Galerius grew quiet and shadow hid his expression. Both listened to crickets and the rustling of trees until Curio decided he had enough to worry about now.

"Show me to your hideout. We can't let the sun rise on us standing out here."

So they threaded back the way they had come, dodging patrols that seemed less alert than before. At points, Galerius became confused about the path back. However, they located the collapsed structure before dawn.

It was a typical two-floor home, only one side of it had collapsed from fire. An overgrowth of weeds in the courtyard and around the foundation indicated it had been long out of use. Surrounding homes were spaced farther apart due to the hilly and rough ground.

"Only rats live here now," Galerius said as he led Curio around the wreckage of the main building. "The other building is still sturdy enough. I think someone hid here not long ago, too."

Curio did not like the restricted space on the bottom floor with only a single door. They could be easily penned inside, though there were cracks in the wall that he and Galerius could fit. However, the house tilted to one side and seemed on the verge of collapse. The interior was devoid of anything other than rotted straw and debris left by other vagrants. While it was hardly splendid quarters, Curio had slept in far worse conditions before. A small fire wouldn't go wrong to chase the chill away and burn off the stale odors trapped in the room. He stretched his tired legs and rubbed his wound, more out of nervous habit than need.

"I wonder what the story is behind this place," he said. "It's strange to leave a city house unclaimed. But I guess it happens all the time."

"No one comes near here," Galerius said. "Maybe people think it's haunted."

"More likely they're wary of criminals or rabid dogs holing up here. I can smell something like wet fur in the air, though there aren't any big animal droppings. In any case, we just need shelter to rest up for tomorrow."

They settled into separate corners, both facing the door. Galerius did not lie down but pulled his knees up to his chin.

"What will we do tomorrow?"

Drawing a heavy breath, Curio sat up and mirrored Galerius's pose.

"Pertinax knows we're here and also knows we want him dead. He's going to try to capture us and ensure we both drink a cup of hemlock. The city will do his dirty work for him."

"We do want him dead." Galerius's voice had hardened, but then he groaned. "But that seems less likely every day. Still, I cannot let Cecelia's death go unavenged."

"Neither can I."

Now Galerius sat up straighter. "But you've been against the idea from the start."

Shifting on the cold dirt floor, he began picking at the hem of his tunic. Cecelia had repaired it for him just before she died.

"The idea has grown on me. I did not know your sister for long, but I did come to love her. To think, I might have been able to marry for love instead of for a more practical reason. Anyway, Pertinax would rather that she die than any other man have her. He said she reminded him of his dead wife."

"Whom he murdered, too." Galerius's fist struck the dirt with a muffled thump.

"Yes, he has a poor record with women. It is not fair that Cecelia should die for his pride. He left her in a bush with his pugio buried in her side. That kind of barbarity deserves punishment."

"Of course he does!" Galerius unfolded his legs and leaned forward. "But how do we make sure he dies for his crime?"

Curio shrugged. "I don't know. He is ready for us. All we have to do is show up near his home, and the Scythians will be upon us. He probably spotted you yesterday and was just waiting for me to show up. If his man had not knocked over something in the alley and revealed himself, we might have been captured."

"Maybe we just need to find something to connect him to Cecelia's murder."

The hope in Galerius's voice brought a bitter smile to Curio.

"We've already done that with his pugio. But I suppose he has bought off that evidence. In any case, who would identify it as his weapon? Besides, I am fairly certain I killed one of his men while trying to escape. I am doubly condemned, and any of my testimony regarding Cecelia will mean nothing."

"But that was in your own defense!"

Curio waved Galerius's voice down, then sighed.

"They were trying to bring me to justice. Remember, we are both banished under pain of death."

The two of them fell into a gloomy silence. Curio stared at the gray earth, trying to frame his thoughts. However, Galerius spoke first.

"I feel as if we have traded places. After tonight, I realize we're not going to succeed in reaching Pertinax. I want to escape now and you want revenge."

Curio smiled. "If I could think of a way that does not end in our deaths, then I'd not give up. Pertinax does not deserve life. But the longer we stay in Athens, the more certain our discovery is. We cannot count on Kinara's help now that she must realize I've left her. I feel bad about betraying her after all she has done."

"Don't feel too bad," Galerius said, his voice stiffening. "She fixed up my nose but then sent me off to die so she could use you to escape her father. She was ready to throw my life away when it suited her."

"To be fair, she didn't send you off to die. She just helped herself by helping you. There's a difference. Though she should know as well as anyone that you would probably die in the attempt, and be completely alone if you succeeded. It does not sit well with me."

"So what are we going to do?"

Curio pulled his cloak tighter. "Rest for now. You seem awake, so take a watch. Wake me when you need to sleep."

"Are we just giving up?"

"No," Curio slipped to the ground, wrapping his cloak over his body. "In the legion, they call it a tactical retreat. We have to stop fighting on his terms and find better ground to stand on. Even if he never leaves the city, there is a way to reach him. We just need to get some distance to find out what it is."

Given his physical and emotional exhaustion, Curio was asleep as soon as he closed his eyes. His dead, dreamless sleep was restful but short. Galerius awakened him at dawn, his own eyes puffy and dark-rimmed.

"I'm hungry," he said. "But I'm more tired. I have some wine here. Let's have a drink before I sleep."

They shared a drink from an old gourd Galerius had stashed in the dark corners of the room. As far as taste went, it was rough but not bad. His stomach growled for something more substantial. Galerius had helped himself to the meager provisions Curio had taken, and so he chewed on a bitter root and some walnuts to calm his stomach. He then set himself by the widest crack in the wall to watch over Galerius's sleep.

He considered their escape options. With the benefit of a rested mind, he realized Pertinax's threats to report him to all gates was mostly bluster. Certainly, he could alert some of the gate watch. However, how vital was their capture to Athen's safety? The guards might be more vigilant for people matching their description and might look more carefully at cargo. Yet they would not conduct a vigorous manhunt. Pertinax couldn't get word to every gate, and enforcement at each would be spotty.

Still, Curio did not like to take chances, particularly when his luck and physical condition were lacking. Pertinax would report them to the most likely gates for their escape. The least likely gates would be last, if at all. As he stared out at the brightening city, he considered what Pertinax would estimate as the least likely gate.

"The port," he said to himself. He would believe, correctly, that they would be looking for Senator Flamininus inland. So no one would think of them leaving by ship. This lifted Curio's spirit and he considered waking Galerius to share his ideas. They could follow the long, walled road out of Athens to its port city and docks. From there, they only needed a short passage north, just enough to set them back on the road to the interior.

Yet as he congratulated himself on the idea, he noticed a gathering of men approaching up the street.

At least one of them brandished a whip.

He grabbed his cane and pack and ensured his daggers and the bone tube were secured to his belt; then, he kicked Galerius awake.

"What? That only felt like a moment."

"The Scythians are coming. Pertinax knows we're hiding here. We've got to go."

To his credit, Galerius was up and ready. Unfortunately, they could only use the door facing their enemies.

"They'll see us if we go out this way," Curio said. "We won't slip them in a straight race."

He scanned the room. The ceiling sagged with black rot worsened by the recent rain.

"Go outside and pretend to just notice them, then lead them back in here. Can you fit through that crack?"

He pointed to the opposite wall where an elongated crack let in yellow morning light.

"I think so. It's not that big."

"We're not that big." Curio stuck his legs into it, and the stone scrapped against his calf. "Lead them in, and then go out that crack. I'll follow."

"What are we doing?"

But Curio guided him to the door and opened it. "Just do what I've said."

He shoved Galerius into the light. He then pulled away a plank of wood from the interior wall. Stucco exploded in black flakes and the scent of mold filled his nose. He pointed it like a spear at the center of the black bulge in the wood ceiling.

Galerius leaped through the door shouting, "They're here!" Then he raced across the room and fit into the crack. He shimmed through, breaking some of the wall as he did.

Curio rammed the bulging ceiling and it shuddered with the blow.

Now the Scythians pushed into the doorway, shouting what must be the Greek command for surrender. But Curio was hard at work with his makeshift ram. He slammed the rotting ceiling as the first of the Scythians stepped over the threshold.

"You've been lucky so far," he shouted. "But no more."

A second impact caused the bulge to buckle and collapse. Having prepared himself, Curio slid back toward the cracked wall as the contents of the top floor dumped into the ground floor.

The Scythians looked up in horror as black water and rotted wood along with dead leaves and other debris fell atop them. Curio even thought he glimpsed a small animal corpse in the mix. They screamed as they shielded themselves, but he did not remain to learn their fates.

Instead, he shoved through the cracked wall. A cloud of dust that smelled of humidity and mold puffed out behind him. He staggered and the twist to his back racked him with pain. But he jammed his cane down to keep from falling. Looking around, he saw Galerius running into the cover of a stand of trees. The Scythians had been so confident in their approach that they had simply charged up to the front door. The rear should have been secured but remained unguarded.

The Scythians choked and sent muffled curses after him, but he pushed off the cane and loped after Galerius. His young friend's face was pale as he peered out from the gray-green bushes surrounding the trees. Curio collapsed into them, and Galerius pulled him across. He now lay on his back facing the gray morning sky.

"You did it!" Galerius brushed Curio's face, apparently dusting off debris that clung to his hair.

"They're only delayed and angrier. We can't waste our advantage."

Galerius helped him to his feet. All the action since the prior night was exacting revenge now. His side ached and his hip jolted him with pain. Yet he could not indulge in suffering. With Galerius's help, he started down the slope toward the more populated streets. They both ran at a crouch so that their heads did not appear above the folds in the uneven ground.

Neither even dared a whisper as they threaded through alleys and paths. They surprised people just emerging from their homes as they raced past. Dogs barked and strained on their chains as they ran by opened courtyards. However, soon Curio's legs and side could handle no more. They headed for the safety of another clump of trees that broke up several homes built around it. Once again, they collapsed into bushes, sending small birds screaming into the sky.

"I think we've lost them," Curio said through his gasping. Sweat rolled down into his eyes as he hung against a bush.

"How do they keep finding us?" Galerius said as he rested beside him. His cheeks were red and shined with sweat, while his mouth hung open for more breath.

"Pertinax must know about that house and he sent the Scythians after us."

Galerius reached for his wineskin and cursed. "Shit, it tore when I went through the wall."

Curio checked his waist, patting around it and finding the bone tube, his daggers, and his pack. The pack was still intact, and he set his head back in relief.

"We've got coins enough to buy us both food and a boat ride out of this fucking place."

Galerius did not immediately reply but lowered his head as he gulped for breath. Curio set his pouch back and used his cane to work himself out of the bushes. His thighs burned from the exertion and he could hardly believe how his abilities had deteriorated since being wounded. Yet he stood straight and looked to the closest houses. They appeared quiet and empty.

"Are we really leaving?" Galerius's voice was weak and low.

"You saw what just happened. Do you think we'll escape a third time?"

"Why not? We've done it twice now."

"Because Fortuna has blessed us, but she will tire of us if we act like fools. We can't remain in Athens. We will find another way to snare Pertinax. Right now, all we are doing is running from one bolt-hole to the next." Curio wiped his hand down his face, then stared at the shining sweat on his dirty palm. "Gods, I need a bath."

Galerius laughed and soon Curio joined him. They rested a while in the bushes, and Curio entertained him with descriptions of the Scythians' dousing with foul water, rotted wood, and other disgusting debris.

"I think the corpse of a small dog or very large rat fell on them, too."

"They're the ones who need a bath!"

Once they had recovered, they carefully emerged from the bushes. They were conspicuous for their dirty and ragged condition, but this only helped them avoid others. The morning sky brightened as they picked a long path toward the port gate.

Curio spent a coin to get them breakfast. It took two tries to find a place that would accept them in their tattered state. It was an open-air vendor who cooked lamb meat skewers. To Curio, it was the most savory meat he had tasted in months. Galerius, however, complained it was too hard and gristly.

"You are a rich man's son," Curio said as they sat in the cool shade and hunched over their skewers. "When you join the legion, you'll have to drop your standards."

"I'll become an officer," Galerius said airily. "And I'll put you in charge of finding us the best meals."

By the time they reached the gate both had relaxed enough to forget the morning's frantic escape. They did not draw any attention as they passed beneath the gate with scores of others heading for the port. They were unique only in that they traveled on foot. However, at points along the road, they stole rides on the backs of carts until someone chased them off.

The walled road was a marvel of Athens. Curio did not know much of its history other than the Athenians built it after their enemies once taught them a harsh lesson about sea access. That was long ago, and the walls showed that age. They were stained black in places and streaks from sun and storm scarred the rock. Some sections were undergoing repairs with cranes set up to lift heavy stones into place. It reminded Curio of the legion engineers and their war machines.

The road poured traffic into the port. Being at a higher elevation at this point, he glimpsed the tops of masts over the end of the wall where the gate stood. Seagulls cried overhead, and the unmistakable scent of the ocean was on the breeze. Curio drew it in, relishing the thought of freedom—from both his infirmities and his obligations. One day, he would give Pertinax what he deserved, but first, he had to recoup and refit for that attack.

"Once we're through that gate, we're free." He walked amid crowds of carts filled with goods to ship or else empty beds prepared to load. Workers chatted as they pushed together into a crowd that would file through the gate to the city and docks beyond.

Yet Galerius stopped and seized Curio's arm.

"Fortuna must think us fools because she has withdrawn our blessings."

Curio instinctively ducked as if a slingstone had shot overhead.

He followed Galerius's staring, expecting to find Pertinax barring in his way. At first, he did not spot the threat, and his eyes glided past it.

But then he focused on the dour-faced soldier and his crew forcing their way through the crowd as if coming directly for them.

Sextus and his men had returned to Athens, and from their hard-cast gazes Curio knew they came with no mercy in their hearts.

17

"What do we do?" Galerius's voice rose with panic, drawing sidelong glances from the press of dockworkers flowing around them. He clung close to Curio, nearly shoving him over as he tried to flee.

Sextus was a tall man, though to Curio that was nearly anybody. He wore a tight-fitting beige tunic with a thigh-high hem like a soldier. It accentuated his muscular build. From this distance, the red scar over his twisted nose was less obvious than his scowl. Stern men of similar builds and dispositions to Sextus followed behind. People seemed to sense they were in no mood for trifles and gave them a wide berth.

"He's coming right for me." Galerius again pushed Curio to the side. "What will happen if he catches me? Dear Jupiter, save me from him."

Curio used his and Galerius's height to their advantage, screening themselves behind crowds and moving to the left of the walled road. Sextus's gaze did not follow, and his apparent fixation on them had been an illusion.

"Don't act so obvious," Curio said more mildly than he felt. "He hasn't spotted us yet."

"But there's no way around him!"

"Stop being dramatic. There are plenty of ways around him. Look at this crowd. Does he know where here? No, and he won't as long as you just act normally."

Sextus was the right-hand of Galerius's father, Cilnius. Curio did not fear him under normal circumstances. He had defeated more menacing opponents before. Yet his injury and the weakness that followed left him unsure of his chances. In any case, he was not going to fight Sextus but leave him behind to chase rumors through Athens.

"Look! He's stopping!" Galerius raised his hand to point, but Curio quickly knocked it down.

"Pointing at someone isn't acting normally. Just relax, and we'll pause here. He's not going to make camp on the road, after all."

They had shifted to the side of the road where vendors set up stalls and shacks to serve the endless flow of potential customers. They shouted for attention at anyone who passed, including Curio and Galerius, and shifted away from anyone who did not respond. So they stood amid these vendors and tried to look as if they were only waiting in the shadow of the wall.

Sextus had stopped his crew, and Curio used the moment to count heads. Even with the swell of people obscuring them, he counted sixteen crew along with Sextus. Of course, he would still have men on the ship to guard it, perhaps four more. He elbowed Galerius.

"If I knew how to sail a ship, I'd steal Sextus's."

"Well, it's my father's ship you'd be stealing. Dear gods, what is he doing?"

From what Curio could determine, Sextus appeared to be gathering his men and speaking to locals.

Galerius stood on his toes to see, but Curio shoved him back.

"Trust me," he said. "He'll walk right past us. Last he knew I was bedridden and you were with me. He doesn't know about Cecelia, either. If he did chase us all the way to Crete and returned, then by now he knows he was duped."

Galerius gave up straining to observe his father's strongman and tilted his head wistfully.

"My father trusts Sextus with his life, but I never liked him. It must have burned him up to sail to Crete and realize we had come and gone."

"More likely he ran into a whole lot of unemployed mercenaries and barely made it out alive." Curio touched his wounded side. "I should know about that."

"Then maybe he's just stopping here like we did." Galerius looked hopeful. "He might not even suspect we're still here. I hope he's just stopping over on his way back to my father."

Together they watched as Sextus worked through an interpreter to speak to locals. They seemed to be getting directions based on how the locals sketched paths in the air, pointing toward landmarks that hid behind the inner walls of Athens.

Galerius chuckled. "Maybe he's getting directions to Pertinax's home. Sextus is not an easygoing man, especially if he thinks someone has made a fool of him. He'll want revenge, I'm sure."

Curio's eyes flicked wide and he gripped Galerius by the arm.

"Of course! That's perfect!"

Galerius pulled back, his round face now scrunched into a frown. However, Curio beamed with a smile.

"Sextus isn't our enemy," he said. "He's our ally. Fortuna has not turned her eyes from us. She still looks down on us, full of pride for recognizing her gift."

Galerius peered skyward as if expecting to find the goddess staring into his face.

"Sextus has been ordered to take me and my sister back home. My father is probably going to sell me into slavery when he learns what happened. Sextus will probably kill you just for being part of it all. How is his arrival good news?"

"I want you to enlist his aid. Approach him alone. You're going to tell him mostly the truth about what happened. Tell him that Pertinax duped him and murdered your sister, then nearly murdered you. He's a madman who tried to destroy what he could not own. You can show Sextus where he is and how to take revenge."

Galerius searched Curio's face as he spoke, concern drawing his brows together.

"Are you sure about this? He'll probably just tie me up on his ship and go after Pertinax himself. Then we'll have a whole new set of problems. I can't go back to my father now. I'm responsible for Cecelia's death."

Curio glanced at Sextus, who still conversed with a local who now seemed to be guiding him toward one of the merchants lining the road.

"Don't act like you want to escape. Beg him to save you and take you away. He'll need you to locate Pertinax, and you'll offer to be the bait in his trap. Just emphasize how Pertinax has been chasing you through the city to silence you since you witnessed him murder Cecelia." Curio imitated a dagger thrust to drive his point home.

"I didn't witness that."

"This isn't a time for truth. Make up whatever story you want. Sextus doesn't know any better. With him and his crew behind us, we'll make quick work of Pertinax. Then you'll flee back to the ship and escape. At least, that's what Sextus will believe since you'll be begging to leave."

"What about you?" Galerius stood on his toes to check Sextus's location. "Sextus will want your head as well."

"Don't worry about me. I'll shadow you and will be with you as bait for Pertinax. Sextus will have to choose either my head or Pertinax's. He'll go for Cecelia's killer, especially since you'll be there to urge him on. But the moment Pertinax is killed, we both flee. We know how fast the Scythians respond to danger, but I doubt Sextus does. He'll be forced to run rather than go after us."

"Then how do we escape?" Galerius folded both hands behind his head in worry. "The whole city will be looking for us."

"Don't exaggerate. The whole city will be looking for Sextus. He's the one who came with more than a dozen men to start a fight in the streets. And news won't travel that fast. We will both head for the northwest gate. If we approach it at different times, we won't match the description Pertinax gave the guard, which must be too general to be of use anyway. I'm telling you, this will solve all our problems. Pertinax will be dead, Cecelia avenged, and we will be on our way to Senator Flamininus's camp, where Varro and Falco are waiting."

Galerius twisted around with his hands still laced behind his head. He again stood on his toes to watch Sextus shoving away from the local who was trying to sell him something.

"I guess it works out. I just need to make sure Sextus doesn't lose his mind and do something crazy. He's got a mean temper."

"Delay Sextus until late afternoon. That way, we can escape the city before the gates close for the night. He'll need to secure clubs or knives, in any case. Don't warn him about Scythians, and don't let him restrain you. Remember, tell him Pertinax hides out in his villa all day and uses his followers to do his business. So, to lure him out, you need to appear vulnerable. Let Sextus know Pertinax controls enough of the elder council that the only way for revenge is to take it yourselves. I'm sure it will appeal to him. Now, hurry. Sextus is on the move. If he tries to grab you, it'll be easier to escape him in this crowd."

"What if he does try? Then what?"

"Head to the docks. We'll get a ship out of here before he can catch us. Don't worry. I've been doing this sort of thing for years. Sextus is no match for me."

Galerius stared after his father's henchman. His profile seemed like Cecelia's, and for an instant Curio believed her shade stood beside her brother in grim determination. Then the illusion dissipated and Galerius nodded.

"This is like the missions you do for Senator Flamininus, isn't it?"

"Something like them, yes. Though it's usually Varro who comes up with all the crazy plans. But this feels like what he would do. Now, go complete your first mission. Your sister is watching."

Galerius balled his fists and whispered his sister's name. Then he resolutely stepped into the flow of traffic and navigated toward Sextus.

Curio followed from the shadowed side of the walled road and used his cane like a prop. He had been a healthy soldier last they had met, and that's what Sextus would be searching for now. His eyes would glide past a hunched man leaning on a cane.

At first, Sextus did not notice Galerius following him. He had to shout his name over the traffic flowing steadily in both directions. Sextus whirled and Galerius raised his hands and ran to him as if reuniting with his lost father.

To Curio's surprise, the dour Sextus broke into a smile when he recognized Galerius. They met in the middle of the road in seeming celebration. Either Galerius had a knack for acting or else he was genuinely glad for the reunion. He nearly leaped into Sextus's open arms.

They embraced, and then Sextus held him back to inspect him. Curio watched the expert eye of the former legionary examine Galerius's face. He touched the recently broken nose and probed the fading bruises. All the while, Galerius spoke. Curio wanted to get close enough to listen in, but he could do nothing to help if Galerius went off the plan.

He had to trust the young man to execute the ruse as they discussed. It had come together so swiftly, driven by the need to overtake Sextus before he entered the city and learned the truth. Galerius would control the narrative and focus Sextus on revenge.

Throughout the reunion, Galerius kept searching the crowd. Curio guessed he was unconsciously seeking him to calm his nerves. When some of the crew seemed to notice this, they also began to peer over the heads flowing all around them. So the moment a cart hauling amphorae passed between them, Curio hurriedly pushed through the crowd so that Galerius would not look toward his location.

Sextus most certainly wanted him dead. Curio knew he considered him a traitor and kidnapper and soon to be awarded the title of murderer, even if he did not deserve it. So he pressed into the traffic, irritating people as he bumped them while trying to monitor Galerius.

The group began to move toward the city again, with Sextus wrapping a muscular arm around Galerius's shoulder as the two walked like old friends. Curio wanted to call out and warn him of a trap. Sextus only had to pull his arm tight to turn that friendly embrace into a headlock. Hadn't Galerius been listening?

Yet the group of Romans pushed through the river of travelers filling the walled road. They stopped at points and, from their angry reactions, had probably learned Cecelia's fate. While Curio had sketched a basic script for Galerius, it would be up to him to make it convincing and coherent. At least he was not straying far from the truth and only presenting the facts to his best advantage.

So Curio returned the way they had come, following the group as they flowed with the traffic headed to the city. The Scythians would be searching for him still, perhaps never realizing he had nearly escaped. Curio considered the madness of returning to such danger.

Then he froze in place at the thought.

He could leave Galerius here. Sextus had manpower enough to challenge Pertinax, especially if he took him by surprise. Cecelia's murder would be avenged. Galerius must return home at some point. Perhaps his father might disown him. However, Cilnius seemed to be a good if misguided man and Galerius's fate might not be as dire as predicted. He owed Doctor Nisos and Kinara for paying their fines, but he could send payment back to them without ever having to return to Athens.

Painful memories would fade in time. Cecelia had not been his actual wife, only the notion of one.

The docks were within reach, and he could leave now. He faced the line of laborers and travelers passing through the gate to where the sky-bright sea beckoned them. How easy it would be to slip a few coins to a captain willing to ferry him some miles up the shore. All his worries would vanish behind him.

It was a practical choice. A safe choice. Indeed, it was a patriotic choice. He had vowed to serve Rome, and his next mission awaited him. Varro and Falco needed him. He had to go.

He searched for Galerius over the heads and carts traveling the road and found him shuffling along with Sextus's arm tightly wrapped over his shoulder. His young friend kept glancing around, probably frantic at having lost sight of the one man he trusted to help him.

With a long sigh, he shook his head. "I wish I could be more like Falco at times like these. He wouldn't even look back."

He decided he was not as practical as he believed himself to be. His word was the measure of his worth, and he had given it to Galerius. He could never live with the practical choice.

As he turned to follow, he stopped cold again.

Cecelia stood at the side of the road, smiling at him. Golden light lit her hair and her soft round face glowed. Curio gasped and staggered back, but ran into someone who shoved him away. He had to lean on his cane to keep himself from landing on the dirt road.

When he looked up again, Cecelia remained smiling at him, only she had become a local girl. She held a basket of white flowers in one arm and more in another basket at her feet. She waved to him, speaking in Greek.

Using his cane to steady himself, he approached the roadside vendor. She repeated herself in Greek until Curio shook his head. Then she held out the basket of flowers and attempted fractured Latin.

"For girlfriend? Very pretty flowers."

Curio examined the flowers, which were freshly cut. They would wilt before the end of the day, and he wondered if the girl would end up throwing most of them away. So he fished out an obol and offered it to her. Her eyes lit up, and she placed six white flowers into his other palm.

He sniffed them to her delight.

"She will like!"

"Yes, she will like these, I'm certain."

Then he set off after Galerius, tucking his cane underarm and carrying his handful of whites back to Athens.

18

Curio shadowed Galerius and Sextus back into Athens. Entering the gates required only a perfunctory search since any weapons and armor would have been surrendered at the initial gate. Still, it was a long journey back and a crafty man could rearm along that road. So, Curio waited his turn for the search and watched Sextus and his crew pass inside without issue. On his turn, the guards looked at the bunch of flowers in his hand and waved him through then moved on to those behind him.

He smiled at the white flowers. He would have to remember this for some future use. A man in a ragged tunic carrying flowers probably appeared harmless. If they had searched him, they would have found his long knife and a bone tube of poison powder. Frankly, in his emotional state, he had not even considered these weapons. Once more, Fortuna looked after him and he began to think Varro was not her only favorite son.

Keeping in contact with Galerius and Sextus soon proved difficult with less traffic for concealment. He used the hood on his cloak to disguise himself as he followed, and sometimes used his cane and at other points walked upright. Sextus's crew were alert to their surroundings and constantly scanned the area. Galerius remained firmly in the center with Sextus fast at his side. He might appear relaxed, but he was taking no chances with Galerius escaping.

They moved slowly through the streets, but this was not Sextus's first time in the city. He led them to a well-appointed inn with signs in both Greek and Latin. Galerius vanished inside along with Sextus and most of his crew. Tellingly, three of them remained outside.

Curio removed his hood and turned into a different street, never missing a stride. None of the crew should have noticed him following, yet Sextus appeared to be a careful man. He could not risk getting closer, particularly by entering a building with them. It seemed they might be there a while and plot their revenge against Pertinax. It was late morning and they had all day to acquire whatever they needed. Curio would have to leave the rest up to Galerius. He simply had to appear eager for revenge, which was no stretch for him.

With nothing more to do for the time being, Curio's focus shifted to remaining hidden. After his encounter with the Scythians this morning, he could not risk venturing into that neighborhood again. He regretted this since he could have used the time to learn the best escape routes and hiding places. Worse still, he might inadvertently give away the impending attack. If Pertinax learned of Sextus's arrival, he would expect trouble.

So, he looked at the flowers clutched in his sweaty hand. He had bought them on a whim, mostly because the girl had seemed so much like Cecelia. However, now he realized why he had purchased them.

The streets leading to the Kerameikos graveyards were nearly empty. It was late afternoon when Curio decided to visit Cecelia's grave, and the flowers he had carried with him everywhere wilted. Grave markers and stelae stretched out in broad avenues, a true city of the dead. His chest tightened when he could not orient himself on where Cecelia's ashes had been buried. While it was not long ago, it felt like an event from another lifetime.

He took several meandering paths, looking for Cecelia's simple stone. The grave had a handful of taller stelae nearby, and he recalled the general direction. However, he discovered many stones had a similar configuration. He chided himself for not setting the location more firmly in his memory.

As he wandered, he watched pockets of mourners murmur over graves. Laborers across the gray distance dug out a new plot while someone looked on. Beyond this, the rows of potters' huts rang with the sounds of their work. Their kilns threw smoke that rolled into the graveyards and down toward the small river that flowed sluggishly by the stone markers.

Cecelia's stone seemed so unassuming and small compared to everything around it. While there might be some order to the graves based on status, he could not determine it. Hers certainly did not indicate a person of wealth or position. He stood over the grave, noting the footprints he, Galerius, and Kinara had left surrounding it. His mind wandered back to that day, and all the bitterness returned to him.

He set the whites across the stone and felt a stinging in his eyes. Folding his hands over his waist, he spoke softly to her grave.

"I hope these freshen up this place. I'm sorry for everything that happened. It was my fault no one was with you. You wanted my protection, and I led you to the grave. I don't know what I can do now."

He looked skyward to hold the tears in his eyes. Why did he care so much for what happened to her? They had barely known each other. People die every day, and many of them do not deserve death. He did not cry for them or even those who fell in battle beside him, true brothers in arms. Now, he could not contain the sadness he felt standing before this pitiful marker for a beautiful woman.

"I will do the right thing today," he said, looking down at the stone and letting the tears release over his cheeks. They rolled into his beard, the thin and tangled mess that Cecelia doubted she could shave for him. He wiped at the tears with the back of his wrist.

"I will keep Galerius safe as long as I can. I have to tell you, your brother can be rash. But I'll do whatever I can to keep him alive. For if he lives, then you will live as well. At least in some way."

Then he balled his fist and narrowed his eyes.

"And I'll avenge you. Once, I just wanted to escape from all of this. That was a mistake. If I could not keep you safe, then I must at least avenge you. Pertinax wanted you, and when you denied him, he took your life instead. Well, I will send him to Hades. Before the sun rises again, he will die."

He imagined himself and Galerius as bait, and Pertinax surrounding them with his henchmen. Then Sextus and his men would emerge to tilt the odds, and Curio would personally drive his knife into Pertinax's heart. He would look him in the eye as he died, and he would know why.

"After he's dead, you can rest and wait until the day your brother joins you in a happy reunion. This is all I can do for you now. I hope it will be enough."

Curio stood a while longer in silence, his shadow falling across the grave. The breeze lifted the wilted white petals and flipped them over the marker. When everything was settled and their names forgotten in Athens, he would help Galerius move her ashes to someplace back home. She deserved better than a forgotten corner of this graveyard.

Then, another shadow overtook his. Someone had come upon him while he was lost in thought. Yet he was not so absorbed that he wouldn't have heard footsteps, meaning someone stalked him. He leaped over the grave and spun just as he felt something swish through where he had been standing.

Pertinax hovered over Cecelia's grave. His face was flushed red, emphasizing the scar that ran from his eye to curve into his nose. A wine-scented cloud billowed around him, flowing into Curio's face with the wind.

"You're a slippery piece of shit, Centurion Curio. I almost had you."

Curio reached for the dagger hidden behind his gray cloak. Pertinax stepped back with a drunken grin.

"You want to die this way, then?" He slipped his hand into his gray tunic and withdrew a pugio. Its honed edge gleamed with the orange sun. "Can't blame you, really. Better than choking to death on poison, which is your other choice. Of course, the elders will give you a burial. When I'm done with you, I'll have to slice you up and throw you in the river. It's your choice."

Curio remained fixed on the white edge of the pugio facing him. Was it the same one he left in Cecelia's body? His own long knife was a poor match for it. He carried the weapon of a thug while Pertinax had one of a soldier.

Pertinax waved the blade before him. "Remembering your legion days? Those are over now. You shouldn't have come back here. You even had the stones to attack me. I admire your guts! But it was stupid."

At last, regaining his senses, Curio raised his knife and pulled his cloak free with his other hand. It could serve as a shield of sorts and give him some advantage against Pertinax's greater size.

Pertinax laughed and stepped forward, pugio still leveled at him. He crushed the whites into Cecelia's marker stone as he forced Curio back.

"Where's your friend? Is he hiding?" Pertinax's eyes shifted from side to side, but he never fully looked away. Even drunk, he was too wary to make that mistake.

Curio inched to the side, probing behind with his heel to ensure he wouldn't fall over. The ground here was treacherous, with loose rocks everywhere. If he fell, Pertinax would finish what that mercenary in Crete could not. A pugio only had to stab the depth of a man's thumb to kill. Like its larger partner, the gladius, it was a horrifically efficient killing weapon. He had to respect it, even in the hands of a drunk brute.

"Well, I'll deal with your friend later. I thought he would show up here, but I found you instead. Call it a blessing. So, here's your last choice, Centurion Curio. Will you give up and take your poison, or do I have to gut you?"

"You murdered Cecelia," he said as he tried to position himself so that Pertinax would have to strike across his own torso. "You'll die for that."

The pugio lowered and Pertinax frowned.

"I didn't kill her. You tried to blame me for it. But maybe it was you, eh, Centurion Curio? They found a pugio in her guts. That's standard legion kit, isn't it? You snuck one in here, just like me, and then went mad and killed her. Do you remember doing it? Kinara fed you so much of that shit that makes men crazy, how do you know it wasn't you? You don't remember anything after Kinara is done with you, and half of what you do remember isn't real. I know all about that."

Curio wasn't listening to this drunken babble. He knew reality from dreams. Instead, he had slowly slipped to the best angle to strike. Pertinax would be forced to block with his bare arm, and his counterstrike would cross his torso, reducing power and accuracy.

He seemed unaware of the threat, perhaps because the adjustments were minuscule and he was drunk. So he bobbled his head as he gloated.

"Well, it doesn't matter who killed her. She was a good-looking woman, but she's dead now. You'll follow her and her brother after you. Thank me later when you all have a reunion in Hades."

Curio struck with all his power. He lurched forward, leading the thrust with his leg, turning into the strike so that it would drive his knife through muscle and ribs and slice into his liver.

Pertinax spun aside with a yelp of surprise.

Curio's blade barely caught an edge of Pertinax's brown tunic, neatly cutting it and lightly scoring the flesh beneath. But Pertinax staggered aside as Curio carried past him.

His heel landed on the flowers now crushed over Cecelia's gravestone, and he slipped. With a curse, he twisted to remain on his feet. Both men had suffered the uneven footing and now regained themselves out of range of their weapons.

Raising his cloak, Curio set himself for another thrust. If he could snare Pertinax in the folds of the cloak then he might be able to bring his weapon to bear.

Pertinax's face reddened and his drunken anger flared.

"The harder you make this the angrier I'll get. You think you have me?"

Rather than answer, he leaped forward and hurled his cloak over Pertinax. He did not expect it, despite the obvious preparation, and the cloak settled over him as Curio swept in from the side.

Pertinax cursed as the cloak wrapped around his head, and he struggled to bat it away with his free hand.

Yet Curio failed to connect. Though he stepped inside Pertinax's reach, his twisting combined with the flying cloak to spoil his strike. Instead, he caught more cloth than flesh.

However, he had Pertinax off balance and so threw his shoulder into his body. The bigger man howled with rage and crashed to the ground, but Curio staggered and collapsed beside him rather than atop him as planned.

Whipping the cloak aside, Pertinax was faster on his feet. Curio flushed with excitement, and it covered all his weakness, but his reactions lagged. Fortunately, Pertinax's intoxicated unsteadiness bought Curio enough time to at least get to his knees.

"You little bastard!" Pertinax's foot connected to Curio's wounded side, and sent him sprawling onto his back. He dropped his long knife and it clattered between two grave markers and out of immediate reach.

Instead, he grabbed a loose rock and hurled it at Pertinax, striking him squarely in the forehead. A fleshy thump preceded garbled curses, and he fell back holding both hands over his face as blood streaked from beneath them.

No amount of battle frenzy could stifle the agony of being struck in his freshly healed wound. He felt as if he had been folded over and tied into place. The pain was too much for him to rise to his feet.

Pertinax started to laugh and was about to speak when he stumbled over a marker and crashed into a man-size stela. He grabbed it like a lover, but the old stone was not properly set. It crashed to the ground and took Pertinax along.

Curio used the moment to groan and stand. He lost sight of the long dagger but knew it was close. However, the gods hid it from him, and he had no time to search.

"Look what you did!" Pertinax struggled up, using the broken stela as leverage to get to his feet. "You made me defile a grave! You're going to pay for that. I won't be haunted because of your stupidity."

Out of breath and weaponless, Curio barely steadied himself to face Pertinax again.

The drunken giant now rose covered in patches of gray dust. Blood flowed from his forehead and around his eyes. However, he was grinning as he patted his waist.

"You lost your weapon," he said. "But not me. Still, I see why you're a centurion. Shitty little cheating fighter you are. Ha! Good for you! But I'm not giving you a chance to get close for another trick."

Pertinax produced a length of leather from his waist. Huffing and hunched over his wound, Curio did not understand until his enemy picked up a rock and fit it into the sling.

"I'll just bash your skull in. Won't take long now."

Curio fled through the graveyard, forgetting all his pain as he did.

The first slingstone zipped past him and shattered the corner of a stela with an explosion of broken rock.

"I'm out of practice," Pertinax shouted. "But I was the best shot with sling or javelin. You're not getting far!"

Curio fled in a zigzag pattern, always looking to put a large marker between himself and Pertinax. The stones sped past, blasting into the ground with bursts of dust or else cracking into nearby markers. One clipped his shoulder, catching in the sleeve of his tunic, which diminished its force. Otherwise, it might have shattered his bones. The sling was the simplest but most devastating weapon in the world. It hardly required any accuracy to stop a man, as a hit anywhere would tear flesh and destroy bone.

Fortunately, Pertinax was drunk and overconfident. He laughed at every miss, promising the next would dash Curio's brains out. However, the boasts grew more distant each time.

He fled for the potter's quarters. The workshops all huddled together in a jumbled mess alongside homes and storefronts, creating a perfect place to lose pursuit. Across the graveyard, he saw people watching from a distance. In any other circumstance, he would beg them to call for help. Yet that was just what Pertinax wanted.

Pain sliced through his calf, and he crashed forward into the sparse grass at the edge of the graveyard. He held both hands out to break his fall but had been running with enough force that he still rolled to a stop.

His left calf throbbed with burning pain, and he touched blood when he reached for it. Again, it had been a graze but far closer. Worse than the cut was being prone. Without his cane and after taking a grievous blow to his wound, standing took all his concentration.

"Aha! The hare is finally run to ground!" Pertinax's voice was a thin echo.

Sweat poured down his face as he willed himself to stand. He screamed as he did, both in frustration and pain. Down the gentle slope, still among the graves, Pertinax laughed in answer and whirled his sling overhead.

Curio bolted away, finding a last reserve to reach the potter district. Despite all the signs of activity, he did not encounter anyone at the edge of these buildings. They were all typical mudbrick constructions with red tile roofs faded to gray. Everywhere were the confusing array of professional tools, carts of clay covered with tarps, barrels and boxes, and an ever-present smoke. He heard people in the distance as he threaded into the narrow alleys. Someone had dumped water into the road, creating a puddle to reflect the orange light of the late afternoon sky.

He cut right as he heard Pertinax's curses growing closer. Before he lost himself in this strange community of craftsmen, he looked behind.

Pertinax might be drunk, but he moved with the speed of Mercury. He was bounding up the patchy slope, his pugio now in hand and his clenched teeth bright against his dark red face.

"Curio! You won't get out of there alive!"

His laughter sounded crazed.

Curio rounded the corner and realized he had entered a maze of walls and workshops. Did Pertinax know this place? That moment of doubt filled him with dread.

To his right, two men vanished behind a building as they chatted. Ahead was a wooden wall anchored in mud. Greek letters were painted on it, seeming to indicate some sort of station. Gray smoke flowed over that wall.

To his left was an open-air workshop with clay set on a wheel and other tools arrayed on a small table. A faded red cloak was draped over the stool.

Pertinax's screaming was closer now. Curio had run himself out of options.

So he did something even he would not expect.

Leaping over the low railing that enclosed the workshop yard, he snatched up the faded red cloak and set it over his shoulders and pulled up the hood. He then adjusted the stool so that his back faced the alley, and he hunched over the clay. His foot felt for the pedal and then pressed to set the wheel spinning.

Pertinax thumped gasping around the corner, and presented with the same scene, stopped.

Curio worked the wheel, dipped his hands in a bucket of slimy water, then began to shape the clay. He didn't know what he was making, but listened intently for Pertinax. To make his disguise more convincing, he gave a slight turn of his head as if acknowledging the visitor.

Pertinax growled and padded forward into the alley, unsure if Curio had gone around the corner, over the wall, or into one of the houses.

He spoke to Curio in Greek.

Not knowing the actual words, Curio guessed his question. He stopped spinning the wheel, but did not turn around. Instead, he waved dismissively with his red clay-stained hand in the direction of the two other men he had just seen.

Pertinax grunted and stomped off.

Curio began working the wheel again, sweat dripping onto the clay deforming in his artless grip. Both eyes strained to watch from the side as Pertinax followed his misdirection. His heart raced at the simplicity of this plan and its startling success. Indeed, show a man what he expects to see and he will believe it. This axiom had saved his life more than once. Now Pertinax rounded the corner. Curio didn't know what was beyond it, and hoped it provided more confusion options.

For his part, he would quietly backtrack and then flee out of the Kerameikos.

Then someone shouted.

Curio nearly fell from the stool as a wiry old man with red-stained hands and wearing a beaten apron appeared in the workshop. He glared at Curio, pointing a bony, clay-crusted finger at him in accusation.

Smiling, Curio backed off the stool and looked back toward the wall where Pertinax had gone.

He reappeared around the corner, and their eyes met.

"Sneaky little shit!"

19

Curio snatched the lump of clay on the wheel before him and flung it at Pertinax as he raced back down the alley. The wiry old man protested, leaping forward as if to catch it.

Unfortunately, he had mistimed the throw and it plopped flat and short of Pertinax, not even delaying his charge.

Curio's strength had drained when he sat down. Standing once more, his body quivered with weakness. His legs, so long out of shape, were like lead and his side throbbed where Pertinax had kicked him.

There was nowhere to flee. Fighting was his only option.

Pertinax crashed through the feeble railing enclosing the workshop. Curio grabbed the wheel from the stand and heaved it overhead.

But before he could bring it down on Pertinax, the old man flailed himself at it with a mournful howl. His bony elbows collided with Curio's face as he seized the makeshift weapon. Pertinax barreled into them, crashing into the melee and sending everyone into the red earth.

The old man screamed and knocked over the water bucket,

sending a wave of cold water under Curio. Pertinax spluttered and cursed as he fought with the old man, somehow having come to possess the wheel Curio intended as a weapon.

Curio grabbed the stool and tried to pull himself up, but his hands were slick with wet clay. He slipped and slammed his jaw on the wooden seat before plowing his face back into the mud.

The old man screeched, and Pertinax roared.

"Look what you made me do! Fuck!"

Curio flipped over and scrabbled aside. Pertinax kneeled in the mud, his pugio bright with red blood. The old potter clutched his broken wheel, his dead eyes as pale as his wispy hair, and stared at the twilight sky. A hole in his side leaked black blood into the dirt.

Now others answered the commotion, not the least those from within the potter's home. A woman and young man emerged from a darkened doorway. The woman screamed and the man collapsed to his knees.

"Fuck!" Pertinax staggered to his feet over the dead man, his pugio dripping blood. "They've seen me!"

Curio pointed at Pertinax. Of course, they did not understand him, but he could think of nothing else in the moment.

"He did it! I tried to stop him!"

Pertinax roared in anger, but rather than charge Curio, he ran at the two witnesses.

As much as he regretted it, Curio used the distraction to flee. Maybe the young man who collapsed at the sight of death would prevail. The woman could also delay him until others arrived.

This was Curio's moment.

However, a shrill cry from a man followed him out of the potter's quarters. He knew that Pertinax was making quick work of the witnesses.

He fled back down the slope toward the graves. The sun cast long shadows, creating a crisscross of darkness.

"Come back here!" Pertinax's voice echoed behind him and was closer than Curio expected.

With renewed terror, he discovered a reserve of strength. He leaped over the low row of stones demarcating the start of the graveyard.

Then he heard a whistling rush of air and pain burst over his left shoulder.

A slingstone had grazed him again, but this time caught enough flesh to spin him around and flatten him. He crashed amid the grave markers, his body slamming atop the hard edges. Bright stars of pain formed in his vision and he stared skyward in a daze.

However, Pertinax's triumphant howl chilled him like the baying of a wolf, and he sprang to his feet. Another slingstone cracked into a grave monument, spraying Curio with grit as he fled past it.

His foot caught on a marker, and he hurled forward. Cursing, he held his arm out to break the fall. This time, he at least landed on an open patch of dirt between grave markers.

But he felt the heavy thumping of Pertinax's feet vibrating through the ground. He barely had time to flip over to face him.

Pertinax's bulky shadow loomed over him against the rose-colored sky. He fell atop Curio, driving the air from his lungs, and howled victory.

"To die among the dead," he said. "That's poetry!"

Gasping and out of strength, Curio stared up at Pertinax as he fumbled to locate his pugio. He held Curio down with his knees, looking like a hunter preparing to skin his catch.

"You're a worthless killer," he gasped as his hand sought the smaller knife he still had in his belt.

"I am a killer," he said, at last pulling the pugio free and then holding it in front of Curio's face. "But I didn't kill the bitch."

An inspiration crashed through Curio's defeated mind and he remembered the bone tube filled with Kinara's poison.

"Now, I'm sending you to meet her." Pertinax raised his pugio.

Curio's hand wrapped around the tube still dangling from his belt. He snatched it free and used his thumb to flick away the stopper.

"This is for Cecelia."

He stabbed the tube forward, expelling a brown cloud of powder into Pertinax's face.

In the middle of his triumph, he inhaled the poison and fell back coughing.

"What's this, you little shit?"

But he had his answer when he slid off Curio, dropped his pugio, and slapped both hands to his face.

Curio would have laughed, but he felt a numbing burn dusting his lips and something land in his eyes.

The poisonous powder had settled over him. He immediately scrabbled back, his eyes watering and throat burning. A tingling cold spread over his skin. He batted at his face, trying to brush away the poison before it took hold.

Rolling onto his back, he crawled forward in the dirt toward the river that now seemed a thousand miles away.

Behind him, Pertinax gurgled and wheezed, his curses reduced to watery gasps.

Despite his own panic and near blindness, he turned to Pertinax. Through the milky haze of his sight, he saw him with his back arched on the ground. His face had turned deep blue and his eyes bulged. From the way he gasped, both hands at his neck, he looked like a fish dying on a muddy bank.

Curio's breathing came in gulps, but he wasn't certain it was due to the poison. He had only suffered a dusting where Pertinax had inhaled a lungful.

The pugio glittered beside him, dull only where his latest victim's blood had dried. He crawled to it, pulling it into his hand as he clawed himself atop Pertinax's body.

"You deserve to choke," he said in a raspy whisper. "But I'm taking no chances."

Pertinax's bulging eyes focused on him and then on the pugio at his neck. A wet scream erupted from his frothing mouth, and he struggled to push away from the blade.

"It...was...her...."

Curio pushed the pugio under Pertinax's jaw, driving the razor-edged wedge of bronze through his throat until it lodged in the depths of his skull.

He squirmed, his eyes rolled back in his head, and then fell flat.

Curio collapsed atop of him, and let the pugio remain buried in his neck. Hot blood pumped into the dirt and soon ebbed as the last of Pertinax's life drained.

"Poetry," he muttered, slumped over the body.

His head rocked, and his vision swam. He wanted to reach that small river and wash this junk out of his eyes. Whatever it was, Curio experienced the familiar dreamy sensation he remembered after taking one of Kinara's draughts.

This powder was a key ingredient, capable of killing in large doses. He hoped he hadn't taken in enough for a lingering death or permanent injury. That might be worse than dying at Pertinax's hands.

So he rolled off the body, feeling as if he were battered around in a high tide surf. The simplest motion set him rocking and spinning.

However, he was determined to leave Pertinax's corpse. He was not so poisoned to forget potters from the workshops would soon follow. Even if they had no love of Pertinax, they would not count him among their allies. After all, he was still banished under pain of death. He could not be discovered inside the city, even in the Kerameikos.

One attempt to rise had turned the world into a whirlwind. Crawling was his most stable option. So he inched along on all fours toward where he hoped the river flowed. By now, the poison was in him, and he wondered what good it would do to wash his face. As he crawled, he realized he might also drown himself accidentally.

So he collapsed to his stomach, balling his fists and laughing bitterly. He patted the cold ground, his body spread across the grave markers. Maybe he was close to Cecelia.

"As promised, you are avenged. I am sorry."

Surrendering to the desensitizing poison, he set his head down. The numbness spread from his face to his limbs. This was how Kinara's draught worked, inducing sleep and stilling the body. Only he might have ingested too much, leading to a more drastic outcome.

Now he was going to dream and perhaps never awaken.

He prayed for good dreams. For all his mistakes and imperfections, he had tried to be a good person. He had offered glory and praise to the gods, remained loyal to his friends, and tried to make the best choices he knew how.

As he rested his head on a cold gravestone, he told himself that he at least deserved good dreams.

His eyelids drooped and he still felt as if he were spinning. He clutched the stones he hardly felt pushing into his body. It was as if a thick pillow sat between him and the ground.

Then he was staring into a golden light. He realized it was the evening sun as it slipped behind the walls of Athens. How had he come to be looking at it?

Someone dragged him by the legs while another took him by the shoulders.

"No, I didn't do it."

He could not hold his head up to see who was carrying him off. Someone spoke to him, but it was so muffled he could not even determine the gender. The voice was thick and muddy, as if he were hearing it from behind a wall and with his head buried under a pillow.

The world swayed and rocked and he felt as if he were flying.

"It wasn't me. Pertinax killed the old man. I was only defending myself."

But he could not have spoken those words, he decided, for he was already experiencing the coldness of oncoming sleep. Bizarre and senseless visions crowded his mind.

So he swayed through the void and tumbled away into blackness.

∽

WHEN HE AWAKENED AGAIN, his head was still spinning, though it was more like the gentle rocking of branches in an evening breeze. He kept his eyes closed against revealing his awakening and to delay seeing where he was. Both prospects filled him with dread.

His mind was clear now, even if still unsettled from the cloud of poison he had inhaled. He suppressed a smirk at his stupidity. In the moment, he hadn't time to consider another option, but of course, throwing powder into the air over his head would be just as harmful to himself. If he hadn't backed up in time, he might have inhaled as much as Pertinax had.

Then, his body tightened at that memory. Pertinax was dead. Cecelia was avenged.

He had been a despicable man, murdering women who displeased him. According to Kinara, he had killed his wife, and that rage manifested in everything he did until this day. He was a beast. In their first encounter, he had beaten Galerius nearly to death for simply bumping into him and causing him to spill wine.

His eyes flicked open remembering Galerius. He was with Sextus, planning an ambush on someone who would never show up. What would he do now?

Forgetting his plan to pretend as if asleep, he now looked up at the ceiling rafters. They were old and stained. Speckles of black mold collected in the corners. He could smell the musty odor. A clay lamp flickered on a table beside him, its flame so low and guttering its light could not reach the edges of the room. From the still and humid air, he guessed it was not a large space, perhaps no bigger than the tiny apartments where he had lived for most of his time in Athens.

No one looked over him. Not Galerius or Cecelia, Doctor Nisos or Kinara. He was alone, at least as far as he could determine. Still, he remained flat and motionless. The poison still echoed through his mind, causing him to feel as if he were on a rocking ship. For an instant, he feared he was, but there was no sound of creaking boards or anything else. More than likely, he was underground.

And this likewise terrorized him. Had he died? Was this Hades? The darkness was oppressive enough to be the Underworld. But what of his judgment and crossing the river? No poison would erase that memory.

Most telling, however, were the ropes binding him to the bed. Shades did not need such physical restrictions. He was alive still.

He had not realized this was what held him in place, instead believing the aftereffects of the poison had weighted his limbs.

For an instant, he almost laughed with relief. After all, he was neither paralyzed nor dead. Instead, he was someone's prisoner.

Lifting his head, he still could not see much beyond his bed. It was a rough wooden palette with a gray wool blanket to serve as a mattress. A pillow that had lost most of its stuffing propped up his head. The ropes were thick and stained deep brown from long use. These pinned his arms and legs to the bed but were not so tight that they restricted his blood flow.

He strained to see beyond the hazy orange glow of the lamp. The walls did not seem far, but he couldn't be certain no one hid in the shadowed corners.

"I'm awake if you haven't discovered it. Do you understand me?"

No one answered his call that echoed off hard, unadorned walls. He rested his head again, and turned to face the clay lamp. As he stared, he realized a small clay vase sat just behind it, obscured by the haze of the flame.

A bunch of white flowers leaned to one side in the vase. The petals were still full and fresh, and only one had fallen to the table.

While these flowers grew everywhere in the city and could just be anyone's attempt to decorate a plain room, Curio's hands and feet chilled at seeing them.

Panic overcame him. Was Cecelia's spirit here, and was she angry with him? He struggled against the ropes, but his senses still reeled from the poison. The bed felt as if it spun from his thrashing and all his shoving against the bonds did not help. They were tied loosely, but well enough to hold him in place. Still, he struggled until he exhausted himself.

Cecelia was not here, of course. But who would know to place those flowers beside his bed?

As he stared at the ceiling and the shifting shadows cast by the lamp, he heard a door rattling in its frame, and then a sliver of gray light appeared. Something passed through the light, and then the door softly thumped shut.

Curio held his breath, straining to see who had entered. Yet the door was just beyond the reach of the lamplight. He only saw the suggestion of a form in the darkness.

"Who are you? Why have you tied me down?"

He listened for a response, but the figure remained silent as a ghost. Curio's hands had now turned to ice, and his poison-addled mind could not escape reaching a supernatural conclusion.

"Cecelia? Have you come to punish me?"

A rich, female laugh rang through the room. The figure stepped closer. The woman hid herself in a black cloak, making her outline hard to distinguish. Yet the golden light caught her face, shining on dusky skin and gleaming from big eyes.

Kinara smiled, the creases between her lush brows darkening with shadow.

"Hello, Curio. I'm glad you are awake."

20

Curio stared at the woman in the black cloak, wondering if Kinara stood before him or if he dreamed of her likeness. The poisonous fog engulfing his mind made it impossible for him to trust his senses, especially as he still felt like he was swaying even when tied to a bed. Yet Kinara entered and settled on the edge of the bed.

He found himself squirming to escape her. She had sat like this scores of times when treating his wounds. Yet somehow, he felt threatened. Perhaps it was guilt at having abandoned her.

"How did you find me? How long have I been here? What about Galerius? I have to get to him."

Kinara laughed again, and set her hand on Curio's knee, just below the rope holding his legs down.

"One question at a time. You've been injured. But why does that not surprise me? You've got bruises and scrapes all over your body. Your shoulder is bleeding and you have a heavy bruise where your stitches were. Did he kick you there?"

"Yes," he said, too quickly for his liking. He did not want to show his fear. Kinara did not respond but remained with her hand resting on his knee and smiling.

"What did I tell you about taking care of yourself? All my good work will be undone."

Curio smiled feebly. Kinara's matter-of-fact demeanor worried him more than if she had been angry at his betrayal.

"Why am I tied down?"

"Because you poisoned yourself. You might spasm and fall out of bed."

Kinara slipped closer, and her hand glided up to his thigh. He still wore his torn and stained tunic. Red mud had dried on his back from the fight at the potter's workshop and now flaked off atop the wool blanket beneath him.

"I still feel sick. How long have I been asleep?"

"A few hours." Kinara flipped her black cloak over her shoulder to reveal her sleeveless arm. She wore her usual stola but seemed to have pinned it to hang loose around her arms.

Curio glimpsed her skin there, then averted his eyes.

"I don't know how you found me, or how you took me to wherever we are, but I am grateful."

Kinara's smile did not shift, but she seemed to be studying him. The lamp reflected yellow points in her eyes as they roved up and down his body.

"It was easy to guess where you would go. You're still thinking about her. Even now, you thought I was her." She giggled. "She is dead, Curio. You have to move on with your life. Our life. You promised to take me to Rome."

"Are you angry?"

"Angry? No. I'm disappointed. I should not have underestimated you."

Curio did not understand what she meant by that, but he contained his accusations at how she had lied about Galerius. He was at a definite power imbalance and was not entirely certain of her intentions.

"Galerius is alive. Somehow, we got the wrong information about him." He hoped his smile looked sincere, for he would have rather demanded an explanation for her manipulation. "He's going to try to kill Pertinax tonight."

Kinara frowned and again shifted closer to him. Her hand shifted up to his waist, settling near his crotch. This made him squirm again.

"You killed Pertinax. I watched you do it and watched you try to reach the river. It gave me the idea to dispose of his body there."

"By yourself?"

"The potters helped me. They were glad you killed him and promised that the river would bury him in mud within days."

"So, you had them bring me here? Wherever we are."

"We're in the place I wanted you to hide the first time. If you had only listened to me then, none of this would've happened. Instead, you made a mess of things. Even after I set everything right, you insisted on returning. I agreed to it, just to get it out of your mind. But then you abandoned me."

"I'm sorry," he said, though he wasn't. Again, he forced something he hoped passed for sincerity into his expression.

Kinara's hand now slipped over his tunic and rested on his lower abdomen. She leaned closer still, and Curio caught the scent of wine on her breath. Her dark eyes were bright with the glowing lamp.

"Don't be sorry." Suddenly her warm hand stroked his cheek, causing him to flinch. Her eyes widened and her hand recoiled. Then she curled her lip. "You've paid the price. And we're going to start a new life together in Rome. You promised."

"Of course we will." The ropes holding him down chastened accusations of deceit and manipulation that he otherwise would've hurled at her. "But what about your father? He won't try to stop us?"

"I've handled things with my father." She set her hand on his cheek, this time with a force that showed she would not be denied. "He won't bother us. At last, things will be as they should be. As I've always wanted them to be."

"Of course they will." He laughed, echoingly false even to his ears. Yet Kinara seemed to drink in that promise, closing her eyes as if imagining this future.

"Kinara, I don't think I need to be tied down now. I'm just a bit dizzy. I'll just lie in bed until you tell me I'm well enough."

Her eyes flicked open and she suddenly loomed over him. Using her thumb, she pulled down on his eyes. The sudden cool air made them sting as she examined him.

"You inhaled a lot of that hensbane powder. I can't give you more, or else I might kill you. So, no, you'll stay tied down for now."

"I promise to stay in bed. Besides, the door is barred. Am I right? Kinara, I'm not going anywhere. I have no one but you now."

His smile hurt from forcing it so wide. Normally, he was a better actor but his nerves and the disorienting effects of this hensbane impaired his technique.

Kinara abruptly rose from the bed and turned her back, pulling the cloak over her shoulders again. She paused before reaching the end of the darkness, then turned to speak over her left shoulder.

"You have Galerius. You still want to find him."

Curio shook his head, though she was no longer looking at him.

"Don't go!" He strained against the ropes and felt the topmost knot slip over his chest.

Kinara turned, one thick brow cocked.

"I am so thirsty. Please, bring me some water."

She stared hard at him, then left, though the door remained cracked open. This was an unexpected boon, and he strained against the ropes to see beyond the door.

The gray light indicated moonlight entering from an unshuttered window or open door. For either to be left open at night suggested the location might be out of the way, which made sense for a hideout. It also hinted that the place might be structurally unsound. The new light spilling inside showed the walls were mudbrick and reinforced with old wood. This was a ruin and not a maintained home, just like the hiding place Galerius had found.

Kinara reentered with a cup brimming with water. She did not speak or smile but sat beside him and cupped his head.

The thirst was real, and he gulped down the water eagerly. Yet before he finished it, he held a mouthful, though careful not to let it fill his cheeks. He set his head back and smiled. Kinara regarded him with hooded eyes and left him on the bed holding the water in his mouth.

Once the door closed and he was again alone with just the lamplight, he struggled upright against the rope. As a child, he used to engage in all sorts of foolish contests with his brothers, one being who could spit the farthest or most accurately. If only his brother could see him now.

He spit the water onto the rope knot, soaking it and his chest with warm water.

Some ropes would absorb the water and become harder to undo. However, this rope was compressed and oily from countless uses. The water instead served as a lubricant.

So he began working against it, pushing with his chest. The bed physically jumped with the force of his attack. Even the flowers on the table beside him shook from his exertions. The knot slipped but remained tied. Still, the constant pressure loosened it.

He would not let Kinara keep him tied up like a pet dog. The poison still rocked his mind, and every shove against the bonds felt like he was spinning in a tempest. But he was determined to gain his freedom.

Though his desire never flagged, eventually his strength did. Combined with the constant sway brought on by the poison, he had to surrender and lie flat. He closed his eyes and felt like he was spinning away into oblivion.

Kinara had not lied to him about the timeline. The draught she fed him would last a full night but vanish by morning. He guessed inhaling the raw ingredient might not last as long, but would linger for several hours.

Therefore, Galerius and Sextus were still preparing to attack Pertinax. He had to meet Galerius at their fallback point. Better still, he had to be there when the attack started. Once Sextus realizes Pertinax won't show, he might grab Galerius and run.

Curio was no longer conflicted about what he had to do. Galerius had proven himself to be a friend worth keeping. He had the potential to grow into more than just another rich merchant's least-favorite son. Besides, Cecelia would have wanted him to protect her brother from their father's wrath. Even though he had failed her in every way that mattered, he would not fail her again.

Yet he remained tied to this bed, unable to fulfill his solemn vow.

As the spinning sensation settled, he began to review all that had happened. The fight with Pertinax had been a chaotic and shameful spectacle. At least he had learned he did not need a cane anymore. He had been developing a dependence on it, using it more for mental comfort than physical aid.

He reflected on Pertinax's final moments choking out his life. It was a fitting end to such a monster.

But what had he said with his dying breath?

"It was her."

What had Pertinax meant by that? Why had he used his dying breath to deny Cecelia's murder? There was no point to it then. Knowing his personality, he should've taunted her death. So perhaps he had not killed her, but who did he accuse?

Curio's eyes flicked open, looking through the dark ceiling above and into his deepest fears.

"Kinara."

His body turned to ice, frozen with the horror of having missed all the signs until this moment. The ropes across his chest seemed to tighten with this realization.

For whatever twisted reason, Kinara had wanted Cecelia dead and had been willing to do it herself.

Now it all came together. Kinara never used Cecelia's name. Even when the two of them sat together, Kinara hardly acknowledged her. Only once had they spent time together, perhaps only for Kinara to pump her rival for information. She seemed to treat her with scorn and showed her no respect.

Curio shook his head, not wanting to remember this.

Kinara had caught Cecelia sleeping with him and had kicked their bed in response. She had never done something like that before.

Now that he thought about it, that seemed like a jealous reaction rather than trying to awaken him.

"No, Curio, don't do this to yourself. She has been taking care of you all this time."

But why? The question bounced around his head. Why had she done so much for him?

The question overwhelmed him, and he tried to resist the obvious conclusion.

Kinara had handled everything for him, ensured no one else saw him, and he interacted with no one but her.

More chillingly, she kept him sedated and malleable with her draughts and the continual pain and weakness he felt. Doctor Nisos had wanted him to exercise and rebuild his strength. She only ever wanted him to lie in bed and rest. She left the stitches in him too long, and this had caused prolonged pain. Looking back now, Kinara's treatments provided fleeting relief, but he always needed more of her draughts to function.

Kinara had been slowly isolating him, becoming the only person he could depend upon.

She always knew where they were. She had conveniently shown up right after Cecelia's murder. But as he remembered it, she had been flushed and sweaty, and her hands clammy. Was it from the rush of having just killed her rival rather than being shaken by the murder? Curio knew now that it was the former.

The pugio had been a convenient prop. Upon seeing it, Curio suspected a Roman was the killer, and Kinara had already painted Pertinax as a murderer. Yet it had been Kinara who presented him with that weapon. Had she wielded it rather than Pertinax? Curio naturally concluded that Pertinax was the killer, given his motivations and history. While she did not name him directly, she did not dissuade Curio from that accusation.

A pugio was uncommon in Greece, but plenty would be in circulation as trophies from old battlefields. Kinara could have acquired one and used it to frame Pertinax. He thought of her dominant strength and how easily she could have cut Cecelia down and dragged her into the bushes. She knew there would be no witnesses when she went to the well in the evening. She might have reported Cecelia's whereabouts to Pertinax and encouraged him to seek her to deepen his connection to the murder. It was no different than the way she had encouraged Galerius to his doom by giving him a feeble means to attack Pertinax.

Curio squeezed his eyes shut, realizing she had set a perfect trap to eliminate Cecelia. However, she likely had not expected them to get arrested for arson.

So when they were caught and taken before the elder council, she knew to bring enough drachmae to bribe their freedom. She had to include Galerius to keep up the pretense of being their benefactor. By paying their fines, Curio became more dependent on her. Of course, she had a different plan for Galerius and later used his pain and rage against him.

Curio wondered if she honestly wanted to go to Rome or if any of that business about her father was true. Maybe that was her response to his banishment. Get rid of Galerius, and then steer him away from anyone, even Varro and Falco, and keep him for herself.

Shaking his head on the bed, he saw the flowers again set beside him. He grew still, eyes widening in realization.

Kinara was trying to take Cecelia's place—from her story about escaping an unwanted marriage to giving him the same flowers. She kept him tied down so he could not escape and would have kept him drugged if he had not accidentally ingested too much of her poison. Yet once the poison wore off, she would be back with one of her draughts.

He might never leave this place. Staring at the vase of flowers, he began to suspect Kinara might keep him hidden here rather than go to Rome.

"Until when?" His voice was a dry whisper. The answer was, of course, until she tired of this fantasy or he displeased her so much that she killed him.

Tears leaked from his eyes, rolling down to his ears as he stared into nothing.

He had killed the wrong person. Pertinax may not have been an innocent man, but he had not been Cecelia's murderer. With his last breath, he told him who was and who needed to pay.

Curio thought he had learned all about deceit from Consul Cato and Centurion Lucian. Yet he had learned nothing. Once more, he had trusted the wrong person and led others to death.

However, rather than pity himself, he gritted his teeth and determined to fix what he could.

Now he understood Kinara's game.

Her evil was not yet done. She would ensure Galerius died tonight, either in a pointless attack on Pertinax's home or by revealing him to the Scythians and thereby ensuring his immediate execution. Worse yet, she might offer him safety in his panic and then poison him. She wouldn't allow him to leave with Sextus. That would be a future threat to her fantasy. Curio had to be completely alone, and then she could easily hide him from Varro and Falco.

Or else kill him and herself if they came too close to discovering the truth. He did not doubt she was mad enough for that.

He lay flat, his senses still rocking gently.

Am I making a mistake? The question rose meekly from his thoughts. Maybe the poison caused visions or altered his memories. It certainly created vivid and convincing dreams when it was mixed into Kinara's draught.

There was only one way to know.

He started jolting his bed, calling out for Kinara. The bed shifted, bumping the table and causing the small clay lamp to wobble and cast dizzying shadows.

Eventually, Kinara slipped inside and rushed to him—a look of concern spread across her face. For a moment, Curio saw the same eyes that had been so intent while treating his injuries. This was Kinara the healer; seeing her now, he could not imagine her killing Cecelia.

"What's wrong? Stop thrashing, or you'll worsen your shoulder."

"I have a question," he said, the words halting and hoarse. Looking up at her, his plan to confront her felt foolhardy. Her lush brow cocked and she tilted her head. She set her hand on his chest as if to comfort him.

"What do you want to know?"

"Will you always take care of me?"

It was not the question he intended to ask, but what felt right to him then. It had the intended effect. Kinara's eyes brightened and her teeth shined through her smile.

"Of course. I will always be here. Haven't I always cared for you?"

"Yes. Are we going to be together in Rome? You won't leave me to start a new life once we arrive?"

"Never!" She sat back and touched her neck in shock. "We will start a new life together."

"Good. That's what I want. A new life. No more secret missions. Killing people. I'm done with all that. I just want peace."

"You'll have it. I will not let you worry about a thing. I will always take care of you."

Curio smiled, uncertain if it was as feeble as it felt to him.

"Why do you love me so much?"

Kinara blinked and her smile assumed the vacancy of someone asked a question too hard to answer. She licked her lips as if searching for a reason.

Of course, Curio knew the reason. She wanted to possess him, to dominate him, to keep him like a pet bird that ate hensbane seeds. None of that had anything to do with love.

"You do love me?" he asked, his voice hardening.

She nodded, but her complexion seemed to pale.

"Don't worry about anything. You should rest now."

"But I can't rest. I keep dreaming about Cecelia."

Kinara froze as if shocked to hear the name, but then darkness crossed her face.

"You don't need to think about her anymore. You have me now. I will take care of you better than she ever could."

"Why did you do it?"

The air became gelid and Kinara glared at him. She seemed to be considering her response. At last, she stood from the bed.

"The hensbane is causing you strange dreams. Pertinax killed her."

"Pertinax denied it with his last breath. Why would he do that?"

Kinara shouted, "Because he's a killer! He killed his wife. How hard is it to imagine he killed her, too?"

"Her name is Cecelia. Her brother's name is Galerius. You never use either one."

Kinara's eye twitched, and Curio was suddenly aware of her strong arms and shoulders compared to his helplessness.

"They are two stupid children who threw away their privileged lives for nothing. They make me sick."

"They're in your way, aren't they? They got between us. And we're not going to Rome. You're going to keep me here."

"Enough of this foolishness." She crossed her arms and glared down at him. "You need to rest, as do I. It is late."

She turned to leave, but Curio shouted for her to stop.

"You're right. My mind is still spinning with strange visions. I'm sorry for babbling like that. Sleep with me tonight. Even if you must keep me tied. I don't want to be alone anymore. Please, Kinara, have mercy on me. Lay by my side."

For all her profession of love, the request did not delay her rejection.

"I will be in the other room. Good night."

The door slammed behind her.

Curio had his answer. That had been as good as an outright confession.

Now, as his head spun from both the revelations of the evening and the lingering poison, he had to figure a way to escape and reach Galerius in time.

21

With little time to formulate a plan, Curio conserved his strength while resting on the bed. The clay lamp continued to flicker in the draft from where the door stood in the darkness. That was another piece of information about his location. If air flowed through the door, he must be above ground, not beneath it as he originally thought.

Yet what did that avail him? The bonds keeping him pinned were loosened but still firm. He pushed against them again. The worn rope bit his flesh and did not yield.

He dropped his head back on the deflated pillow. How had it come to this, he wondered. Kinara, for whatever bizarre reason, was trying to insert herself as Cecelia's replacement. She planned to keep him drugged and locked away here, probably for as long as his body could tolerate it. He shuddered at what would follow when he could no longer.

He resolved to not let that moment come. Galerius was in danger from her now. Curio had made a desperate bid to get Kinara to lie with him and perhaps forget about Galerius for a while. That might have been enough time for Sextus to realize his target was dead and then take Galerius away. At this point, he was safer being hauled back to his home than remaining in Athens.

But Kinara had seen through that ruse.

Now it was up to him to save himself and his rash, foolish, but beloved friend. Curio had placed him in danger, even if only through attacking the wrong threat. He would do everything possible to save him.

"But what is that?" He groaned and would've slapped his forehead if his hands were free.

There seemed no possibility of escape. Once Kinara determined enough of that hensbane seed had worn off, she would force another draught on him. From that point, she could time his draughts so that he never recovered. Perhaps she had a way to keep him on the edge of consciousness, living in some sort of fever dream for the rest of his days. Any hope of escape would vanish, and he would grow physically incapable of defying her.

"Gods, that's worse than death."

Whatever he would do, it had to be soon for both his and Galerius's sakes.

He fought a rising panic that clouded his thinking. Kinara was not going to untie him until he was under the power of her draught. He tried to enumerate the situations where she would have to let him out: washing and sanitation, basic exercise, and maybe eating. None of these were urgent enough for release tonight. He could not imagine if he asked to use the latrine that she would untie him. If he tried that tactic and failed, then she might conclude the poison had cleared enough to administer another of her draughts.

Even if he did manage to free himself, he was sore and exhausted from his fight with Pertinax. Kinara was full of vigor and a strength possibly augmented by her madness. If he did not secure some sort of advantage, she could wrestle him back into his restraints. He remembered how easily she flipped him around when she had cared for his wound.

Biting his bottom lip, he turned his head aside in shame. Was there no chance, after all? He stared at the flame dancing in the lamp. Its amber haze grew brighter, obscuring the wilting whites behind.

Then he knew what to do.

There was one thing Kinara valued above all, at least for now, and that was himself.

His idea was madness and might end in death. Yet either way he was as good as dead if he did nothing.

He tested his bonds a final time just to be certain they couldn't be slipped. While he had loosened the top rope, those pinning him around the wrists and legs held fast. He couldn't wrest an arm free, and even if he eventually did, he would be too late to help Galerius. Something had to be done now.

"Kinara?" he called out. "I'm thirsty again. Please!"

She did not answer, but he continued to cry out for her until she opened the door enough to allow in faint light.

"I told you to rest. Stop exerting yourself."

"Please, just another cup of water."

"I've used it all up for today. Tomorrow, I'll draw more. Now, don't disturb me again."

The door clapped shut.

Curio gave a short sigh. She had not left to confront Galerius. Perhaps she did not need to and instead sent intermediaries like the Scythians to apprehend him. The point of his request had been to confirm she was still present. Otherwise, his plan would certainly end in a horrific death.

"Very well," he whispered to himself. "Either the gods love you, or they don't. Let's find out what they think about me."

First, he twisted as far as his bindings would allow, which for his upper body was enough. He bit at the dry, deflated pillow under his head. He imagined he must look like a dog trying to bite its tail as he struggled to snag it.

His teeth caught the dry cloth, and he managed to tug the pillow from beneath his head. Now holding it in his mouth, he shimmied with his shoulders to the edge of the narrow bed. He then stretched his neck over it and released the pillow. Being mostly empty of all but a handful of feathers, it settled lightly on the hard-packed dirt floor.

Now he lay still another moment, both letting his stiff neck recover and preparing for the next step. It was easier than falling on a sword, but still, self-preservation instincts fought him. He gulped a breath and held it as if he were about to dive into a lake.

He bumped his shoulder against the table. In his earlier thrashing, the bed had shifted up to the small table so they touched. Now, he could hit it with enough force to shake the lamp.

The flame shuddered as if irritated at being disturbed. Of course, lamps were designed to resist being knocked over. So he renewed his attack, thrusting his shoulder against the wood table and shaking the lamp toward the edge.

It now hovered there, the yellow light swaying seductively as if begging to be set free. He stared at it, reciting a prayer to Vulcan in his head.

Let it burn swift and bright and consume all that is evil. He closed his eyes to focus himself as if it were the spiritual equivalent of shouting his prayer. Then they flicked open, and he amended it.

Of course, keep me from burning alive, and I will make you an offering on this day for the rest of my life.

Satisfied he had done all he could, he bucked the table and the lamp tumbled to the pillow below.

It landed softly and did not break, which Curio had hoped for. If Kinara heard the clay shatter, then she could stop the fire before it caught.

He had aimed well, and the oil spilled out to the dry pillow. The innocent, dancing flame of before now spread across the pillow like an eagle freed from a cage, casting a bright light into the corners of the small room.

Curio's satisfaction vanished. First, the light would give away the fire before it could spread, and he had not considered this. Next, the fire was dangerously close, and the heat flashed under his right side with unexpected intensity. He had not counted on his primal reaction to an uncontrolled fire being so close.

The flames crawled up the table legs and spread to the bed frame. Curio contorted and screamed as the intense heat scorched his exposed flesh.

The door slammed open and Kinara shrieked.

The flames now spread across the small table, burning up the whites that crumbled into glowing ash. The timeworn ropes that lashed Curio to his deathbed caught fire.

He realized now Vulcan had not heard his prayer. He had condemned himself to death in the flames.

Then water splashed over him, and sour smoke and steam gagged him. His eyes burned from it, but the heat had withdrawn.

"What happened?" Kinara held a clay water jug in hand, one she had lied about being empty. Her eyes were bright with terror. The fire still twisted around the table, and she had no time to wait for an answer.

Curio spluttered and coughed, but he had survived. He offered a mental apology to Vulcan for his doubt.

Kinara splashed more water at the fire, but it was not enough. The flames had retreated from the bed but were now crawling up the bracing timbers and heading for the rafters. Despite the mold and humidity, the wood was dry enough to burn. Kinara had to act fast to stop the spread.

"I'm fine," Curio choked out. "Let me out so I can help."

But Kinara ignored him. The fire lit her face, and whether it was from the strange light cast by runaway fire or something worse, she wore an expression of sheer madness.

"What have you done?" She repeated the question as she fruitlessly sprinkled more water from the jug. Only then did she cast it aside, so it shattered against the wall, and changed her tactic.

She seized the wool blanket that had been stuffed under Curio to make a mattress. It was wet and singed, but large enough to smother the flames on the table.

This minor shift in bulk, combined with the age of the rope, the fire, and Curio's exertions, created slack he instantly felt.

He extracted his arms while Kinara was busy patting out the flames beneath the blanket.

Smoke coiled thick along the ceiling and the sickening stench of burned and rotted wood filled the room. Both Curio and Kinara were coughing, and blinking away tears.

But Kinara did not see him pulling the rope from his waist. It had been burned the worst and broke easily.

Then he tugged out his right leg.

Kinara whirled around, her face a rictus of hatred. Her teeth and eyes flashed in the unstable light of the fire.

"You did this on purpose! Are you trying to kill me?"

Curio answered with the heel of his freed foot. It slammed into her stomach, knocking the wind from her and slamming her against the opposite wall.

"Just as you killed Cecelia!"

Kinara tripped over the blanket and struck one of the burning beams supporting the mudbrick wall. One of the rafters above her had caught fire and now drizzled flaming ash. Her stola caught fire around her neck, and she screamed in terror as the flames licked up her neck and cheek.

Curio wrestled with the last bond, his foot stuck in a rope that had somehow become tighter when the others had loosened.

While Kinara had doused most of the flames, the fire was rallying as burning ash settled on other flammable wood.

She spasmed and shrieked, desperately trying to pat out the flames that had caught her at a difficult angle.

Now Curio popped his foot free, and he leaped off the bed and for the opened door.

"Don't leave me here!" Kinara shouted. "Help!"

But he slipped out the door and into air that felt impossibly cool and fresh. He immediately slammed his back against the door, just in time to feel Kinara slam against it. Such was the force that he nearly fell over.

Now he looked around for something to brace the door, and

hopefully leave Kinara to choke to death on the smoke that rolled out from the top of the frame.

He was in a larger room, and immediately aware of two unshuttered windows that flanked a closed door. Moonlight streamed in from them to illuminate the room.

In his life, he had witnessed up close the horrors of combat, the viscera and blood that turned the landscape red. He had huddled in the ghost-haunted darkness of primal Iberia, terrorized by both the angry gods of its forests and the monstrously twisted barbarians who worshiped them. Yet none of that was as bizarre and chilling as this moonlit room.

As Kinara pounded on the door, screaming his name and crying out in pain, he struggled to understand what he saw.

To his left, just before the door, was a bedroll that Kinara had obviously occupied. Beyond it was a room that reminded Curio of his father's cubiculum from when he was a boy. However, this was old and rotted, covered in dust and webs.

A bed like the one he had been strapped to dominated the wall to his left. A corpse, skeletal and shrunken, lay on it. A wisp of dark hair still clung to the scalp. The mouth hung open in an endless scream and eyeless sockets stared up into nothing. Ropes had once held down a fuller body, for now death and decay had wasted the flesh so that the ropes hung free.

Curio detected the scent of rot beneath the acrid smells of the fire behind him.

Kinara continued to pound at the door, cursing him in between her terrified screams.

But Curio had not yet absorbed all that he witnessed.

Seated in a heavy chair beside the bed, set at an angle as if it were used by someone who might be consoling the corpse, was a man.

Doctor Nisos sat there, dressed in his white night tunic. His face was bluish in the moonlight, and his head hung down over his chest. He sat upright in the chair, held in place by a single length of a familiar old rope. Both hands were set on the armrests, and one held a bouquet of white flowers, still fresh but wilting from lack of water.

His eyes were half-opened, and froth had dried around his mouth. He seemed to be staring right at Curio.

"You'll pay for this!" Kinara shouted behind his head. She continued to batter the door, and Curio knew the moment he released she would burst through. He couldn't tell if the fire was spreading, but smoke still rolled into the room. He had to barricade it and then find Galerius before it was too late to help him.

He looked to his right.

A Roman soldier waited for him in the darkness. Curio's automatic reaction was to lift his arm in defense.

Kinara threw all her force into a kick, and the door exploded open and flung Curio to the ground.

He landed on a hard mosaic floor of faded ochre and brown patterns. A cloud of smoke expelled into the room, heralding Kinara's entrance.

Wasting no time, he flipped to his back and realized the soldier was nothing more than a centurion's muscled breastplate and helmet kept on a rack. A light pilum was set beside it, and a harness completed the image of a real soldier. Gladius and pugio were both in the correct places.

Kinara snatched the pilum and lowered it at Curio as he lay on the mosaic.

"You traitor! I saved your life, and look at how you repay me!"

Curio crawled back on his arms. "What have you done? That's your father!"

"You don't deserve the life I saved for you!" She jabbed the pilum at him, the point threatening his neck. Behind her, orange light gleamed from the makeshift prison room.

"You're mad," he said. "You hid it well. But you're fucking crazy."

Kinara shrieked. "It was not supposed to end like this!"

She charged at him, and Curio rolled away as the pilum struck the mosaic. Like a good Roman pilum, the iron head bent into uselessness as it scored the stone.

Curio pounced to his feet. Kinara's strike had carried her to block the door, and he had one chance to skirt past her.

But either his reactions were still sluggish or she was faster than he thought. She whirled and slammed the pilum butt directly into the wound she had so carefully tended.

This brought Curio to his knees, painfully crashing on the stone mosaic floor.

"You ingrate! You pig! You betrayed me!"

The pain radiated through his body and numbed his limbs. He had never experienced anything like it. Yet Kinara knew just where he was weakest.

She clubbed him on the head, and he collapsed flat. The world rocked and the floor felt as if it was spinning.

Grabbing him by the hair, she used her uncanny strength to raise him to his knees.

Whatever appeal she might once have had was now subsumed into a twisted visage of hatred. She spit in his face.

"I did so much for you. For us! We could've been together in peace. But look what you did to me!"

She turned her head to display the black and burned flesh of her neck and cheek and part of her ear.

"Suits your personality."

With a roar of fury, Kinara flung him back toward the door where smoke poured out.

"We were going to start a new life together." Some of the madness faded from her voice, but she still held the bent pilum like a club in white-knuckled hands. Her face gleamed with sweat as she stepped closer. "You were my champion, Curio. How can you hurt me so?"

He struggled to his feet, blood dripping from his head. The room swayed, but it was different from the effect of the hensbane seeds.

Kinara pressed closer, herding him toward the burning room and the destroyed door. The smoke blurred his eyes and burned his throat. Fortunately, it did the same to Kinara and she paused to cough.

"Was I going to be your champion, like that poor skeleton on the bed?"

Kinara struggled with her cough, trying to form a retort. But she looked toward the skeleton in the bed.

And a lifetime of training took over Curio's body.

In one deft motion, he plucked the gladius from its sheath hanging from the armor rack.

He turned on the ball of his foot and stepped forward with the other for a punching strike.

Kinara turned back, her eyes running with tears. Her lush brows shot up in shock.

The gladius plunged into her gut just below the ribcage. Curio drove it with all his force until the blade ran down to the handguard.

He released the blade, and Kinara stumbled back. Her eyes were wide, her dark irises like two pinpoints. She opened her mouth, and bright blood vomited onto her chest.

She wavered, blinking in confusion, reached for Curio, and then collapsed at his feet.

He stood over her, his breath ragged and raw from the smoke. The fire had not become a blaze, but it persisted in creating sour ash and smoke. Even if her screaming had not attracted others, the fire would bring the Scythians. He could not be here for that.

"You got overconfident," he said. "You didn't realize that poison had worn off. Pity for you."

He set his foot on her body, then dragged out the gladius. He wiped it on her stola, just as he would for any defeated enemy. Then, he took the harness from the rack and returned the sword to its sheath. The pugio sheath was empty, which did not surprise him.

Looking over the corpse on the bed, he could determine nothing of the identity. It appeared to be the corpse of a younger man of his own size. He had no time to dwell on it. If he had time to explore the home he might learn more. Instead, he turned to Doctor Nisos.

"I'm sorry." It was all he could think to say, then he brushed the doctor's eyes closed.

To the corpse on the bed, he nodded. "Whoever you are, thank you for your sword. It has avenged you."

Outside, the air was even colder and fresher. He was somewhere on the far outskirts of Athens. This was the outer walls, and perhaps near the Kerameikos.

For the moment he had only to escape the scene, but he would soon need to reorient himself and find Galerius. By now, he and Sextus were about to learn their plotting had been for nothing, and Curio wanted to help him escape.

He had promised this to Cecelia, and even if she no longer had ears to hear it, he would keep it.

22

Curio had wandered the nighttime streets of Athens for too long. Kinara's hideout had been across the city in a mournfully lonely place, but still inside the main walls. Once he heard distant alarms, he followed them to Pertinax's home, and the results of a battle were plain to see. The Scythians had arrived and encircled the area. Once more, concerned neighbors watched from their windows or else gathered in small groups by street corners.

Now, he watched from the shadows of an alley. Several bodies were gathered into a pile, and a whip-carrying man stood guard over them. As hard as he tried, he could not get close enough to see if Galerius was among the dead. He decided that Sextus would've prioritized Galerius over revenge. If things went badly, then he would have grabbed Galerius and ran.

Of course, there was always a chance that Galerius escaped and was waiting at their rally point. Curio spent the rest of the night navigating to it while avoiding patrols or anyone else. Along the way, he upset several watchdogs but otherwise revealed himself to no one.

Galerius was not at the point.

Curio had done all that he could. At last, he was exhausted and hungry. Thirst raked at his burning throat. He smelled like smoke and was covered in ashes and blood. He disgusted even himself.

But now he had a gladius at his side, and that made the world a safer place.

He curled up in a ditch and covered himself with rotted boards and trash, then fell asleep. Even had he wanted to remain alert for Galerius, he could not help it.

The next morning he extracted himself from the muck and crawled up from the ditch. A small field gave a home to several trees where black birds darted between branches. The sun was already up and people were on the roads.

He realized he would be a horrifying sight to anyone finding him now. If he intended to escape with Galerius, he had to find a bath. Of course, he had no money left. He had lost everything but had gained a weapon. Perhaps it was not a bad trade. He would have to become a thief and brigand long enough to restore himself. The gods would forgive him later.

Water was easiest to come by since the Athenians kept their jugs stacked just inside the walls of their homes. It took patience and cunning, but Curio had both. He snagged a jug and was able to clean most of the dirt and blood as well as soothe his thirst. He stole a Greek-style tunic from another home, a gray cloak from another, and then pinched apples from a street vendor.

He hid the harness and sword under the cloak as he made his way toward the docks. Thievery might become a way of life, he mused. Of course, thieves were despicable people, but he was beginning to understand how some fell into the life. For many, there was no other way to survive.

He only wished he knew the language better. If he had studied Greek like the sons of the wealthy, then he could have learned what happened last night. Instead, he gambled that Sextus was also heading to the docks this morning and hoping to escape with Galerius.

Progress was slow, for the beating Kinara delivered had hobbled him. Last night he had been carried by rage and desperation. Today, being calmer, all those pains returned and bent him over.

But he did not need another draught and never would allow anyone to give him another. Nor did he need a cane. That had been something Kinara pushed on him, ensuring he felt as weak as she wanted him to be. All the way toward the gates and down the walled road leading to the port, he kept thinking of that skeleton strapped to the bed.

He would never learn the corpse's story. All he could guess was that Kinara would do to him what she had done to that corpse. If he had not acted as he did, one day, someone would find his bones in a bed next to that one.

Passing out of the city with a weapon was easier than entering with one. So when he crossed to the docks, he realized to return he'd have to surrender the sword or else leave by ship. If Galerius was not here, then they might never meet again.

Among the bustling docks, he watched ships pulling in and out of the harbor. It was a familiar sight. Everywhere, commerce was the same, with crewmen shouting to each other and dockworkers pushing through the crowds. Crates, barrels, and amphorae were stacked everywhere. Nets were spread all over like the walls of a great city. People of every country milled through on their business, and woven among them, Athenian soldiers watched with hooded eyes.

Curio blended in here and did not need to worry about his weapon being discovered. Many others carried swords and daggers, for these were surrendered at the gates and not on the docks themselves.

The crowd was more cosmopolitan here, and Curio was able to ask around in Latin without drawing undue attention. The few people who had news only described a debacle of some kind among Roman crime gangs, but they had no more details. The leaders were dead, and the matter settled. Curio was not sure if that meant Sextus. Details were impossible to come by, and those he spoke with were impatient to get on with their business.

He checked on the departure of Roman ships, but without coins to bribe the authorities they did not release anything more specific than some ships had left for Rome.

At last, by noon, he had despaired of finding Galerius. The gods had taken him home.

This hit him harder than he expected, and he found an upturned barrel that had been a seat to countless sailors and sat down. Seagulls danced around him, sizing him up for something to steal. He stared back at them and then began to weep.

He hid his face from onlookers, but no one cared. The world was busy with its own concerns.

But for Curio, he felt as if his world had ended.

All of his friends were gone now. How would he ever find Varro and Falco without any means to pay for his travel? He didn't even know where to search. If he did not become a brigand himself, he would probably be enslaved to a brigand group before long.

Yet more keenly he felt the loss of the twins. Even if it had been circumstance that kept them by his side, they sat with him throughout his long recovery. At the time, he had over-credited Kinara and overlooked the power of their love and friendship. That had been what healed him, and not draughts or canes. He only understood it now that both were gone.

The seagulls decided Curio wasted their time and flew off.

He stifled his sobs under his hand and tried to think of what to do. Maybe if he could get back to Rome, he might be able to claim his money from this place called a bank. He had trusted the men called bankers because Varro trusted them. But without anyone there to mind his money, what would stop the bankers from stealing his wealth?

Even Servus Capax was destroyed. He had not a shred of anything left. No family. No friends. No home.

The self-pity washed over him in wave after wave. The crowd flowed around him, only glancing at him as they passed.

Then he heard his name.

He dropped his hand to his lap and sat upright.

"Curio, it's me."

The harsh whisper came from the darkness between a stack of crates. A heavy cart sat nearby and cast dark shadows over everything Galerius squatted between them.

Curio immediately sat upright, wiped his face, and put on a scowl.

"For the love of Jupiter, you were supposed to meet me by the northwest gate."

"I know," he whispered, still crouched in hiding. "But things went wrong. Pertinax never showed up and we got ambushed. Sextus fought a retreat, and was going to take me home."

"And what? Your new home is between two stacks of crates? Get out of there and sit with me."

He fought every urge to grab Galerius into a teary hug and instead shifted on the barrel to make space. Galerius looked both ways, his eyes wide like a suspicious cat. But Curio urged him out, and he slipped over to sit beside him.

"I just don't want us to get caught."

"Where's Sextus now?"

"Gone," Galerius said brightly. "He got me on the ship, and of course, I got right off. He had to sail or else face the Athenian navy. That's right, not those men with the whips but real soldiers on warships. I guess they got word Sextus was a troublemaker. So he had to leave or else face capture."

"What do you think he'll do now?"

Galerius shrugged. "Probably lie to my father that Cecelia and I are both dead. Of course, that will just mean my father will want to kill you and the others for kidnapping us. But maybe I'm wrong. Maybe he'll keep searching. Sextus seems to be enjoying his time as the big boss. That'll end fast if he goes home without me, at least."

Curio admired Galerius as he stared out at the sea, his youthful face free of worry. He seemed oddly contented despite all they had endured. Perhaps he could learn something from his young friend.

"Well, we've got to sneak out of this city somehow. We're still wanted men."

"That's why I was hiding. Don't you think we're taking a chance sitting here?"

"We're fine. No one looks for a man hiding in the open, just as long as we blend in."

Galerius looked around and then examined themselves.

"You're wearing Greek clothes. And you've got a cut on your head. What happened?"

"It's a bit of story," Curio said. "But I'll tell you all about it once we're out of here."

"That'll be easy."

Curio lifted a brow at this, and Galerius smiled.

"You said we only have to go up the coast a short distance. I've got two drachmae I lifted from Sextus. I figure that should pay for a short trip, and there are plenty of Roman captains here. It won't be hard to sail off to our new lives."

"Don't talk about new lives," Curio said with a shudder. "I'll explain it later."

"If you say so. I found a few ships ready to cast off. I bet if we hurry, we'll catch one of them willing to take us a half day up the coast."

Curio slapped the gladius hidden under his cloak. "Good, and after that, we'll live on our wits and by this sword I found last night. We've got to link up with Varro and Falco. The two of them can't function without me."

Galerius faced back out to sea and sighed.

"It's hard to believe Cecelia isn't coming with us. She would've loved an adventure like this."

"Adventure," Curio repeated the word. How long had it been since he thought any of this was an adventure? Maybe when he had just joined the legion, but no more. Still, he slapped Galerius on the back and laughed.

"Yes, onto another adventure, and we'll carry Cecelia in our hearts for it."

AUTHOR'S NOTES

There is little in terms of actual historical significance contained in this story. It takes place on the eve of the Roman-Seleucid war, which resulted after a long cold war. As such, we find Curio in Athens at the crossroads of history. Much will change over the ensuing years as larger conflicts reshape Greece.

Perhaps one point needing clarification is the Scythians. The Scythian Archers were supposedly three hundred public slaves employed by Athens as a sort of police force. Though the Scythians were most famous for their archery, they did not employ bows to enforce peace and safety within the city. For this, they either used clubs or long whips as described in the story. Bows would have been inappropriate for a crowded city like Athens.

Of course, the Scythian "police force" is not an established fact. They are known to us from their depictions in plays and as artwork on ancient vases. There is little else to support their existence. Also, the Scythians were employed centuries earlier than their appearance in this story. No one is certain exactly when the Scythians began their role as enforcers or when this enforcement ended. However, by the time of this story, they probably would have been disbanded. So, their appearance here is an anachronism.

The Scythians had little authority of their own and reported to a council of magistrates who enforced public order and criminal punishments. It is an open question as to why Athens would employ foreign "barbarians" as enforcers. However, one theory is that a foreign enforcer would be more impartial and have no connections within the city to corrupt them.

Now Curio and his new friend, Galerius, must reconnect with Falco and Varro. The Roman-Seleucid war is about to begin, the fate of Servus Capax remains to be seen, and a whole new world of adventure awaits all of them.

NEWSLETTER

If you would like to know when my next book is released, please sign up for my new release newsletter. You can do this at my website:

http://jerryautieri.wordpress.com/

If you have enjoyed this book and would like to show your support for my writing, consider leaving a review where you purchased this book or on Goodreads, LibraryThing, and other reader sites. I need help from readers like you to get the word out about my books. If you have a moment, please share your thoughts with other readers. I appreciate it!

ALSO BY JERRY AUTIERI

Ulfrik Ormsson's Saga

Historical adventure stories set in 9th Century Europe and brimming with heroic combat. Witness the birth of a unified Norway, travel to the remote Faeroe Islands, then follow the Vikings on a siege of Paris and beyond. Walk in the footsteps of the Vikings and witness history through the eyes of Ulfrik Ormsson.

Fate's Needle

Islands in the Fog

Banners of the Northmen

Shield of Lies

The Storm God's Gift

Return of the Ravens

Sword Brothers

Descendants Saga

The grandchildren of Ulfrik Ormsson continue tales of Norse battle and glory. They may have come from greatness, but they must make their own way in the brutal world of the 10th Century.

Descendants of the Wolf

Odin's Ravens

Revenge of the Wolves

Blood Price

Viking Bones

Valor of the Norsemen

Norse Vengeance

Bear and Raven

Red Oath

Fate's End

Grimwold and Lethos Trilogy

A sword and sorcery fantasy trilogy with a decidedly Norse flavor.

Deadman's Tide

Children of Urdis

Age of Blood

Copyright © 2024 by Jerry Autieri

All rights reserved.

No part of this book may be reproduced in any form or by any electronic or mechanical means, including information storage and retrieval systems, without written permission from the author, except for the use of brief quotations in a book review.

Printed in Great Britain
by Amazon